PRAISE FOR

Murder Unmentionable

"Sweet iced tea, a cast of charming Tennessee characters, and a vintage-lingerie store help this debut go down easier than a mint julep in July. Readers who like their cozies with a Southern flavor will enjoy getting to know Emma and her aunt, Arabella, as they try to catch a killer as slippery as a satin peignoir."

—Lila Dare, author of the Southern Beauty Shop Mysteries

"Filled with Southern charm, this is a flirty mystery you're sure to find alluring."

—Riley Adams, author of the Memphis BBQ Mysteries

"Meg London has hit the right note with the characters . . . and the setting . . . Vintage-lingerie details and Southern charm add to the atmosphere of this appealing first cozy."

—*The Mystery Reader*

"Entertaining . . . Meg London captures the essence of a small Southern town's quirkiness."

—*Genre Go Round Reviews*

"Like the name of the store, this mystery is very sweet. With a very interesting cast of characters . . . this was a fun debut into the life of Emma and the town of Paris, Tennessee, and I'm looking forward to more books in the series."

—*Cozy Mystery Book Reviews*

Laced
WITH POISON

MEG LONDON

BERKLEY PRIME CRIME, NEW YORK

THE BERKLEY PUBLISHING GROUP
Published by the Penguin Group
Penguin Group (USA) Inc.
375 Hudson Street, New York, New York 10014, USA

USA I Canada I UK I Ireland I Australia I New Zealand I India I South Africa I China

Penguin Books Ltd., Registered Offices: 80 Strand, London WC2R 0RL, England
For more information about the Penguin Group, visit penguin.com.

LACED WITH POISON

A Berkley Prime Crime Book / published by arrangement with the author

Berkley Prime Crime Books are published by The Berkley Publishing Group.
BERKLEY® PRIME CRIME and the PRIME CRIME logo are
trademarks of Penguin Group (USA) Inc.

For information, address: The Berkley Publishing Group,
a division of Penguin Group (USA) Inc.,
375 Hudson Street, New York, New York 10014.

ISBN: 978-0-425-25214-7

PUBLISHING HISTORY
Berkley Prime Crime mass-market edition / July 2013

PRINTED IN THE UNITED STATES OF AMERICA

10 9 8 7 6 5 4 3 2 1

Cover illustration by Nathalie Dion.
Cover design by Rita Frangie.
Interior text design by Laura K. Corless.

ALWAYS LEARNING   **PEARSON**

To my wonderful husband, two beautiful daughters and the best sister in the world. Your never-ending support and encouragement mean the world to me.

Acknowledgments

I would like to thank my editor, Faith Black, who takes my raw material and helps me turn it into a book, and my agent, Jessica Faust, who helped me fulfill my dream of becoming an author.

I'd also like to thank my friends Laura Alden, Janet Bolin, Krista Davis, Kaye George, Daryl Wood Gerber and Marilyn Levinson for their brainstorming, hand-holding and support.

Chapter 1

EMMA Taylor stood behind the counter of Sweet Nothings, her aunt's vintage lingerie shop in downtown Paris, Tennessee. It was almost the end of September, and Emma was reviewing the month's sales before opening for business. She twirled a piece of dark brown hair around her finger as she studied the black-and-white figures on the computer printout. Sales had been good. Customers were coming from as far away as Nashville and Memphis to check out their one-of-a-kind pieces, and they were doing a brisk online business, too, since Emma's friend Liz had gotten their web site up and running for them.

Unfortunately, though, they were still in something of a hole. Emma worried her lower lip between her teeth. Someone had thrown a brick at their front window—the police were never able to discover who, although Emma and Arabella suspected it was someone whose feathers they'd riled

while investigating the murder of Emma's ex-boyfriend—
and replacing that enormous pane of glass had cost a small
fortune.

Emma ran a finger down the column of numbers. Things
were definitely improving, though, and hopefully a robust
Christmas season would put them back in the black again.

Emma glanced at her watch. Almost time to open. She
looked around the shop. Everything seemed to be in order—
stock was tidied and ready, a Lucie Ann gown hung from
the open door of one of the white distressed armoires Emma
had ordered for the shop when they renovated and a Jenelle
sheer lace nightgown in a soft rose graced the mannequin.
Sweet Nothings was ready for business.

Emma unlocked the front door, switched the sign from
closed to *open* and was putting away the computer printouts
when she heard the front door ping. "Can I help you?" she
said, looking up.

"It's just me, dear." Arabella bustled into the shop, two
enormous shopping bags in one hand and the leash for
Pierre, her French bulldog, wound around the other. She had
the jacket of her pale gray pantsuit over her arm and had
untied the bow at the neck of her cap-sleeved white blouse.
"It's getting quite warm. There's not a cloud in the sky and
that sun is still strong even if it is September." She tucked
a strand of her silver hair back into her French twist.

Emma's aunt might have been in her late sixties, but she
was as stylish as anyone Emma knew half her age. Emma
had always been intrigued with her and remembered spending many pleasant evenings on Arabella's porch listening
to tales of her travels to Europe, India and the Far East.
Emma never knew what had made her aunt decide to return
to Paris in the '70s, settle down and open her lingerie shop.

Emma indicated the two shopping bags. "Let me take those for you."

Emma took the bags, and Arabella bent down to unclip Pierre's leash. He made a beeline for his black-and-white toile dog bed where he immediately stretched out, the occasional twitch of his black ear or white ear his only movement.

"Wait till you see what I have in there." Arabella grinned and pointed at the bags.

"Did you and Francis go shopping?"

Arabella had spent the weekend in Jackson, Tennessee, about an hour away, where Francis Salerno lived. He was an agent with the TBI—Tennessee Bureau of Investigation— and Arabella had met him when he was helping the local police look into the murder of Emma's ex-boyfriend. Arabella had had to brave the wrath of her old friend Sally Dixon when Francis began asking her out. Sally thought she was owed first dibs, but it wasn't Arabella's fault that she had been the one to catch his eye. He was tall, with dark hair streaked with gray, and always reminded Emma of the actor who used to play the star in *Magnum P.I.*

Arabella shook her head. "No, but we did catch a wonderful movie, although I've already forgotten the name of it, and had a great steak dinner at that place, whatever it's called. We even had a picnic yesterday!" she finished triumphantly. She looked at Emma over the rims of her reading glasses. "And don't worry. Francis made a reservation for me at the loveliest bed-and-breakfast."

Emma smiled to herself. Arabella had obviously fallen hard for Francis. She was glowing and walked around in a perpetual haze, unable to remember names, places or much of anything else.

Emma straightened a peach 1930s negligee on one of the mannequins. "So, no shopping?"

"Not with Francis, no. He's not much of a fan, I'm afraid. But I did stop at a wonderful estate sale on my way back yesterday. Wait till you see what I bought!" She reached for the nearest of the shopping bags.

Emma felt her stomach clench. They really couldn't afford to purchase more stock at the moment. The figures she'd been perusing earlier that morning swam before her eyes in a dismal sea of red.

Arabella must have noticed the look on her face. "Don't worry, dear Emma." She put a hand on Emma's arm. "We'll sell these things in no time. Besides, I've had the most wonderful idea."

"What is that?"

Arabella winked and shook a finger at her playfully. "Let me show you what I've got first."

She pulled a beautiful flowered peignoir set from the first shopping bag. It looked brand-new, although Emma could tell by the style that it was vintage. Arabella arranged it carefully on the counter and stood back with the air of a parent presenting a clever child's best trick.

"It's early 1950s," Arabella said, running the fabric through her fingers. "Crepe de Chine, bias cut and pleated all around. The skirt on the robe has a sweep of one hundred and two inches!" She finished triumphantly. "It has French seams throughout and they're all pinked."

Emma admired the print of tiny roses and other multicolored flowers. It was beautifully delicate and feminine. "Oh, look." She fingered the three Lucite buttons that closed the robe at the waist. "These are so perfect."

Arabella nodded as if to say *I told you so*. "And you won't believe what else. The ensemble was made in-house at Henri

Bendel, the exclusive New York City department store. It's really one of a kind."

Arabella put a hand inside the shopping bag. "But that's not all." She pulled out an off-white robe and nightgown set. The robe had cream-colored lace from the neck to the waist and also around the waist, and a sweeping skirt. The negligee had matching lace creating a V under the bust. "This set is from the 1940s," Arabella said as she spread the two pieces out on the counter. "It was made by Tula, but the rayon crepe de Chine is by Narco—the North American Rayon Corporation. The fabric was highly prized during the World War Two era for its exotic feel."

Emma held the luxurious fabric reverently in her hands. She could imagine how wearing a gown and peignoir set like this would make any woman feel glamorous.

"There's more." Arabella dove back into her two shopping bags and pulled out several additional nightgowns, another peignoir and negligee set and a gorgeous bed jacket.

"These things look almost brand-new," Emma said as she helped Arabella fold the garments up and put them back in the bags.

"They do, don't they?"

Emma slid the last of the garments in. "Okay, now that we've looked at your purchases, are you going to tell me what your wonderful idea is?"

Arabella clapped her hands. "I think you're going to love it!"

Emma raised her eyebrows and waited.

"A trunk show!" Arabella declared with all the vigor of a game show host announcing the winner. "What do you think?"

"A trunk show?"

Arabella nodded. "Yes. It's like a party—like the ones

where your friends try to sell you jewelry or makeup or things for the kitchen that you don't even recognize. The hostess invites all her friends and provides refreshments, and we show off our wares."

"But who would we get to host it?" Emma ran through her mental list of friends.

"That's the best part!" Arabella was nearly bouncing in her excitement. "Deirdre Porter has agreed to host it for us! I called her on the way back here on my cell. She's going to e-mail an invitation to all her friends today. It's perfect."

"You're right." Emma began to smile. "It is perfect." Deirdre Porter was the daughter-in-law of Alfred Porter, the mayor of Paris, Tennessee, and his wife Marjorie, who came from one of Paris's oldest and wealthiest families. Deirdre would attract the A-list to their trunk show.

"We'll make a fortune!" Arabella assured Emma, patting her on the arm. "Meanwhile, let me put these bags in the back. Our first customers could be arriving shortly."

An hour later, after a dark-haired, fortyish woman left with a glossy black-and-white Sweet Nothings bag dangling from the crook of her arm, Arabella stood in the middle of the shop and looked around.

"Some days I honestly cannot believe what you've done with the shop." She turned and smiled at Emma. "The pink walls, the black-and-white toile . . . it's all perfect," she said with a slight catch in her voice.

"So you don't miss your pea green shag? Or the fluorescent pink and orange accents?" Emma had stripped the shop of everything that had screamed '70s in exchange for shabby chic décor.

"Not a bit!"

Arabella was straightening the gown on the mannequin and Emma was flipping through a catalogue when they heard a strange noise coming from outside. It sounded like someone yelling for help. Arabella glanced at Emma with her eyebrows raised. Emma ran to the door and yanked it open.

She stepped outside, stood under the black-and-white Sweet Nothings awning and looked up and down Washington Street—the main shopping area in Paris, Tennessee. At first things looked just as usual, but then she noticed someone coming down the sidewalk. She squinted slightly. It looked like Sylvia Brodsky, who lived over the Taffy Pull a few doors down and worked at Sweet Nothings as a saleswoman and bra-fitting specialist. She'd moved with her son and daughter-in-law from New York where she'd spent several decades working in lingerie at Macy's department store. Emma had often heard the term *crusty New Yorker*, but she'd never quite understood what it meant before meeting Sylvia.

Emma looked again. It *was* Sylvia. She was waving her arms and calling for help. Emma couldn't imagine what the emergency was. Washington Street looked as peaceful as ever—no flames shooting from any of the windows, and no one chasing Sylvia. Emma started down the street toward her.

They met in front of the Meat Mart, where Emma occasionally went to treat herself to a good steak or some loin lamb chops. Emma glanced at the window and saw Willie Williams, the butcher, tip a figurative hat in her direction. She smiled in return and turned her attention toward Sylvia.

Sylvia tended to cultivate a somewhat unusual style of dress, and today was no exception. She was wearing a bandanna that had gone askew, leaving one eye nearly covered, like a bizarre pirate's patch. Her gray hair bristled out around the edges. She had a trench coat over a pair of purple fleece pajama pants and was shuffling along in fuzzy pink slippers. Something had obviously sent her fleeing to the street still in her nightclothes.

"What is it?" Emma asked.

"Help!" Sylvia gasped. "You've got to help me." She grabbed Emma by the arm and began to drag her down the street.

Shopkeepers were peering out their doors now, and some had come to stand on the sidewalk, arms folded across their chests. Angel Roy stood in front of her beauty salon, a comb in one hand and a can of hair spray in the other. Today her fire-engine-red hair was teased high in front and gathered into an asymmetrical ponytail that complemented her one-shoulder cotton top. She looked quizzically at Emma as she and Sylvia marched toward her. Emma gave a quick shrug as they came to a halt just beyond Angel Cuts, Angel's salon.

A red truck was pulled up to the curb, the back doors yawning open. *We Move You* was written on the side in white block letters. Two men came out of the door next to the Taffy Pull, which led upstairs to Sylvia's apartment. They muscled a large, floral-patterned recliner through the door, set it down on the pavement, tilted back their ball caps and swiped a hand across their sweaty foreheads.

"What's going on?" Emma asked again.

"It's not fair," Sylvia protested, plopping down onto the temporarily abandoned recliner. "They didn't even tell me. These men"—she gestured toward the two who were still breathing heavily after their trip down the stairs with the enormous chair, and the one who was waiting by the truck—"just showed up and started heaving my furniture around."

"What?"

Sylvia nodded so vigorously, her hoop earrings slapped

against the side of her face. "I told them I didn't want to move, but they went ahead and did it anyway."

"Who is doing this?" For a moment Emma wondered if Sylvia hadn't paid her rent and was being evicted.

"My rotten kids. My son and that princess he's married to. They've been trying to get me to move to that old folks home, Sunrise or Sunset or something like that, over on Harrison, near the cemetery, for a year now. Pretty convenient. First the home, then a short trip to a plot and gravestone." Sylvia crossed her arms over her chest and set her jaw. "This is a sneaky, nasty, underhanded maneuver if you ask me." Her chin quivered, and she dashed a hand across her eyes. "They sent these moving men without even telling me. I was making my tea when they barged in."

The two men in ball caps looked at each other. One began to open his mouth, then closed it again and shrugged.

"I've heard that place is actually quite nice." Emma remembered one of their customers talking about it.

"It's for old people!"

"It's called Sunny Days, isn't it? And it's not just old people. There's independent living as well. I'm sure that's what your kids have arranged for you."

"Yeah, could be." Sylvia looked warily at Emma from under lowered brows. "Don't you go telling me to move there, too."

"Well, it looks rather nice. I saw a copy of their brochure at the grocery store. It's a pretty place, and everyone looks like they're having a good time."

Sylvia snorted. "Doing what? Playing bingo?" She shuddered. "Please."

"Maybe you could entertain them with your tarot reading."

Sylvia fixed Emma with a beady stare. "The cards aren't for entertainment, you know. They're a serious business. Besides, I've got my little side business going here. Who's going to come to Sunny whatever you said it was to have their cards read?"

"Oh, I don't know. It's a mile or two outside of town. Not that far for anyone with a car."

"Uh, lady?" The taller of the two men approached Sylvia. His T-shirt, like the truck, was red, with *We Move You* screened onto the front. It stretched across an abdomen as round and big as a watermelon. "We've got to get moving here, no pun intended. You going to let us put your stuff into the truck or what?"

"Why don't you give it a try?" Emma said. "If you don't like it, you can always move back. I doubt the landlord is going to rent that apartment anytime soon." She sensed Sylvia softening. "You might actually like it."

Sylvia scowled. "It's all on account of me forgetting I was running a tub. So a little water overflowed and ran downstairs. What's the big deal?"

"A couple of thousand dollars in repairs, that's what's the big deal."

Emma hadn't heard Angel come up behind her and whirled around when she heard her voice.

Sylvia looked at Angel, then at Emma, then back at Angel again. A look of defeat settled on her face. "All right, all right, I'll go. As my uncle always said, you can't fight city hall. Just bury me over at Sunny Poop or whatever it is you call it. Just close the lid and dig me in. I'm done fighting." She put her hands on the arms of the recliner and shoved herself to a standing position.

"Come on." Emma linked an arm gently through Sylvia's.

"Let's go back to Sweet Nothings, and I'll make us both a cup of tea while the men load the truck."

"Not that green stuff you drink?" Sylvia shuddered.

"I've got some Lapsang souchong you'll love."

"Oh, all right." She shook her finger at Emma. "But I'll be back bright and early tomorrow morning, don't you worry."

Chapter 2

THE first Sweet Nothings trunk show was scheduled for the following Saturday afternoon. Invitations had been sent, and Deirdre had already planned the menu—champagne punch along with plenty of lemonade and sweet tea for the non-drinkers; a selection of cupcakes from Sprinkles for dessert and some savory appetizers from Let Us Cater to You, including Lucy Monroe's cheese straws, without which, as Lucy often boasted, no party, special event, wedding or christening could possibly take place in Paris.

Arabella spent the intervening time examining all her new purchases, cleaning them and making any small repairs, which were remarkably few given the age of the garments.

Finally, the big day arrived, dawning bright and sunny with a light breeze.

"Let's hope the weather is a good omen," Arabella said,

as she helped Emma assemble the things they would be taking to Deirdre's. Arabella's Mini was too small to transport all their merchandise and supplies, so Emma had arranged to borrow Sylvia's Cadillac as well.

They piled what they could into the Mini, and Arabella and Emma gave each other the victory sign when they were able to close the trunk. Emma waved as Arabella pulled out of the driveway.

Moments later, Sylvia arrived in her Cadillac. Emma watched as she pulled into the parking lot, narrowly missing the sign at the entrance. She shuddered. Sylvia really shouldn't be driving, and it was probably only a matter of time before her kids intervened and took away her license.

Emma had everything at the ready. She grasped her cargo and headed toward the open door of Sylvia's Cadillac. "Thank goodness her legs bend," she called to Sylvia as she approached the car.

"Whoa! Who on earth is that?"

"Arabella thought it would be nice to have a mannequin dressed in one of the vintage ensembles. We call this one Melanie because Arabella thinks she looks like that woman who played Melanie in *Gone with the Wind*."

"She does kind of. Do you need a hand with that?"

Emma had opened the back door and was struggling to get the five and a half foot tall "Melanie" in the backseat.

"Would it be easier if she rode up front?"

"It might be. Do you mind?"

"Not at all." Sylvia got out of the car and watched as Emma went around to the front passenger seat. She slid Melanie into place and touched up her vintage '40s pageboy, which had become slightly messy in the struggle to get her into the car.

"Don't you think we ought to put something over her? I

mean, if we're going to drive through town with her in the front seat."

Emma frowned at the mannequin propped in the seat, her gaze focused out the front window.

"No, I think it'll be okay. I don't think anyone will notice."

"Okay by me, then." Sylvia slid into the backseat, on the opposite side from Melanie. "I'll let you drive if you don't mind."

Emma didn't. In fact, she was relieved. Riding with Sylvia was an experience—one that she had no immediate desire to repeat. She was pleased to note that the car drove relatively smoothly. She checked the brakes several times, and they were fine.

"Tom Mulligan gave my baby a complete overhaul," Sylvia said, slapping the seat cushion affectionately. "She drives really good now, doesn't she?"

"Yes. She certainly does," Emma said, wondering why cars were always considered feminine.

Feeling more confident about the Cadillac, Emma pressed down on the gas pedal, and they picked up speed. They were heading out of downtown Paris when Emma noticed lights behind her and heard the brief blare of a siren.

"What! I don't believe it! I wasn't speeding. What on earth could the police want?"

Sylvia gave a noncommittal shrug, and Emma thought she heard a choked-off laugh.

Emma eased the Cadillac onto the gravel shoulder and slowly came to a halt.

"Ma'am." A long, lanky policeman who didn't look any older than eighteen approached Emma's open window.

"What is it, Officer? I'm quite certain I wasn't speeding. Do I have a taillight out or something?"

"No, ma'am. Everything is fine, ma'am. But you need to tell your friend there," he gestured toward the passenger seat, "we've got laws here in Paris against public nudity. I'll let it go this time, but don't let me catch it happening again."

Emma had to squeeze her eyes shut and bite her lip to keep from laughing. She didn't dare turn and look at Sylvia, although she thought she heard an aborted chuckle coming from the backseat.

"Yes, Officer, I will certainly do that. We're not more than three or four minutes from our destination, and I'll be sure Melanie"—she nodded her head toward the silent mannequin—"puts some clothes on."

"Thank you, ma'am. And you be careful now."

Emma waited for the traffic to clear, then pulled the Cadillac back out onto the road. As soon as they were a safe distance away, she and Sylvia burst into laughter.

"I don't think Melanie gets the joke," Sylvia said, indicating the silent mannequin, who continued to stare out the front window, with a wave of her hand.

That induced a fresh fit of giggling, and she and Sylvia were still laughing and wiping tears from their eyes when they arrived at Deirdre Porter's house.

It was an imposing-looking brick, Georgian-style home. All the windows gleamed in the sun, and the brass knocker on the front door had been polished to a high gloss. A small, man-made brook ran in front of the house with an ornate bridge over it. Emma stopped in the middle and stared down at the water.

"Are those koi?" Sylvia pointed to several fish that swam past and disappeared under the bridge.

"I think so," Emma said as she reached for the door knocker.

Arabella had arrived ahead of them, and it was she who opened the door to their knock.

"What's the matter? Were you crying?" She peered at Emma's face.

Emma bit her lip. "No, laughing. I'll tell you about it later."

Arabella gave her a strange look but didn't ask any further questions.

"Deirdre wants us to set up in the living room." Arabella indicated the direction with a nod of her head.

Emma carried Melanie into the room in question. Deirdre had a coatrack set up, and Arabella had already arranged all of the Sweet Nothings pieces on it. Emma reached for the vintage gown they'd decided to dress Melanie in, but she stopped with her hand halfway to the hanger. Deirdre's living room was gorgeous, and she paused to take it all in. The ceiling was at least twelve feet tall with floor-to-ceiling windows draped in luxurious fabric in a soft, neutral color edged in gold trim. The sofa and round, tufted ottomans were the same color, creating a harmonious look that was both sophisticated and soothing. A fireplace with an ornately carved mantelpiece was the crowning touch.

"Gorgeous place, isn't it?" Catherine "Bitsy" Palmer said as she went past with a box of cupcakes from her shop, Sprinkles. Bitsy was anything but, at six feet tall. And she was every inch the Southern belle with long, blond hair and enormous blue eyes. She was friends with Emma's oldest friend, Liz, and was as nice as could be. "Deirdre did a lot of the decorating herself," she called over her shoulder on her way to the kitchen.

Emma slipped the matching peach silk peignoir onto the mannequin and carefully tied the sash at the waist in a floppy bow. She stood back to admire the effect.

"Looks great!" Emma's best friend Liz Banning came up behind her and gave her a quick hug. "I hope you sell a lot today."

"Me, too," Emma said, brightening at the sight of her friend with her warm smile and wide-open, freckled face. They had known each other forever, having grown up in Paris together. Emma had practically lived at the O'Connell house where Liz's older brother, Brian, had treated her like another kid sister. Their relationship had evolved, however, with Emma's return to Paris, and Emma realized she'd had a crush on Brian for a long time. They'd been dating for the last few months, and Emma was excited to see where things would lead.

By now the doorbell was ringing every few minutes, and guests had begun to drift into the living room, glasses in hand.

"I think everyone is here. Are you ready?" Deirdre Porter, the hostess, put a hand on Emma's arm. She looked effortlessly beautiful, as usual, in well-fitting trousers and a low-cut pink cashmere sweater, her long hair brushed to a sheen and held with a clip at her nape. Everyone in Paris had been surprised when Peyton Porter had returned from college engaged to her. It had set more than one person's teeth on edge that he'd thrown over his local girlfriend for someone no one knew and, worse, no one knew anything about.

Emma glanced around the room. Four women were seated on each of the sofas that faced each other across a glass and chrome coffee table, and all the other chairs and ottomans were occupied as well, with a group of three women leaning against the wall by the fireplace.

Arabella was in her element. Emma watched with admiration as she showed off each of the garments they'd brought in turn, extolling the virtues of each piece as well as giving a brief history of vintage lingerie in general and these specific items in particular. She finished with a flourish, and applause immediately broke out.

Arabella waited for the room to quiet down again and then spoke. "If anyone is interested in trying on any of the garments, please feel free. Emma or Sylvia"—she nodded in their direction—"or I will be glad to help you. Deirdre has graciously made her powder room on this floor available as well as the *salle de bain*," Arabella used the French term with relish, "on the second floor if you want to see how you'd look in any of the negligees."

"I'd like to try this robe on," said a woman with dark hair cut as short as Emma's but lacking her sassy style.

"Certainly." Emma took the garment from her and held it up for her to slip into.

"I'm Jessica Scott by the way. Deirdre and I were in the same sorority. I'm the administrator at the Sunny Days Retirement Community." She stuck out a hand and gave Emma's a sharp shake.

"Our friend Sylvia just moved in there."

"Really?" Jessica glanced around the room.

"She's over there. The one with the gray bob and silver hoop earrings."

Jessica narrowed her eyes. "I don't think I've met her yet."

She slipped into the robe that Emma was holding out. Her short and slightly stout figure did nothing for the beautiful garment.

"What can you tell me about this piece?" She scowled at herself in the standing mirror Emma and Arabella had brought along for the occasion.

"It's early 1950s and is made of rayon satin." Emma began reeling off the facts she'd memorized about the piece in a silvery blue floral fabric. "There are attached waist ties"—she reached inside the robe and pulled them taut—"that you can tighten for a perfect fit."

Jessica turned around and admired herself in the mirror. "I rather do like it," she announced to the small group that had gathered around her. "What do you think?"

"I think it's positively lovely," one of the women gushed. She looked to be in her mid-thirties and had mousy blond hair teased into a style that seemed too old considering her age.

"This is Crystal Davis," Jessica said, frowning at the woman. "She's my secretary."

"And distant cousin," Crystal piped up. She pulled the sleeves of her blue cardigan down over her hands.

Jessica renewed her appraisal of herself in the mirror. "I think you're wrong, Crystal. It makes me look short and slightly dumpy."

Emma noticed Crystal's face fall and wondered whether Jessica was always so blunt, or did she dislike Crystal for some reason?

Jessica stuck her hand into one of the robe pockets and turned this way and that in front of the glass. She pulled her hand from the pocket and held something up. "What is this?"

The others strained to see. Emma held out her hand, and Jessica placed the object in her palm. It was a small blue bead with the capital letter *P* on it. She held it up for the others to see.

Conversation around the room had fallen silent, and the other women gathered around to examine the tiny item.

"It looks like a bead from one of those hospital identification bracelets they used to make years ago," said a woman in an elegant pantsuit who also had teased gray hair. "My mother saved mine, and it was made with beads like that, only in pink, of course. It was," she cleared her throat, "sometime in the 1950s. I refuse to say exactly when."

The other women laughed obligingly. Emma wasn't particularly sensitive about her age—she was only twenty-nine, but she realized that it was merely a matter of time before people would begin reminding her of her ticking biological clock.

"That reminds me of an amazing story I just heard," Jessica said in the kind of loud, commanding voice that made everyone stop talking and turn in her direction. "I heard it from one of the residents on our nursing floor. She had been a nurse herself at one time and worked in the Henry County Hospital here in Paris. The hospital was even smaller then, this was around 1954, and on this particular night, there was a terrible storm and accidents all over the roads. People on stretchers were lined up in the halls of the emergency room, and the doctors could barely keep up. Fortunately, the maternity ward was empty except for two women in labor. Rose took care of both of them."

Jessica paused as Emma helped her out of the vintage robe, and Deirdre handed her a glass of punch. She took a sip before continuing.

"One of the women was very poor, married to a farmer and having her tenth child or something like that." Jessica scowled, and it was obvious she disapproved. "According to Rose, they could ill afford the other nine, let alone a new baby. I don't know why people do that, but . . ." She shrugged. "The other laboring woman was very wealthy. Rose referred to her as 'Cat.' She was either forty, or nearing it, I don't quite remember what Rose said, but this was her first child. She and her husband had been married since their twenties, but she had been unable to get pregnant. Finally, the long-awaited heir was about to arrive. But," Jessica took another sip of her punch, and the room was completely silent as they waited for her to continue, "the baby was stillborn."

Several women gasped, and they all looked at one another.

"Go on," Crystal said, and Jessica scowled at her again.

"As I said, it was a stormy night, and all the doctors were busy in the emergency room. None of them was paying much attention to what was happening in labor and delivery. Rose had an idea. She decided to switch the babies."

Here the women gasped again, and even Crystal was silent.

"Rose gave the rich woman the other woman's baby to raise it as her own."

"Was it a boy or girl?" an older woman with fading red hair called out.

"According to Rose, it was a boy," Jessica said with a look of triumph on her face. "I'd say that little baby sure lucked out."

Marjorie Porter's laugh rang out loud and clear. She was wearing a perfectly tailored suit that was obviously expensive but also very subdued. Marjorie came from the sort of old Southern wealth that felt showing off was for the lower classes. "Honestly," she said in condescending tones, "you don't believe every single thing someone tells you, do you? Don't you think the old nurse must be demented and made the whole thing up?" She looked around the room for approval. "I mean, who would do such a thing? It was probably something she saw on television."

Chapter 3

STUNNED silence greeted Marjorie's pronouncement, then everyone began talking at once. Deirdre went from group to group urging everyone into the dining room where the food had been set out.

Emma felt a prickle of envy when she saw Deirdre's dining room, but then she reminded herself that she was perfectly content where she was in her little apartment over Sweet Nothings with its darling window seat and view of Washington Street below. If she and Brian O'Connell got married, she doubted they would be able to afford anything so lavish as the house Deirdre lived in, but with Brian's architectural knowledge and carpentry skills, they would certainly be able to create a nice home.

A blush crept up Emma's neck to her face. Here she was fantasizing about marrying Brian when they'd barely begun dating. She knew he was beginning to see her as girlfriend material, but he needed time to heal from a failed engagement that had left him scarred and somewhat wary.

Emma glanced around the dining room admiring the beautiful carved marble fireplace, the arched windows partially concealed behind plantation shutters and the exquisite antique dining table and chairs.

The caterer, Lucy Monroe, had created a gorgeous spread for the occasion with her famous cheese straws taking pride of place. She was one of Emma's mother's oldest friends. Emma had grown up knowing her as Aunt Lucy, and no Taylor occasion had been complete without some goodies created by Lucy. Emma took one of the small plates Deirdre had set out and helped herself to an assortment of hors d'oeuvres. She had just taken a bite of a deliciously light mille-feuille wrapped around some kind of mushroom mixture when Jessica came up to her.

Jessica's face was the picture of dissatisfaction—brows lowered threateningly, mouth turned down and eyes narrowed. "How dare that woman! Who does she think she is." She glared at Emma as if Marjorie's outburst had been her fault. "Just who is she anyway?"

"Marjorie Porter," Emma mumbled around the bit of pastry in her mouth. She swallowed quickly. "Our hostess's mother-in-law. She's the heir to the Davenport fortune."

Jessica wrinkled her brow. "Why does that sound familiar?"

"After the Mitchums started the Paris Toilet Company and created the antiperspirant, which they named Mitchum after themselves, the Davenports started a line of bleaching creams that made them almost but not quite as much money," Emma explained.

Jessica snorted. "Still doesn't give her the right to browbeat other people. I feel sorry for poor Deirdre having *that* woman as a mother-in-law. Deirdre and I were sorority sisters—did I tell you?"

"Yes."

"Phi Mu. My mother was a Phi Mu and her mother before her. I always knew I would join as well."

"Really?"

"And Rose isn't in the least bit demented, although I hate to use that term. We prefer to talk about memory issues rather than dementia. No, Rose is perfectly fine in that department, but she does suffer from severe osteoporosis and is all bent over, the poor dear."

"Oh," was all Emma could think to say.

"Look, there's Charlotte Fanning. I must go say hello."

Jessica walked off toward a tall, exquisitely coiffed, champagne blond woman who was dripping with expensive jewelry. Emma watched idly as she chewed on one of Lucy's cheese straws. The blond woman stiffened when she noticed Jessica approaching her. Jessica smiled and held out her hand, but instead of returning Jessica's handshake, the woman ignored the proffered gesture and instead, turned on her heel and stalked away. Jessica was left standing with her hand stuck out in midair.

What was that all about? Emma wondered. But before she could think about it any more, Bitsy came up to her. She had a plate of hors d'oeuvres as well and was nibbling on the end of a cheese straw.

"If I had known *she* was going to be here, I wouldn't have come." Bitsy tipped her head toward Jessica, who had recovered her aplomb and was filling her plate at the buffet table.

"Jessica?" Emma said, to be sure.

Bitsy nodded. "I can't stand that woman. When we were in college—"

"Excuse me, dear, but could you lend a hand?" Arabella

put an arm around Emma. "Hello, Bitsy. I'm looking forward to your delicious cupcakes."

"I'm sorry, Aunt Arabella." Emma put her plate down and dabbed at her lips with her napkin. "I'll be right there."

"That's perfectly all right, dear. I'm glad you're enjoying yourself. Sylvia and I have made any number of sales." Arabella's cheeks pinked up from excitement. She wound the long blue and white print scarf she was wearing through her hands. "I'm very, very pleased. But we do need some help getting that nightgown and peignoir off dear Melanie for the trip home."

Emma couldn't help it. She started to laugh.

"What's so funny, dear? I do wish you'd let me in on the joke," Arabella said dryly.

Emma related the incident with the police on the way to Deirdre's house, and soon Arabella and Bitsy were joining in the laughter.

Arabella dabbed at her eyes. "Perhaps we should leave the garments on poor Melanie then. We don't want the dear girl getting a ticket for being a public nuisance. That would be rather harsh, don't you think?"

By the time Emma finished helping Arabella and Sylvia pack up, Deirdre was clearing the food from the table.

Emma picked up a platter that was empty save for a few curls of parsley.

"Oh, don't bother," Deirdre said from across the table where she was stacking dirty plates. "Gladys can take care of it." Deirdre motioned toward a timid-looking red-haired girl skulking in the corner. Her face was ghostly white except where peppered with ginger-colored freckles.

"It's no problem," Emma said. "I'm happy to help."

"Thanks." Deirdre smiled. "You can leave it on the counter. Gladys can load the dishwasher after everyone is gone."

Emma leaned against the swinging door to the kitchen and pushed it open. Deirdre's kitchen was as exquisite as the rest of the house with a huge island in the center, granite countertops, a brick fireplace and a huge, antique dresser against the far wall displaying an impressive collection of china and pottery. French doors led to a brick terrace surrounded by well-tended gardens.

Gladys came into the kitchen behind Emma, her hands full of precariously balanced plates. Emma took a stack from her quickly.

"Don't want these to fall."

Gladys smiled her thanks.

"Have you worked for Deirdre long?" Emma tried to draw the girl out.

She nodded mutely. "I help out a few of the other ladies, and I work part-time at Sunny Days as an aide."

She clamped her thin lips closed as if she'd already revealed too much.

Emma left the dishes on the counter as instructed. Gladys was already rinsing the stack of plates she'd brought in from the dining room.

Emma noticed that three white boxes, tied with string, were stacked on the island, and she recognized them as coming from Sprinkles. They must be Bitsy's cupcakes. Bitsy made delicious cupcakes in all sorts of unusual flavors and decorated them with edible flowers that Liz provided from her garden. Her shop was full all day long with people looking to satisfy their sweet tooth.

Emma put a hand against the door to the dining room, but it wouldn't budge. She stepped aside, perplexed, but a second later the door swung to and Marjorie stepped into the kitchen.

"I'm so sorry," she said, sounding anything but. "Were you trying to get through the door?"

Emma nodded and smiled to show that she hadn't taken offense in any way and then pushed her way through the door and back into the dining room.

Everything had been cleared, and Deirdre was putting out cups and saucers for coffee and tea as well as delicate porcelain plates for dessert. Some women had drifted back toward the living room, while others were still standing around, nursing glasses of punch or nibbling on the last of their hors d'oeuvres.

Emma chatted with a few of the women, and several asked for her business card. Many had never been to Sweet Nothings before, and she was happy to have the opportunity to spread the word.

A few minutes later, Marjorie came back through the swinging door with a platter of cupcakes in her hand.

"I do hope you don't mind, Deirdre. I thought I would make myself useful and put these out for you."

Deirdre gave a tight smile. "That's fine, Marjorie. Thank you for your help."

"I thought I would pass them around, if that's all right with you."

Deirdre nodded, her smile getting even tighter.

Marjorie held the tray toward Jessica.

"Oh, those look delicious," Jessica said, peering at the display in Marjorie's hand. "Are those flowers edible?" She pointed at the multicolored pansies, violets and other small flowers adorning the tops of the cupcakes.

"They are." Bitsy piped up from where she was standing near the entrance to the dining room. "There are a number of edible flowers, but they must be grown organically without pesticides."

"I can vouch for these." Liz stepped farther into the room. "I grew them myself in my garden."

"I can't wait to try one," Jessica said, her hand hovering over the platter. "Mother always said it was rude to reach across a serving plate to select an item from the back." Jessica reached for the closest cupcake.

"My mama would have slapped my hand if I'd done that," a woman in a bright magenta silk blouse said as she, too, selected the nearest cupcake when Marjorie approached her with the tray.

While Marjorie handed round the rest of the cupcakes, Emma helped Deirdre pass out cups of tea and coffee. Emma was stirring a spoon of sugar into her tea when someone grabbed her elbow.

It was Jessica. Her face was the color of oatmeal, and there were drops of perspiration on her forehead.

"Do you know where the powder room is?"

"Yes, it's just down the hall there." Emma pointed toward the corridor. "Are you okay?"

Jessica shook her head. "I must have eaten something that disagreed with me. I'll be fine." She moved at a quick pace in the direction Emma had indicated.

"Is she okay?" Deirdre said, coming up behind Emma.

"She said she thinks she ate something that didn't agree with her."

"She looked terrible." Deirdre furrowed her brow. "I'll give her a few minutes and then go check on her."

Emma milled around, chatting with different people, but always with an eye out for Jessica. Suddenly she realized it had been ten minutes since the woman had disappeared in the direction of the powder room. The same thought must have occurred to Deirdre, because just then she came up to Emma.

"Has Jessica come back yet? I don't see her."

Emma shook her head. "No, I don't think so."

"I'm going to check on her." Deirdre put down the cup she was holding and walked purposefully toward the hallway.

Emma wondered if she ought to follow, but before she could decide, she heard a scream, and Deirdre burst into the room.

"Someone call nine-one-one! Jessica has taken ill, and we need to get help right away."

"Is there anything I can do?" Emma whispered to Deirdre.

She shook her head. "I don't think so. She's unconscious, and it's obvious she's been very sick." She wrung her hands together. "I've covered her with a blanket and put something under her head, but there's nothing more we can do. I have no idea what happened to her." She looked around. "Oh, I do wish the ambulance would hurry."

Just then the wail of a siren pierced the Saturday afternoon quiet.

"I'd better open the door." Deirdre headed out toward the front hall.

All conversation stopped as they watched a man and a woman wheel a stretcher down the hall toward Deirdre's powder room. Conversation resumed, but in hushed tones, as they waited for the ambulance crew to reappear.

Fifteen minutes later, they heard the sounds of wheels on the wood floor, and within seconds the stretcher was being wheeled past the dining room on the way to the front door, only this time a passenger was strapped to it, shrouded in blankets.

Deirdre chewed on the skin on the side of her thumbnail. "I hope she's going to be okay," she whispered to Emma as if it had suddenly become improper to speak out loud.

Conversation broke out again as soon as the door closed behind Jessica and the stretcher.

"Do you think it was something she ate?" a woman suggested.

"We all ate the same thing," Deirdre pointed out.

"It could have been some kind of allergy," the woman shot back.

"I wish we knew what was going on," someone else wailed plaintively.

"We could call the hospital," another suggested. Emma noticed it was the woman with the washed out–looking red hair.

"I don't think they're going to tell us anything, our not being relatives," the woman in the expensive-looking pant-suit said.

"It might be best if I handle this." Marjorie drew herself up to her full height, head high, bosom thrust forward. She looked annoyed, as if Jessica had ruined Deirdre's party on purpose. "I'll get my things, and then I'll be off to the hospital to find out what is going on. I'm on the board. They'll have to talk to me."

They all watched as Marjorie marched out the front door a moment later. Groups clustered here and there in the living room and dining room. Everyone was obviously reluctant to leave until they heard about Jessica. Deirdre put on another pot of coffee, but no one was anxious to touch any of the leftover food.

Finally, after what felt to Emma like an eternity of small talk, the front door opened and Marjorie walked in. All heads turned immediately in her direction. She very deliberately removed her jacket, put down her handbag and then stood in front of the group.

"I'm afraid I have very bad news."

A gasp went through the crowd at her words.

"I'm sorry to have to tell you that Jessica did not make it."

A half dozen women began shouting questions, but Marjorie held up her hand, and they quieted down.

"The cause of death is currently inconclusive. There will be an autopsy at which point we will all know more. The doctors have said, however, that it seems to have been something to do with her heart."

Chapter 4

EMMA spent an uneasy Sunday unable to settle down to anything. She would pick up a book or turn on the television, but soon her concentration was diverted by thoughts of what had happened at Deirdre's party. She felt terrible about Jessica even though she hadn't really liked the woman all that much. She hoped they would soon find out what went wrong. Perhaps Jessica had had some kind of heart condition that no one knew about?

It was something of a relief when Monday morning arrived and she was able to go down to Sweet Nothings and start a new day.

"For once I'm glad it's Monday," said Arabella, who arrived shortly after Emma. She unclipped Pierre's leash, and Pierre made a dash for his dog bed.

"I feel the same way."

"I can't get that poor girl out of my mind."

A long, drawn-out cough heralded Sylvia's arrival, and both Arabella and Emma turned toward the door. Sylvia yanked her portable oxygen tank over the threshold and parked it in the corner. "What a weekend," she said as she tucked her purse under the counter. "First all that excitement on Saturday at Deirdre Porter's, and then yesterday, bingo with the ladies in the home. My head is reeling," she commented dryly.

Arabella took off her jacket and went into the back to hang it up.

"I know what you mean. My head is reeling, too. And on top of it," Arabella said as she stuck her head around the corner, "I had a call from Les."

"What? Is he asking you out again?" Emma went to stand in the doorway. Les was Arabella's longtime on-again, off-again beau. He ran the Toggery, the oldest shop in Paris. She had been spending less and less time with him since meeting Francis.

"Yes." Arabella sighed. "I managed to put him off by saying I had to check my calendar." She fiddled with the button on her blouse. "I do like Les, it's just that . . . Oh, I don't know! It's because of Francis of course."

"Well, if you're not planning to marry Francis, then why not go out with both of them?"

"Do you really think that's okay?" Arabella looked unsure. She tipped a bag of dog food into Pierre's empty dish. At the sound of the nuggets hitting the metal bowl, Pierre roused himself from his bed and ambled over to see what was on offer.

Sylvia snorted. "Why not?"

"It's just that I feel guilty."

"It's not as if you were stringing either of them along," Emma said. "You've always been open about not wanting a serious relationship."

"That is true," Arabella said, although she didn't look completely convinced.

Sylvia shrugged and went back to straightening a drawer full of camisoles. "Everyone in the retirement home is talking about that girl, Jessica, dropping dead at our trunk show."

Emma noticed Arabella cringe slightly at Sylvia's blunt statement and gave a small smile. New Yorkers weren't known for sugarcoating their words, whereas Southern ladies employed so much sweetener it was enough to give anyone cavities.

"Does anyone at Sunny Days know Jessica well?" Emma asked. "Was there something wrong with her that might have caused her to take ill suddenly?"

Sylvia blew out a puff of air. "Don't know, really. I don't think anyone was all that close to her. And believe me, no one is crying in their soup to see her go."

"That's awfully harsh." Arabella put down the garment she was examining.

Sylvia shrugged. "I'm only repeating what I heard."

Emma was thinking about that when the bell over the front door tinkled and two women entered.

"Can I help you?" Emma said.

The taller of the two shook her head. "We're just looking, thanks."

Emma went back to arranging some of the new stock that had just come in. She removed one of the vintage peignoir and negligee sets from where it was hanging on the door of one of the open distressed white armoires, and she replaced it with the bed jacket Arabella had picked up at the estate sale.

The bell tinkled again, and two more customers arrived. By the time Emma had waited on them, several more had arrived, and they did a brisk business all morning.

Finally, the last woman left, swinging a black-and-white shopping bag printed with *Sweet Nothings*. It was almost noon.

The bell over the front door pinged again, and Emma stifled a groan. *Would she never get a chance to sit down?* She looked up to see Brian O'Connell pushing open the door. She felt a smile broaden across her face. She hadn't expected to see Brian today. He had his hands full pitching in at his father's hardware store, across the street from Sweet Nothings, while getting his architectural renovation company off the ground.

"Hello, ladies." Brian's blue eyes crinkled with pleasure as he ran a hand through his brown hair, leaving it adorably mussed. His tall frame seemed to fill their small shop.

"Brian!" Arabella said, grasping his arms and giving him an air-kiss on both cheeks. "What brings you to Sweet Nothings?"

"Just checking up on some of my favorite ladies."

His smile made Emma feel warm all over.

"I also wondered if Emma"—he smiled in her direction—"might be free for some lunch. I have time for a quick bite at the Coffee Klatch."

"I'd love to, but I hate to leave Aunt Arabella and Sylvia alone."

Sylvia gave a sound like a water buffalo snorting, and Arabella said, "Don't be ridiculous, dear. We can handle things on our own. You go ahead."

Emma felt a warm glow as she retrieved her jacket from the stockroom and slipped into it. *Lunch with Brian.* Things were certainly looking up.

THE Coffee Klatch had started life as the Paris Diner, and despite new, young, hip owners, a fancy espresso machine and a different name, it was still essentially the Paris Diner as far as the townspeople were concerned.

It was a few minutes before noon, but all the booths and tables were already taken and a handful of people were milling around the hostess stand waiting for something to open up. When you got up before dawn and had breakfast by six a.m., you were pretty darned hungry by noon. Emma thought back to her days in New York when no one booked lunch before one thirty and you made dinner reservations for eight o'clock or later.

The hostess, a tall, blond girl wearing a pair of cowboy boots with a long black skirt and white blouse, and with a stack of menus tucked under her arm, led the first group of four toward a booth near the kitchen.

"It shouldn't be too long," Brian said as he smiled down at Emma.

Emma didn't care how long it took—she was enjoying being with Brian.

Finally, the hostess came back, led them to a small table and laid two menus down. "Waitress'll be with you in a minute," she said, and she turned her back quickly, heading toward the front of the Coffee Klatch.

Before Emma could say anything, Mabel sidled up to their table, pencil and pad at the ready. "Something to drink?" she said economically. Mabel had started at the Coffee Klatch's previous incarnation, the Paris Diner, right after high school, and now, twenty years later, the place wouldn't be the same without her.

Brian looked at Emma inquiringly.

"I'll have a glass of sweet tea, please."

Mabel scribbled on her pad and then looked at Brian. "Drink?"

"I'll have the same." Brian smiled at Mabel, and her face softened.

"Gotcha." She scribbled on her pad again and started to turn away.

"How is Marshall?" Brian asked, referring to Mabel's young son.

The way Mabel's face changed, it was as if the sun were coming out. "Oh, he's doing so well in first grade! The teacher put him in the Lions group—that's the advanced reading group. My Marshall is that smart!" And she headed toward the kitchen with a huge grin on her face.

"Now that that's settled . . ." Brian said as he looked at Emma, and she smiled back. Brian shook his head. "I've been so busy, I've barely had time to breathe. Every time I passed Sweet Nothings I wanted to stop in and say hello. Bobby Fuller has done an admirable job of overseeing the hardware store, but there are still some things I need to take care of myself, and I was either needed there, or I was under the gun on one of my renovation jobs." He touched the back of Emma's hand. "I've missed you. Tell me what's been happening."

Emma tried to ignore the sensations the touch of his hand on hers was causing. She took a deep breath and told him about the trunk show and Jessica's death.

Brian let out a soft whistle. "Certainly sounds like you've had your share of excitement. How is Miss Arabella? And Sylvia?"

Brian had come to know them both during his recent renovation of Sweet Nothings.

"They're fine." Emma explained about Sylvia's move to Sunny Days.

Brian laughed. "I can imagine she's keeping them on

their toes there." He looked Emma in the eye. "And how about you? Everything okay?"

"Sure. Fine."

Mabel arrived with their drinks, and they were momentarily silent as she slid them onto the table. "Ready to order?" She pulled her notepad from the pocket of her frilly apron.

Brian frowned and glanced at the menu quickly. "Do you know what you want?" He lowered it and looked at Emma.

"I'll have the turkey club."

Mabel nodded, jotted something on her pad and looked at Brian with her penciled eyebrows raised.

"I'll have the pulled pork with extra barbecue sauce on the side." Brian handed his menu to Mabel.

"Fries?"

"Yes, please."

Mabel replaced the pad in her pocket and headed toward the kitchen.

"I've been meaning to call you." Brian took a long sip of his iced tea. "I was hoping we could go to dinner or catch a movie or something. It's been too long."

Emma was surprised to note that Brian seemed a bit . . . shy?

"I've just been so darned busy. All I can manage when I get home at night is to fall asleep on the couch watching television." He picked up the salt shaker and began to twirl it between his fingers. "I've got something to ask you," he said finally.

"Yes?"

"This college buddy of mine is getting married this weekend. His name's Chip. We played soccer together. He's a good guy. He and Megan have known each other forever."

Brian took another long sip of his tea. "I sort of hoped you wouldn't mind going to the wedding with me. It's at the Beauchamp Hotel and Spa. Hopefully it shouldn't be too boring."

A wedding! Brian was asking her to a *wedding*. Emma felt a rush of warmth flood her face. She tried to maintain some semblance of cool, but it was an epic fail.

"Yes," she gushed without even thinking.

"Thanks." Brian looked relieved. "I'd hoped you'd say yes. As a matter of fact, I already told them I was bringing someone." He grinned. "I kept meaning to call, but it's always so late when I get home. Besides, I was half afraid you'd say no." He wiped a hand across his forehead. "You're doing me a huge favor."

EMMA pushed open the door to Sweet Nothings. Arabella was standing behind the counter turning the pages of a magazine. Sylvia was sitting on one of the toile-covered love seats, chin on chest and eyes closed. They both jumped to attention when they heard Emma enter.

Sylvia gave a deep rumbling cough, and Arabella said, "How was your lunch?"

"Okay, I guess." Emma slipped out of her jacket and went into the back room to hang it up. When she emerged, both Arabella and Sylvia were looking concerned.

"Didn't you have a good time?" Arabella fiddled with the ends of the black-and-white scarf she was wearing.

"Oh, it was fine."

"Okay, out with it," Sylvia barked. "Tell Auntie Sylvia what happened."

Emma slumped against the counter, her chin propped in

her hands. "Brian asked me to do him a favor and go to a friend's wedding with him."

"But that's wonderful!" Arabella crowed.

"Don't see anything wrong with that," Sylvia concurred.

"There isn't anything wrong with it. Not really," Emma admitted. "It's the way he put it. I thought he was asking me on a date . . . to a wedding . . . but then he thanked me for doing him a favor." She appealed to Arabella and then Sylvia. "I really thought he was beginning to see me as something more than just his kid sister's best friend."

"Well, he will soon," Arabella said briskly. "This is your chance. A wedding is the perfect romantic occasion to turn things around. There'll be champagne, and dancing, and candlelight . . ."

Sylvia nodded her head in approval. "It will give you the chance to wear a spectacular dress. Something that will really make Brian sit up and take notice."

Emma felt her spirits rise. "You're right." She gave a wicked grin. "Brian isn't going to know what hit him."

"Go get 'em, girl," Sylvia said before lapsing into a coughing fit that sent Arabella running for a glass of water.

Emma was musing on what she might wear to the wedding when the door slowly opened and a gentleman stuck his head into the shop. He had dark hair and eyes, and when he smiled, Emma almost found herself forgetting all about her date with Brian.

"Can I help you?" She stepped out from behind the counter. Men were sometimes their best customers, opening their wallets wide to please a wife or girlfriend.

"Detective Bradley Walker, ma'am. I was hoping you might be willing to answer a few questions."

"About what?" Emma's hand flew to her throat, and she

turned to look at Arabella and Sylvia. "Where is Chuck Reilly? Doesn't he usually—"

"Detective Reilly is on vacation, ma'am," Walker answered smoothly.

"Oh," Emma said. Not that she wanted to encounter Chuck Reilly ever, ever again! They'd dated briefly in high school, but Emma had soon come to her senses and realized that Chuck's good looks were only skin-deep. He'd been especially obnoxious to her during the investigation into her ex-boyfriend's murder, and if she never set eyes on him again, that would be fine!

"Detective Walker," Arabella said smoothly, gliding forward with her hand outstretched. "Please come in. We'd be more than happy to answer any questions you have if you would be so kind as to tell us what this is all about."

"I gather you attended a party on Saturday at the home of . . ." He consulted his notes briefly. "Mrs. Deirdre Porter?" He looked up at Emma.

"That's correct."

"Actually, Detective, we all did." Arabella made a gesture that encompassed Emma, herself and Sylvia.

Walker looked up from his notebook and smiled. "Thank you, ma'am, that's most helpful to know."

"But what is this all about, Detective?" Arabella drew herself up and gifted Walker with her most imperious look.

"Well, ma'am, as I'm sure you are aware, a young woman took ill at the party and subsequently died. We're in the process of looking into the events leading up to her death."

Arabella's eyes widened. "Good heavens! You don't mean the death is suspicious?"

"I'm sorry, ma'am, but I'm not really at liberty to say. Could you tell me"—he glanced at Arabella, Emma and

Sylvia in turn—"did you all partake of the food offered at Mrs. Porter's party?"

"Why, yes," Arabella said immediately.

Emma and Sylvia both nodded.

"And the cupcakes?"

"Of course. They were delicious." Arabella looked offended that he even had the nerve to ask.

"I see." Walker made some notations in his notebook. "And I presume none of you suffered any ill effects after the party?"

Emma, Arabella and Sylvia all shook their heads in unison.

"Did you know the victim, Jessica Scott, well?"

Emma answered first. "I didn't know her at all. We met at the party."

Arabella shook her head. "Same here."

Sylvia gave a bark of a cough before answering. "I didn't know her, but I know she runs the old folks home my kids have stuck me in."

Walker nodded and added to the notes he'd already taken.

"Did any of you ladies help prepare or serve the food?"

Once again all three shook their heads.

"I helped clean up," Emma clarified.

Walker nodded. "Who did serve the food, do you know?"

"Most of it was already out on the table when we went into the dining room."

Walker's eyebrows rose a fraction of an inch. "Where were you before that?"

"We were in the living room." This time Arabella answered. "The party was actually a trunk show, and we were doing our presentation. Everyone except our hostess had gathered together at that point."

"So no one slipped out?"

Arabella shrugged and looked at Emma and Sylvia.

"All I can say is I didn't see anyone leave," Sylvia piped up.

"Me, neither," Emma agreed, and Arabella nodded her head.

"How about the dessert—the cupcakes. Were they out on the table as well?"

Emma shook her head. "No. Marjorie Porter, Deirdre's mother-in-law, passed those around."

Walker's eyebrows rose another fraction of an inch, and he quickly jotted another note.

"I do wish you would tell us what this is about." Arabella sniffed.

"I'm sorry, ma'am, I'm sure you'll be told in good time." He slapped his notebook closed. "Thank you for your time."

Heavy silence hung over Sweet Nothings as the door closed on Detective Walker's departure.

"I can't imagine what that was all about!" Arabella stalked toward the stockroom. "I could use a big glass of sweet tea right about now. Anyone else?"

Emma and Sylvia murmured their assent, and Arabella disappeared into the back room.

Emma was unpacking a box of new lingerie she'd ordered from Monique Berthole in New York when the door to Sweet Nothings was flung open so hard it nearly ricocheted off the wall. Arabella had just come out of the stockroom with a pitcher of tea and a tray of glasses. They all looked up, startled.

Bitsy stood in the doorway, drawn up to her full six feet. Her eyes were red and puffy, as if she'd been crying, but the look on her face was one of pure anger.

"What's wrong?" Emma dropped the panties she was folding and rushed over to Bitsy.

"Oooh, I am spittin' mad right now!" She thumped her fist in the air like that scene in *Gone with the Wind* where Scarlett O'Hara vowed never to be hungry again.

Arabella was her usual cool, calm self. She poured a big glass of sweet tea and advanced on Bitsy. "You sit yourself down, missy, and take a sip of this. And then you tell us exactly what is going on."

Bitsy took a couple of gulps of the iced tea and slowly her breathing became more regular. "Oh, that is good." She put down the glass and sighed.

"Now, what is it that has you so upset?"

"Well," Bitsy began, and Emma noticed two bright red spots appearing on her cheeks. "This policeman came around to the shop. Said he was a detective." She tossed her blond mane contemptuously. "Started asking me all these questions."

"I imagine he's the same one who came around here. He asked us a passel of questions, too," Arabella said.

"At first it was about this and that, nothing much." Bitsy took a long sip of her tea. "But then he started talking about the food at Deirdre's party. Who prepared it, who served it, things like that. And then"—the red spots on her cheeks intensified—"he told me that Jessica was poisoned!" She drew the word out slowly and furiously. "And he thought my cupcakes were responsible!"

"But your cupcakes were only one of the many things eaten at the party," Arabella said.

Bitsy raised an eyebrow. "That obnoxious detective said Jessica had been poisoned by foxglove."

"Foxglove? What's that?" Emma asked.

"It's a common plant. All of it is poisonous—the leaves, the stalk and the flowers. The flowers are very pretty. That detective seems to think that I somehow mistook a foxglove flower for something harmless and put it on one of those cupcakes!" Bitsy exhaled furiously.

Emma froze. All the flowers for Bitsy's cupcakes came from Liz's garden.

Had Liz made a terrible mistake? One that had cost Jessica Scott her life?

Chapter 5

IT took several glasses of sweet tea to calm Bitsy down. Arabella had to make a fresh pitcher. For once, Emma was grateful that the shop was empty. She glanced at Arabella and was concerned to see that she looked rather shaken.

"Aunt Arabella, let me pour the tea and why don't you go sit down?"

"Thank you, dear, I don't mind if I do." She eased herself onto the love seat next to Sylvia, who was the only one who appeared to be taking things in her stride.

Emma took over pouring refills on the tea, glancing from time to time at Arabella to make sure she was okay. All of this coming on the heels of the murder at Sweet Nothings in June might be too much for her.

Arabella took a long sip of her tea, and Emma was pleased to note that a soft blush of color appeared in her previously ashen cheeks. Arabella put her glass down suddenly. "But you didn't even know that woman. What was her name again?" she appealed to Emma.

"Jessica. Jessica Scott."

"You didn't even know her before the trunk show, did you? Why would the police think you had any reason to harm her?"

Bitsy looked down at her lap. She reached for her tea, and Emma noticed that her hand shook slightly. "Right now they seem to think the whole thing was an accident, but . . ."

"But what?" Arabella sat up slightly straighter. "It's best to tell us everything, then we can decide on a course of action. I can always speak to Francis if need be."

Bitsy heaved a sigh and stretched her long legs out in front of her. "Jessica and I actually knew each other in college."

"UT? University of Tennessee?"

Bitsy nodded. "We were both rushing the same sorority, Phi Mu. There was only one spot open, and we both wanted it. Jessica's mother had been a Phi Mu and her grandmother before her."

"She told us that," Emma said.

Arabella nodded. "At least twice, I'm quite certain."

"I certainly didn't have any such illustrious heritage." Bitsy rolled her eyes. "My parents didn't even go to college, and they weren't particularly keen on my joining a sorority for fear I wouldn't fit in with all those *snobby girls*, as they always called them." She sighed again. "I don't know if you remember it or not, but around that time there was a case involving a man named Gerald Palmer—same last name as mine but absolutely no relation—who was wanted for embezzling a huge amount of money from some charity." Bitsy paused and had a sip of her tea. She closed her eyes and let out a huge breath. "Well, Jessica started a rumor that

that man—Gerald Palmer—was my father. He wasn't, but it didn't matter. She was voted in, and I wasn't."

"Oh!" Arabella half rose to her feet in indignation.

"What a dirty deed!" Sylvia exclaimed.

"It was, wasn't it? She apparently thought it was perfectly fair in order for her to get what she wanted."

"But that's terrible," Sylvia said. "I mean it's terrible that she did that to you, but right now, the bad news is"—Sylvia shifted around in her seat—"it makes you prime suspect number one as they say on those cop shows."

"I know." Bitsy hung her head.

"You know what I would like to know?" Arabella turned toward Bitsy. "Where do those flowers come from anyway? The ones you put on your cupcakes."

Bitsy shot a panicked glance at Emma and bit her lip before answering. "They come from Liz Banning's garden."

"Liz, did you say?" Arabella put a hand to her ear.

Bitsy nodded.

"Our Liz?" Arabella turned to Emma for confirmation. "Liz Banning?"

Bitsy nodded again, her mouth pulled down into a frown.

"Oh dear!" Arabella jumped and tea sloshed out of her glass and down the front of her dress.

"We've got to warn Liz." Emma grabbed her purse and began digging for her cell. "Did you tell the police the flowers came from her?"

"I had to." Bitsy's tone was apologetic. "They asked me. I couldn't lie."

"You're absolutely right." Arabella got up from her seat and went to put her arm around Bitsy's shoulders. "They would have found out anyway."

"We've got to warn Liz," Emma repeated as she upended

her purse and dumped the contents onto the counter. She grabbed her phone and began punching in Liz's number. Suddenly she stopped abruptly.

"It might be better if I drove out there and talked to her in person." She looked to Arabella for approval.

"I think that would be very wise, dear."

AS soon as the Sweet Nothings *open* sign was flipped to *closed*, Emma jumped in the bright yellow used Volkswagen Beetle she'd bought several months after arriving back home in Paris. After driving Arabella's Mini, she didn't want to try maneuvering around town in some hulking SUV. The Bug, as she referred to it, was just the right size.

Liz lived outside of town in her childhood home, which she and her husband had renovated and expanded. Emma suspected they might all be sitting down to dinner, and she hoped she wouldn't be interrupting them.

Liz's station wagon was pulled up to the garage when Emma got there, but she was relieved to see that Brian's red pickup truck wasn't. He spent a lot of time at his sister's, and she didn't feel up to facing him at the moment.

Liz had an apron tied around her waist when she answered the door.

"Emma! How nice to see you." Her freckled face broke into a huge grin. "You're just in time for supper. Nothing special, I'm afraid. The kids wanted mac and cheese, although I did make it myself, and not from a box. And don't tell them," Liz's voice dropped to a whisper, "that I added some Asiago and Parmesan to the usual cheddar."

"I don't mean to intrude," Emma protested.

"Nonsense. You know Ben and Alice will be thrilled to see you."

Just then Ben skidded into the hallway and came to a stop in front of Emma. "Aunt Emma!" He jumped up and down in his stocking feet.

Liz ruffled his hair affectionately. "I heard Brian asked you to Chip's wedding." She couldn't hide her smile.

Emma shrugged. "He asked me to do him a *favor*." She made a face.

"A favor?" Liz laughed. "Don't kid yourself. It's a date. I assume you're going." There was no doubt in Liz's voice.

"Of course."

"Do you have a dress? We could go shopping in Memphis and find something that will make my thickheaded brother sit up and take notice."

Emma thought about her closet stuffed full of clothing and the plastic storage bins under her bed. "Yes, let's."

Emma hated having to bring up the reason for her visit, but there was no getting around it. "I have something to tell you," she said in a low voice to Liz. "Could we . . ."

"Ben. Go wash your hands." Liz pointed down the hall, and after a feeble protest, Ben obeyed.

"Let's sit in here." Liz led the way into the living room.

The living room had a high, beamed ceiling and a window seat that ran beneath the bay window. Comfortable, overstuffed chairs and sofas were grouped in front of the stone fireplace.

Emma perched on the edge of a chair and waited while Liz took a seat on the sofa. She looked at her friend's face and hesitated. She wasn't sure how to begin.

She cleared her throat. "Bitsy had a visit from the police."

"What?" Liz's face collapsed into lines of worry.

"They told her that Jessica died from foxglove poisoning."

Liz's hand flew to her mouth. "Foxglove is a plant. Everyone knows it's poisonous. How did—"

"They think a foxglove flower was used to decorate one of Bitsy's cupcakes."

"But all those flowers come from me, and I would never, ever use foxglove." Liz glanced toward the window. "I don't even grow it in my garden. Heaven forbid the children would get into it." She shuddered, and Emma noticed her clasped hands tighten. She looked at Emma. "There's got to be some explanation."

"I'm sure the police will figure it all out. Fortunately, Chuck Reilly is away on vacation. Another detective came to see us at Sweet Nothings, and he seems much more on the ball."

"The police have been to Sweet Nothings?" Liz's eyes widened in alarm.

Just then the doorbell rang, echoing three or four times before dying away.

"Honey, will you get it?" Matt, Liz's husband, called from the kitchen.

Liz turned to Emma with a look of panic on her face. "Who could it be? We're not expecting anyone."

"Maybe it's Brian?"

Liz's shoulders relaxed slightly. "You're right. It's probably Brian. He has a knack for knowing when I'm about to put dinner on the table." She smiled briefly.

Emma followed Liz to the door and held her breath while Liz pulled it open.

Detective Walker was standing on the steps. "Mrs. Banning?"

Liz nodded, her eyes round with fear.

"Could I have a word, please?"

Chapter 6

"LIZ? What is it? Who's here?" Matt Banning strode down the hall toward the front door.

Emma knew he worked as a software designer, but to her, he looked every inch the cowboy from his boots to his checked shirt. He was drying his hands on a towel, and his eyes were dark with concern.

He put his arm around Liz and looked Detective Walker up and down. "What can we do for you?"

Walker pulled out an identification card and handed it to Matt. "We're investigating the death of a Ms. Jessica Scott at a party that your wife attended on Saturday afternoon."

Matt looked from Walker to Liz, his eyebrows raised. "Quite a lot of people were at that party. Why are you questioning Liz?"

"Ms. Scott apparently ingested foxglove, a highly poisonous plant. The hostess served cupcakes that were decorated with edible flowers apparently grown by Mrs. Banning. We are looking into the possibility that foxglove was mistakenly used as one of the decorations."

"Liz would never make a mistake like that!" Matt stood even straighter, and Emma thought he looked taller than his normal six feet, four inches.

"I understand how you feel, sir," Walker said diplomatically, his gaze sweeping the foyer and the living room beyond. "We would like your permission to search your yard and garden if you don't mind."

For a minute it looked as if Matt was going to say he minded very much, but then his shoulders slumped and he said, "Fine. If that will prove to you that my wife had nothing to do with this tragic mistake, go right ahead."

Walker nodded, turned on his heel and called out to several men who were waiting in the driveway. He spoke briefly to them, and then they all disappeared around the edge of the garage, into the backyard.

Matt shut the door with a little more vigor than was necessary, exhaling so forcefully that Emma couldn't help but think of a bull blasting air from its nostrils prior to charging the matador.

"They have a lot of nerve!" he declared. His face had turned a dark, dusky red, and his eyes were sparking.

Liz linked her arm through his. "You were right, dear. Best to let them get on with their search. They're not going to find anything. I'm confident of that. Let's not let it spoil our dinner." She turned toward Emma. "You are staying, aren't you?"

Emma nodded and followed Liz and Matt into the kitchen where Liz bustled around setting a place for Emma and dishing out portions of macaroni and cheese. The children had already eaten, and Matt removed their plates from the table and put them in the dishwasher.

Emma's appetite had deserted her, and she pushed her portion around and around on her plate hoping Liz wouldn't notice she wasn't eating. When she looked up, she saw that Liz was doing the same thing, and the only one eating with any gusto was Matt.

The kitchen table was in a niche created by a large bay window that overlooked the backyard and Liz's gardens. They could see the policemen traipsing up and down the rows of flowers in the fading light. Emma glanced at Liz. Liz smiled, but Emma could see the worry in her eyes and the tightness of her expression. She balled her fists in her lap. How could the police possibly think Liz had made such a criminal mistake?

"Mommy, Mommy." Alice came running into the kitchen, her blond ponytail flying, her face puckered with concern. "What are those men doing in our backyard?"

Emma noticed Matt's jaw tighten threateningly.

"It's okay," he said soothingly, "Mommy and Daddy know they're here, and it's okay."

"Okay. Can I have a cookie?" Alice pointed at a fat ceramic jar in the shape of a cat sitting on the island.

"Only one," Liz warned.

They all waited as she retrieved an oatmeal cookie and dashed off toward the family room clutching it possessively.

Twenty minutes later, both Liz and Emma had given up all pretense of eating, and Matt was on his second helping. The doorbell rang, and Liz jumped up, banging her leg against the table. Tears came into her eyes and she dashed them away quickly.

"You stay here." Matt threw down his checkered napkin. "I'll get it. I'm sure they're satisfied now and will go away and leave us alone."

Emma and Liz stayed in their seats at the table, listening to the murmur of voices drifting down the hall. Suddenly Matt raised his voice. They couldn't hear what he was saying, but it was obvious he was upset.

Liz bit her lip. "I'd better go see what's going on."

"I'll go with you." Emma pushed back her seat and jumped up.

Liz hurried toward the front door, her arms crossed protectively over her chest. "What's wrong? What's going on?" She turned to Matt and saw the look on his face. "Oh."

Walker was standing in the foyer holding what looked like a small plastic bag in his hand. He turned toward Liz. "We've searched the gardens, and while we did not find any foxglove plants within their confines," he paused momentarily, "we did find several plants beyond your property— certainly near enough to give you easy access." Walker brandished the bag he was holding, and Emma could see it contained a flower of some sort.

"But I didn't . . . I had no idea . . . that's ridiculous," Liz stammered. "Besides why would I . . ." She looked around her frantically. "I didn't even know the woman."

"What does this mean?" Matt demanded, his brows lowered threateningly.

Walker looked serious. He turned to Liz. "I have to ask that you don't leave town without letting us know."

Liz's hand flew to her mouth. "Oh."

"We appreciate your cooperation." Walker nodded toward Liz and Matt. "Good day."

* * *

ARABELLA arrived at Sweet Nothings the next morning with her usual hustle and bustle. Pierre's collar and leash jangled as she pulled him into the shop.

"Pierre! Come on," Emma coaxed.

"It's that annoying dachshund, Bertha." Arabella tut-tutted as she yanked on Pierre's leash. "Pierre has already escaped twice to see her, although it's been almost two months since the last time he managed it. Mr. Zimmerman was absolutely furious. But Pierre is quite determined to woo his Bertha, which is ridiculous. There's no way either Mr. Zimmerman or I would allow it. Can you imagine? A French bulldog and a dachshund mating?" Arabella shuddered. "It would be World War Two all over again." She laughed. "Pierre comes from a championship bloodline, and nothing must be allowed to sully it. If I ever do breed him, it will be carefully thought out."

Pierre finally gave up the tug-of-war the two of them were engaged in and skulked off toward his dog bed.

"He looks as if he imagines himself as Romeo to her Juliet."

Arabella laughed. "Romeo and Juliet indeed. Star-crossed lovers, right, Pierre?" She chucked him under the chin and scratched his back. Pierre gave a sigh of contentment, the love of his life momentarily forgotten.

Arabella wound Pierre's leash into a coil and stowed it beneath the front counter. "So tell me. How did you make out with Liz last night?"

Emma shook her head and shuddered. "Not well. I had barely gotten there when the police showed up."

Arabella gasped.

Emma looked down at her clasped hands. "They insisted on searching the Bannings' garden, but they didn't find any foxglove."

Arabella's face started to light up, and Emma held up a hand.

"But they found some very close by on the neighboring property. Within easy reach of Liz's garden."

"Oh, poor, dear, Liz! But the police couldn't possibly think that—"

"They haven't made any accusations, but they did ask her not to leave town."

Arabella gasped again. "Oh, but that sounds as if they must be serious."

Emma shrugged. "I don't know. Liz was devastated. When I left she was sitting in the dark in the living room just . . . staring. I offered to stay and help get Alice and Ben to bed, but Matt said he could manage. I wish I could do something."

"So do I." Arabella frowned. "Liz wouldn't have mistaken foxglove for an edible flower."

"Absolutely not. She's had years of experience and has taken dozens of classes. She's a Master Gardener. But if it wasn't an accident, that means someone did it on purpose to make Jessica ill or . . . or to kill her."

"That's so hard to believe!" Arabella sagged against the counter. "Liz didn't even know that woman, did she?"

"That's what she said, but other people at the party knew Jessica. And maybe one of them had it in for her for some reason."

"How will we ever find out who that might be?"

"We could start with her colleagues. She worked at that retirement community Sylvia moved to."

Arabella gave a glint of a smile. "I think it's high time we checked out Sylvia's new apartment, don't you?"

Emma smiled back. "Brilliant idea. Let's ask her when she comes in for her shift later."

"We could have a pizza party!" Arabella enthused. "It would be fun."

SUNNY Days Retirement Community did everything possible to live up to its name, Emma noticed when she and Arabella pulled into their driveway early that evening after work. The façade—a main building with several wings branching off of it—was a bright red brick, and brilliantly colored asters and mums bloomed in pots on either side of the front entrance.

Emma turned into the parking lot and found a spot for the Bug, the interior of which was perfumed with the mouthwatering aroma of freshly baked pizza. Emma grabbed the pizza boxes, and Arabella clutched a box of Bitsy's devil's food, vanilla and carrot cupcakes as they made their way back toward the entrance.

"The place looks cheerful enough," Arabella said as they entered the small lobby filled with furniture covered in a bright floral fabric. She took an experimental sniff. "And there's no smell except for that lemon air freshener."

Emma looked around. Arabella was right. The place looked comfortably homelike and very clean. She approached the front reception desk where an older woman with a halo of thin white hair and imperfectly applied red lipstick sat reading a magazine. A name badge with *Volunteer Resident* written on it was pinned to her gray cardigan. She looked up at Emma and smiled.

"Can you tell me how to get to Sylvia Brodsky's apartment?" Emma asked.

Emma was surprised when the woman smoothly typed Sylvia's name into the PC on the desk. Emma realized it was vanity to assume that only the young knew how to use computers.

The woman smiled again. "She's down that hallway toward the end. Number 204."

Emma thanked her, and she and Arabella began the journey down the long hallway, trailing the scent of pizza behind them. Most of the doors had some sort of decoration on them—a seasonal wreath, bells or fake flowers. All in all, Emma thought the place was rather nice. They passed a room with *Activities* written on a plaque next to it. The scene outside the door reminded Emma of the time the Hells Angels rode into town and stopped at the bar on Route 69, although instead of a mass of Harleys parked at the curb, here it was a tangle of walkers, wheelchairs and motorized scooters.

They found Sylvia's apartment easily enough, and Sylvia's deep rumble greeted their knock immediately.

"Come on in." Sylvia was wearing a rich burgundy caftan and had a paisley scarf tied around her hair. Her bright gold hoop earrings caught the light from the hallway and reflected it back.

"This is very nice." Arabella stopped on the threshold and took in the small living room, neatly arranged with Sylvia's things—her silver samovar taking pride of place on a round table covered with a brightly colored fringed cloth.

To Emma everything looked almost the same as it had in Sylvia's old apartment over the Taffy Pull but without the sickeningly sweet smells of sugar and vanilla permeating the air.

"Eh, it's not bad," Sylvia admitted.

An older gentleman with an ebony-topped walking stick stuck his head through the open doorway. "Oh, you've got company. Pardon me."

Sylvia patted her kerchief. "Don't be silly, Earl. Come on in. These are a couple of friends of mine. Arabella"—she swept a hand in Arabella's direction—"and her niece, Emma."

"Pleasure to meet you, ladies." He gave a sharp bow. "Don't let me disturb your party. I'll see you later tonight at cards?"

"Sure." Sylvia waved good-bye and shut the door as Earl ambled away.

"Everyone seems quite friendly."

"Bunch of nosey parkers you mean," Sylvia grumbled, but Emma noticed the smile hovering around her lips. "You want a tour before we eat?"

"We'd love one, wouldn't we, Emma?"

"There's not a whole lot to see." Sylvia grabbed her keys from the small desk by the door and tucked them in the pocket of her caftan. She led them out to the hallway. "This wing is all independent living. A lot of us still have cars, and we can all manage without any help."

"Yes, but if you need it, it's close at hand, I imagine," Arabella said.

Sylvia nodded. "Now on the other wing you've got your assisted living types. We have a kitchen in our places, but they don't. They take their meals in the main dining room. Some of them may need help bathing or dressing or have to have someone remind them to take their pills. Thank God I'm not there yet."

"What's in the main building? I noticed it must be four or five stories." Arabella glanced through the open door of an apartment.

"That's your nursing." Sylvia led them around the corner toward the reception area. "The poor stiffs there need a lot more care than the rest of us. Frankly, I'd rather check out than end up there. Half of them don't even know where they are."

They were about to head back to Sylvia's apartment when they heard shouts coming down the corridor.

"Thief! Stop! Thief!" A woman in a pair of mint green pants, a matching print top and white flats yelled at the top of her lungs. Her head of teased white hair quivered with indignation.

Sylvia turned to stare in her direction, and Emma took a step forward. Before anyone else could move, a woman in a pleated plaid skirt, cotton crew neck sweater and loafers came out of one of the rooms marked *Office*. Emma thought she looked familiar but couldn't immediately place her.

The woman stared at Emma, Arabella and Sylvia for a moment, a horrified expression on her face, before turning her attention back to the resident in the mint green outfit.

"What's wrong, Mrs. Decker. Has something happened?"

"Has something happened?" Mrs. Decker spit out furiously, her white frizz bobbing with each indignant shake of her head. "My brooch has been stolen! The one Arthur gave me for our fiftieth. It's gold with diamonds and pearls. Arthur always knew what I liked."

"Are you sure you didn't misplace it?" the woman, whom Emma finally recognized as Jessica Scott's secretary, who had been at their trunk show, responded soothingly.

"I most certainly did not." Mrs. Decker's delicate coif swayed mightily. She turned around and pointed a finger at Sylvia. "You!"

Sylvia pointed to her own chest. "Me?"

"Yes, you! Nothing ever went missing before you got here. And now my brooch is gone, Mrs. Henry has lost that new radio thingie her grandson bought her, and Mr. Mason's Korean War medals have disappeared."

Chapter 7

"I'M so sorry," Jessica's secretary said as soon as she got Mrs. Decker calmed down and back to her own room. She smiled at Emma and Arabella. "I'm Crystal Davis. We met at Deirdre's party. Jessica Scott is . . . was . . . my cousin." She gave a delicate sniff and wiped a hand across her eyes.

"We're very sorry for your loss," Arabella said. She dug in her purse, produced a clean, hand-embroidered handkerchief and held it toward Crystal.

Crystal shook her head. "I'm fine. Thank you."

Arabella looked at her doubtfully. "Are you going to allow that woman"—she pointed in the direction Mrs. Decker had taken—"to make accusations like that?"

"Oh, she doesn't mean anything by it. She's getting a little dotty, I'm afraid." Crystal made a circular motion with her finger by her temple as she said this.

"Still! What about Sylvia's reputation?"

"And to think I was almost starting to like it here," Sylvia said.

Crystal glanced this way and that, like a cornered rat. Finally, she excused herself and scurried back toward the safety of her office.

"Useless!" They heard someone snort behind them.

They turned around to see a very tall, imperious-looking woman with a dark gray chignon headed toward them. She was wearing silver flats, black slacks and an oversized, tailored white shirt with the collar turned up. She was the most elegant-looking older woman Emma had seen other than her aunt.

She pointed a red-tipped finger in the direction of Crystal's closed office door. "That woman is totally useless." With an effort she changed her frown to a smile and held out her hand. "Eloise Montgomery."

They made introductions all around. Eloise turned to Sylvia.

"I'm so sorry that happened. Mrs. Decker is not, contrary to what that sniveling idiot Crystal said, dotty in the least. She's a nasty piece of work, that's what she is. Every time someone new moves in, she comes up with some slanderous rumor to spread."

"You would think Crystal would be onto her by now," Arabella said.

Eloise shuddered. "Not that girl. If brains were leather, she wouldn't have enough to saddle a June bug."

"I supposed being Jessica's cousin . . ." Arabella said, and Emma had to hide a grin when she saw the sly look on Arabella's face.

Eloise swallowed the bait smoothly. "I don't know why Jessica kept her on. Treated her downright poorly, too. Always yelling at her, telling her to hurry, making her run errands. Once she even insisted poor Crystal polish her shoes. I can't imagine why Crystal put up with it."

"Maybe she couldn't get anything else," Emma suggested.

"Rumor has it," Eloise lowered her voice, "that she's embezzling from Sunny Days, and that's why she stays. Frankly, I don't think she'd have the brains to pull it off unless she's the best actress to come along since the Barrymores." She glanced at her watch and smiled. "I must be off. Lovely to meet you. Sylvia, I hope I'll see you at cards tonight?"

"Sure. Why not."

Emma was glad to see that Sylvia's expression had lightened slightly.

"Our pizza must be getting cold," Arabella said.

"Let's go back to my place." Sylvia turned toward the hall. "I've got some vodka on ice, and we can pop the pies in the oven to warm them."

They followed Sylvia down the hall and back to her apartment.

"You know what I'm wondering?" Arabella said after they'd been settled on the sofa and Sylvia had poured out tiny glasses of iced Stolichnaya. "I'm wondering if Crystal didn't have a good reason for killing Jessica. Polishing her shoes, indeed! I would have felt like killing her, too."

"I know." Emma took a cautious sip of vodka. "Talk about nerve!"

Arabella put her empty glass down on the coffee table. Her cheeks were tinged with pink and her eyes were bright. "Sylvia, maybe you can do a little snooping?"

"Sure."

"And I had an idea while I was walking down the hall." Emma turned toward Arabella. "There was a sign up asking for volunteers to help with activities, game night and other things. I could sign up, and it would give me an excuse to talk to both the staff and the residents."

"That's a wonderful idea! Let's get you signed up right away."

"Pizza first," Sylvia called from the kitchen, where she was pulling the pies from the oven. "Who knows what you'll uncover around this place. Maybe you'll even find Mrs. Decker's missing brooch."

EVERYONE was on tenterhooks for the rest of the week wondering what the police might find next. Emma jumped every time the door to Sweet Nothings opened, and she could tell Arabella felt the same way.

Finally the week went by, and it was Saturday. Emma woke early, yawned, stretched and slipped into the window seat that looked down over Washington Street. She lifted the edge of the curtain and peered out. The skies were blue with huge, puffy clouds floating past. The perfect day for a wedding.

Emma felt butterflies stir in her stomach at the thought. She would be spending the whole afternoon and evening with Brian. Who knew what might happen?

Emma and Liz had hoped to take a shopping trip to Memphis, but Ben came down with strep throat, and Liz couldn't leave him. Besides, the police had asked her not to leave town for the near future.

Fortunately, Emma's closet was well stocked from her days as a fashion stylist in New York City. She stuck her head into its depths and began sliding garments along the rack. After five minutes, she had four *possibles* strewn on the bed.

She tried on each of the dresses in turn and settled on a pale pink sheath with a pearl embellished neckline. She'd bought it to go to another wedding held at the Hamptons country house of a big fashion executive at Donna Karan. It hadn't been the most memorable evening. One of the groomsmen got drunk and followed her around all night until she finally hailed a taxi to take her to the train station before the wedding cake had even been served. She hoped this wedding would prove to be more fun.

Emma was too nervous to eat much for breakfast or lunch. Instead, she had a long soak in the tub and took her time getting dressed. She slipped the pink sheath over her head and examined herself in the mirror. The outfit needed . . . something.

She dove into her closet and poked around on the shelf, finally unearthing the item she was after—a broad-brimmed straw hat with a pink ribbon. She slipped it on. Perfect!

Emma was ready when Brian knocked on her door. He appeared even taller and broader shouldered standing in her tiny apartment. She was momentarily tongue-tied again, like the adolescent she was when she first developed a crush on her best friend's older brother. But then he smiled, and she found herself relaxing.

"I have to apologize." Brian tugged at the blue and white striped tie he was wearing. "I'd hoped to borrow Liz's station wagon for the day, but it's in the shop for a tune-up. I'm afraid we're stuck with my pickup truck, but"—he held up a hand—"I've cleaned it inside and out so you don't have to worry."

"That's fine." Emma answered his smile with one of her own.

GRACE Episcopal Church was built in 1896, making it the oldest church building in Paris. It was notable for its stained glass windows by Tiffany and its welcoming bright red door.

Brian parked the truck, helped Emma down from the passenger seat, and, with a hand on her elbow, led her around to the front of the church. A handful of people had gathered on the steps waiting to enter. Emma counted three hats among the four female heads, in shades of pastel such as pale pink and creamsicle orange.

"Hey, Brian!" A young man in khakis and a navy blue blazer stepped away from the crowd. He waved a hand in their direction.

"That's Tyson," Brian said, steering Emma in the young man's direction. "We were in the same fraternity at UT."

Emma suddenly realized how little she really knew about Brian.

Brian and Tyson clasped hands and shook heartily. Both had wide grins.

"I didn't know you were going to be here," Tyson said, glancing at Emma with an inquiring look on his face.

"I'm sorry." Brian grinned sheepishly. "Emma, this is Tyson. Tyson, this is Emma Taylor. She's Liz's best friend," he added awkwardly.

Was that all she was to Brian? Liz's best friend? The look Tyson gave Emma let her know that he certainly found her attractive. She stood a little straighter. She would just have to get Brian to see her in the same light.

A few moments later, they filed into the stark white church and found a seat. The organ wheezed to life and the music swelled to fill the nave. The bride entered, a vision in white organdy, on the arm of an older gentleman in a dark suit. Emma watched the ceremony through a veil of tears that blurred the plum-colored bridesmaid dresses to a misty swirl. She glanced up at Brian. His gaze was on the couple at the altar, but there was a preoccupied look on his face.

Finally, the newly married bride and groom sprinted back down the aisle, hand in hand, to the strains of Beethoven's "Ode to Joy." The congregation rose to its feet and slowly made its way out the doors, down the front stairs and through the reception line that had formed around the couple.

Emma's head swirled from all the new names and faces. Brian looked at her and grinned.

"I could sure do with a big glass of Tennessee Tea right about now."

"That makes two of us."

The air was pleasantly cool, but the setting sun was aiming its rays at the small group gathered on the lawn, and Emma let her wrap slip from her shoulders as she and Brian made their way back through the milling crowd toward Brian's truck.

In less than fifteen minutes, they were pulling into the parking lot of the Beauchamp Hotel and Spa, or "the Beau" as it had become known locally. It was a low-lying modern building with large windows all around. Beside the entrance, varicolored striped ornamental grasses swayed in the breeze.

The lobby was as soothing as Emma had remembered from her last visit to the Beau—painted a restful pale green with light wood floors, Oriental rugs and a reception desk that was part waterfall. She and Brian followed signs down a lushly carpeted corridor to the Grand Ballroom.

The room had expansive windows that looked out over beautifully manicured lawns and gardens and an enormous crystal chandelier that was suspended from the cathedral ceiling. It would have been impressive under any circumstances, but today it had been turned into a fantasyland of trees outlined in twinkling lights, flickering candles and luscious bouquets of flowers.

Soon the newly married couple had been introduced, the first course served and plenty of bubbly champagne poured. The band started to play a song that had been popular when Emma and Brian were in high school. Brian looked at her and raised one eyebrow. "Want to dance?"

"Sure." Emma hadn't been dancing in ages, and she felt her spirits lift to the beat of the music.

Brian was a smooth dancer but without being a show-off. Emma was sorry when the song ended and segued into a slow number that had been playing on the radio recently. She was surprised when Brian held his hand out.

"Want to give this one a try?"

Emma gladly accepted and slid into his arms. Up close, she could smell a hint of his aftershave and the scent of his freshly starched shirt. It was intoxicating. Brian tightened his arm and pulled her closer, and a sigh escaped Emma's lips. It felt so right. She let her head drop against his shoulder as they swayed in time to the music. The song ended, and Brian didn't let go. The next song was also a slow one, and Emma relished the extra few minutes wrapped in Brian's arms.

But eventually the song ended, and they drew apart. As they made their way back to their table, the band leader announced that the bride would be throwing her bouquet. Emma froze. Should she go up with all the other single women? What would Brian think? On the other hand, it might seem churlish of her to stay in her seat.

She was hesitating when a crowd of women surged past her. It was easier to join the throng heading toward the front of the ballroom. Emma made sure to position herself in the back. She didn't want there to be any chance she would catch the bouquet. The mere thought made her face go hot.

With an appropriate amount of fanfare, and a burst of festive music from the band, the bride launched her flowers high into the air. Emma watched, panicked, as the bouquet scaled the heads of the crowd and headed straight toward her. Her first instinct was to duck, but she wasn't fast enough. She put up a hand to ward off the floral missile but ended up catching it instead.

"Well done," Brian said when Emma returned to their table. He pointed toward the flowers. "Doesn't that mean you'll be the next one to get married?"

Emma felt her face burn. She quickly put the bouquet under the table by her feet. "Just a silly old superstition." She laughed to show Brian just how silly she thought it was. The heat in her face lingered, and she fanned herself with her hand. "Is it hot in here?"

"I'll say." Brian looked around. "People have been going out on the terrace. Want to see if it's any cooler out there?"

"Sure."

They wove their way among the round, linen-covered tables toward the French doors leading outside. Brian twisted the gold lever on the nearest one and pulled it open. A welcoming rush of cool air enveloped Emma.

"Oh, that feels good."

They stepped outside. The terrace was lit by tiny white lights wound in the surrounding bushes and a few strategically placed spots, leaving pockets of shadowy darkness. Brian led her toward one of the less well lit patches. He loosened his tie.

"This is much better. I could hardly breathe in there."

They stood in their darkened corner listening to the

haunting hoot of an owl in the distance. The breeze had an edge of coolness to it, and Emma shivered suddenly.

"You're cold," Brian said. His voice had a note of concern to it.

Emma wrapped her arms around herself. "A bit. It feels good."

"Here. Take my jacket." Brian slipped out of his blazer and placed it around Emma's shoulders.

She could feel the warmth of his body contained within the fabric and could smell the combination of his tangy aftershave and the sharper smell of soap. She closed her eyes and inhaled deeply.

When she opened her eyes, Brian was watching her intently. "I want to thank you for coming with me tonight. I hope you're having a good time." His voice dropped to a husky level, and he said softly, "I am." He tilted his head slowly and moved it toward Emma's. She closed her eyes again.

And then she felt his lips on hers.

Chapter 8

EMMA could still remember the first time she flew on an airplane. Her parents were taking her to Florida for winter break. She remembered looking out at the fluffy, white clouds and wondering what it would be like to float on one of them.

Now she knew.

Brian's kiss had transported her into another world where everything was light, bright and weightless. The feeling stayed with her all day Sunday.

"You look different. Something's happened," Arabella declared as soon as she walked into Sweet Nothings on Monday morning and saw Emma's expression.

"Nothing's happened. Why?" Emma could feel the smile spreading across her face.

Arabella laughed as she unclipped Pierre's leash. "It's written all over your face. Something happened. Something good."

Emma momentarily buried her face in her hands. It seemed so ridiculous all of a sudden—to be excited because a boy had kissed you. That was high school stuff.

"I gather you had a good time at the wedding on Saturday," Arabella said, her tone drier than the Sahara.

"Oh yes. It was lovely." Emma turned around and busied herself with sorting out one of the drawers.

Arabella sighed. "My weekend wasn't as good as yours obviously was."

"Oh no." Emma spun around.

Arabella shrugged. "I had dinner with Les on Sunday night."

Emma saw Arabella roll her eyes, an uncharacteristic gesture for her aunt.

"It was rather tedious. We had an early dinner at Ruggero's Italian Bistro—you know that place out at the Paris Winery?" Arabella fiddled with the strand of amber beads around her neck. "Dinner was lovely, but Les made it clear he's hoping for some sort of . . . commitment . . . from me." Arabella laughed. "I've managed to avoid that sort of responsibility all my life. As soon as a man got too serious," she snapped her fingers, "I said good-bye and good luck." She smiled fondly at Emma. "Had I known it might have been possible to have a dear daughter like you to share my life with, perhaps I wouldn't have run away from marriage quite so fast." She sighed. "But at this time in my life . . ." She shrugged. "There's no point."

A thud against the front door startled them both.

"Sorry. It's just me." Sylvia pushed the door open and wrangled her oxygen tank over the threshold.

Arabella put down a lacy camisole she was folding. "How's life at Sunny Days?"

Sylvia made a rude noise. "Some things are okay, but I

swear I'm going to deck that Decker woman if she keeps telling people I'm the one stealing things."

"That doesn't sound too good," Arabella said.

"Eh." Sylvia shrugged a shoulder. "Could be worse. My new friend Earl's got a real head for cards, so we've been partnering up. So far we've won a free lunch in the dining room, a rubber jar opener and a bright yellow umbrella with *Sunny Days* written on it."

"I still don't like the fact that that woman is going around bad-mouthing you." Arabella frowned.

"I signed up to volunteer," Emma said. "I'll go over after work and see if they have anything for me to do. Maybe I can help Sylvia get to the bottom of things."

"Believe me," Sylvia said, "I'd be eternally grateful. The place is growing on me, and I'd hate to be thrown out on account of that loony tune Decker woman."

THE parking lot at Sunny Days was almost empty when Emma pulled in after work. She'd grabbed a quick bite to eat at the Coffee Klatch and had then headed away from downtown Paris toward the retirement community.

"This your first time?" The woman behind the desk was much younger than the one who'd been there when Emma and Arabella had visited. She looked to be in her thirties, had mousy brown hair and was wearing a pair of glasses whose lenses were extremely smudged.

"Yes."

The woman consulted some papers on her desk. "Why don't you go on ahead to the activity room." She pointed down the hallway. "Our residents are having their ice cream social. I know Crystal could use some help."

Emma's spirits perked up at the thought of some ice

cream. She headed in the direction the receptionist had indicated and quickly found the room in question.

A long table was placed in the middle of the space and covered by a plastic cloth. Two women stood behind three tubs of ice cream—Emma recognized one of them as Crystal. Smaller tables held bowls of what Emma assumed were toppings.

She pushed the door open quietly and headed toward Crystal.

Crystal looked up and clamped a hand over her mouth in surprise. "Oh, I didn't expect to see you back here. Is there something you wanted?" She stood poised with her ice cream scoop over the container of what looked to Emma like butter pecan.

"I've volunteered to help."

Crystal gave a twitch of annoyance. Her blond hair had deflated slightly, and she'd tucked one side behind her ear. A dribble of ice cream snaked down the front of her white blouse.

"Hey, kid. What are you doing here?" Sylvia sidled up to Emma and patted her arm. "Good to see you. You here to volunteer?"

Emma nodded.

"Good." Sylvia lowered her voice. "Keep your eye on that Decker woman." She indicated the lady Emma had met on her earlier visit. "I'm beginning to think she's the one lifting the stuff from the residents' rooms. You know that line from Shakespeare? 'The lady doth protest too much, methinks.'"

Emma nodded. This might turn out to be more interesting than she expected.

She spent the next forty-five minutes dishing out ice cream. By the time she was finished, she had rejected her earlier thought about the evening turning out to be interesting. Her hands were sticky with chocolate fudge and vanilla ice cream, and she longed to escape to the ladies' room to wash up.

Five minutes later, when all the residents were happily in possession of a bowl of ice cream, she slipped into the hall and went in search of the restrooms. She was coming out when she nearly ran into Liz.

"Emma, what are you doing here?"

"I've been volunteering." Emma gestured toward the activity room. "Dishing out ice cream."

"I understand the ice cream socials are a huge hit. I've tried to get Dad to go, but he says he hates the way the women all cluster around him trying to get his attention."

"It does seem rather uneven, doesn't it?"

Liz nodded. "It's paradise for any man interested in finding a date. Dad just isn't one of them." She glanced at her watch. "I'd better hurry. I'm just dropping off some homemade soup." She brandished the plastic grocery bag she was carrying.

Emma gave her a quick hug and continued down the hall, nearly colliding with the tall, silver-haired woman she and Arabella had met on their first visit to Sunny Days. The name came to her suddenly. Eloise Montgomery.

Eloise put a hand on Emma's arm and pointed down the hallway toward the direction Liz had taken. "That woman"—she paused and watched as Liz disappeared around the corner—"had an absolute knock-down, drag-out fight with our administrator Jessica Scott one day. We all came out of our rooms to see what was going on. It was like one of those big fights in Vegas, although instead of fancy furs and diamonds, we were all in fleece sweatpants and terry cloth robes."

"What were they fighting about?"

"Beats me. But let me tell you, it was a real banner night around here." She hesitated then leaned toward Emma. "I heard there was something suspicious about Jessica's death. Makes you kind of wonder, doesn't it? That woman sure looked mad enough to kill."

Emma made her escape and went back to the activity room to retrieve her purse and say good-bye to Sylvia.

"You come across any good clues?" Sylvia asked.

Emma shook her head.

"Better luck next time. I'll see you tomorrow."

Emma made her way down the hall and toward the double doors in the lobby. She pushed one open and stepped into the cool night air. She was headed toward the Bug when she noticed Liz's station wagon with the *Ballet Mom* sticker in the rear window.

Eloise's words, *That woman sure looked mad enough to kill*, echoed in Emma's ears as she drove out of the parking lot and headed back toward town.

EMMA got back to her apartment and changed her clothes. She flipped on the television, but nothing held her interest. She couldn't settle on anything. All she could think about was what Eloise had said about Liz. The words *mad enough to kill* went around and around in her head like some kind of crazed mantra.

She had to see Liz tonight and talk to her. Liz needed to know what rumors people were spreading about her. Emma knew Liz had had nothing to do with Jessica's murder, but they had to come up with a plan to stop the people in the retirement home from talking as if she had.

Emma grabbed her keys, slipped into a light jacket and

headed down to her car. She wasn't sure whether she was relieved or disappointed to see that Brian's truck was absent from Liz's driveway when she pulled in fifteen minutes later. Liz answered the door almost immediately. Emma noticed a book open on the coffee table in the living room beside a glass of water. Liz had obviously been sitting alone, reading. Sounds of the television drifted down the hall from the family room where she supposed Matt and the children were gathered.

Liz looked drawn and tired, and the usual luster was missing from her hair.

"Emma, come on in." Liz held the door wide. "Would you like some tea or a glass of wine?"

Emma shook her head. "I'm sorry to show up like this, but I had to talk to you."

"That sounds so serious." Liz smiled, but the light failed to reach her eyes.

"It is. Can we go in there and sit down?" Emma indicated the living room.

"Sure. What is all this about?"

Emma perched on a chair opposite Liz. Liz took a sip of water, and Emma noticed that her hand shook slightly.

Emma wet her lips. She wasn't sure how to begin. There was no real way to sugarcoat it. She might as well come right out with it. "A woman at Sunny Days, Eloise Montgomery, said you had a huge fight with Jessica Scott before she died. She said everyone in the hall heard it."

A dark, dusky red crept up Liz's neck toward her face. For a moment Emma thought she was going to deny it.

"Yes, I did." Liz hung her head so that a curtain of hair fell over her features. She was quiet for a minute. "Are you accusing me of murdering Jessica Scott?" Her voice was bitter.

"No!" Emma exclaimed.

"It certainly sounds like it." Liz's gaze bore into Emma's.

"I'm sorry." Emma looked at her hands. "I didn't intend to upset you. I thought you ought to know that people are talking about you."

"A lot of other people have argued with Jessica as well. I've seen and heard it myself." She looked up defiantly.

"But you said you didn't know her," Emma said as gently as possible.

Liz's back stiffened, and she took another sip from her glass. "I don't." She looked Emma square in the face. "I don't . . . didn't . . . know her. At least, not in the way you meant."

Her words hung in the air for several seconds. In the silence, Emma heard shouts and gunshots coming from the television down the hall.

"What did you argue about?"

Liz tossed her hair back. "Things were missing from Dad's room. At first it was little things—the new box of tissues I'd brought or the tin of cookies for his afternoon tea. But then his hearing aid went missing . . . the new one we'd gotten him."

"What did Jessica say about it?"

Liz rolled her eyes. "She said that perhaps Dad had misplaced it. Which was ridiculous. Matt and I searched that room high and low. We looked all through his chest of drawers and even through his pockets. Besides, Dad may need some help getting around, but he's not suffering from memory loss! Although Jessica hinted at that, too." Liz looked down at her hands then back up at Emma. "I guess I blew my top."

"It's too bad that so many people heard you. Now rumors are spreading that you may have had something to do with Jessica's death."

Liz stifled a sob. "The hearing aid was so expensive." She was crying openly now. "And we can hardly afford to replace it. We've spent so much on the renovations to the house." She waved a hand around the room. "And Matt . . ." She stopped and buried her face in her hands.

"What is it?" Emma slipped out of her chair and went to sit next to Liz. "Is something wrong with Matt?"

Liz shook her head. "No, it's just that business has been slow lately. He lost the bid on a big contract that we were so sure he was going to get." She tried to smile. "Things will pick up, but right now, money is very, very tight. I guess I took it out on Jessica that day. Especially when she refused to do anything about it. She actually didn't believe me." Liz's cheeks flamed pink. "And now that odious woman is going around telling everyone about our argument. How long before the police hear about it?"

"Let's hope it doesn't get that far."

"But what if it does?" She turned toward Emma. "What am I going to do?"

"I'm going to look into it. I'm sure we can get to the bottom of this ourselves before it goes any further," Emma said with way more conviction than she felt.

Chapter 9

EMMA slept fitfully, worrying about Liz and thinking about Brian. She was exhausted by the time she got down to Sweet Nothings on Tuesday morning. She was early, and the shop was quiet. Emma turned on the lamp over Arabella's desk and powered up her laptop. The screen sprang to life, and soon Emma was staring at the numbers on Sweet Nothings' balance sheet. Sweet Nothings was inching its way toward being in the black. The trunk show had brought in some much-needed revenue, and as long as sales stayed much the same, they would be okay.

Boxes had arrived from New York—some of the latest items in Monique Berthole's line. Emma had chosen the garments she thought her customers would like—nothing too racy or uber-fashionable. As far as she could tell, *pretty* was what sold best in Paris.

Arabella arrived as Emma was slitting open the first box.

She removed several tissue-wrapped bundles and laid them out on the counter—matching camisoles and panties in gorgeous hues of shell pink, blush, peach, aquamarine and white.

"Oh, these are beautiful," Arabella said as she regarded the delicate lace and silk creations. "Where are you going to display them?"

"I think I'll put them on the shelves in one of the armoires so people can see all the pretty colors."

"Good idea."

Emma emptied the box and retrieved the envelope inside with *invoice* stamped on it in red. She ripped it open and spread it out on the counter. The numbers made her gasp. There must be some mistake. She would never have placed such an expensive order.

Emma felt sweat break out along her upper lip, under her arms and on the back of her neck. She had to get this sorted out right away, before Arabella found out. Had she misread the prices? Had she inadvertently ordered twice as much as she intended?

"Emma, dear, is something the matter?" Arabella was looking at her with her face creased into lines of concern.

"Oh no," Emma said breezily, trying to ignore the feeling that her stomach was plummeting on the final leg of a roller-coaster ride. "I think the eggs I made myself for breakfast this morning didn't quite agree with me."

"Do you want to go back upstairs—" Arabella began when the front door to Sweet Nothings swung open and Sylvia entered, even more breathless than usual.

"You won't believe it!" Sylvia slammed her purse down on the counter and stood with her hands on her hips.

"What?" Arabella said smoothly, casting a glance at Emma.

"Sunny Days is crawling with police!"

Sylvia's eyes were bright, and she was standing straighter than she had in days. "It's right out of one of them cop shows."

"Police?" Arabella and Emma echoed together.

"They asked all of us to stay in our rooms, but I did manage to get a peek into the hallway. That sourpuss Crystal Davis was keeping watch, but there wasn't much of anything to see. I gather all the action was up on nursing. Earl said he saw someone taken out on a gurney earlier. He couldn't tell if they were dead or alive—the blanket was pulled so far up it might have been either. But it was an ambulance waiting and not a hearse from McEvoy's Funeral Home." Sylvia pursed her lips. "Of course, they might have passed at the hospital."

"But the police—" Arabella stopped and put a hand to her mouth. "It can't be another murder. Things like this don't happen in our little town. Why, it was only recently I even started locking my front door."

"I wonder what happened." Emma chewed her bottom lip. "As a new volunteer, maybe I should go over there and see if they need any help?"

"Great idea! Sylvia and I can handle the shop. You go get the scoop!"

THERE was only one police car in the lot at Sunny Days when Emma got there. She wondered if Sylvia had been exaggerating the scene earlier that morning. Emma had meant to head to Sunny Days right away, but Sweet Nothings had suddenly gotten busy, and she'd ended up staying until after lunch when things quieted down again.

She noticed a familiar station wagon in the far right

corner of the lot and wasn't surprised when she ran into Liz in the lobby.

"Emma." Liz grabbed her by the arm. "The police have been here all morning. I came to check on Dad and make sure everything is okay."

"Is he on the same floor—"

"No. He's in assisted living, and I gather the police have been up on the skilled nursing floor. Still, I was worried."

"Sylvia came in this morning positively bursting with the news."

"I do suppose it's more exciting than hearing about everyone's grandkids, or worse, their hemorrhoids."

Emma laughed. "Let's see if Crystal is in her office. Perhaps she can tell us what's going on."

They approached the closed door with the sign *Office* on the front. Emma knocked briskly, and they waited for a response.

Nothing.

Liz put her ear to the door. "I don't hear anything. Either Crystal isn't in there, or she's taking a break and is ignoring us." She tried the door handle, but it was locked.

They started down the hallway toward the activity room. All apartment doors were shut, and it was very quiet. They peered through the glass into the activity room, but it was empty.

Liz looked at her watch. "They must all be napping after their lunch."

They heard a noise coming from the end of the corridor and turned in that direction. Mrs. Decker came around the corner, her cane thumping the ground indignantly with every step. Light coming from the windows lining the hall shone through her halo of white hair, making it look even more transparent than usual.

She stomped toward Emma and Liz, her mouth moving before she even got there.

"They're trying to murder us in our beds! You've got to get me out of here." She plucked at Emma's sleeve.

"I'm sure they're doing nothing of the kind," Emma said gently. "Why don't you go back to your room and get some rest?"

"I know for a fact that someone has been murdered. The police are here, aren't they?" Mrs. Decker punctuated her sentence with several thumps from her cane.

"Just because the police are here—"

"Someone on the nursing floor has been murdered," Mrs. Decker insisted. "I saw it with my own two eyes. They wheeled her out a couple of hours ago, and then suddenly we have the police going over the place with a fine-tooth comb." She glared at Emma and Liz as if daring them to disagree.

"Mrs. Decker!" someone called from down the hall.

Eloise Montgomery was floating down the hall in a purple silk caftan. She motioned toward Mrs. Decker. "Come on, Mrs. Decker. Let's get you back to your room."

"Thinks she runs the place," Mrs. Decker muttered under her breath. She shook off Eloise's arm and obligingly turned around and thumped her way back down the corridor toward her room.

"What nonsense has she been filling you with?" Eloise asked when she came abreast of Emma and Liz.

"She seems to think someone's been murdered," Emma said.

Eloise rolled her wide-set blue eyes. "If that useless Crystal Davis would come out of her office and handle things, absurd rumors like that wouldn't be spreading around." Eloise fiddled with the large pendant she wore from a silk

cord around her neck. "I do hope they hire another administrator soon. I gather that Crystal's thrown her hat into the
ring, but if anything, this whole episode certainly proves
she isn't worthy of the position."

"Well, we didn't get anything new from her," Liz said to
Emma as Eloise continued on her journey down the
corridor.

"I'm not so sure. What if Crystal has been after Jessica's
job for a while? Maybe she decided to take matters into her
own hands and make it easier by getting rid of Jessica?"

"Could be." Liz punched the up button on the elevator.

The fourth floor was quiet with several medication carts
parked outside of the residents' rooms. Emma didn't immediately see any police but then caught a glimpse of Detective
Walker at the end of the floor. He had his notebook out and
appeared to be writing something down.

"There's Detective Walker. I'm sure he can tell us
something."

Walker looked up as they approached, and there was no
mistaking the admiring light in his eyes. Liz poked Emma
surreptitiously, and Emma shot her a dirty look.

Emma started to introduce herself, but Walker inter-
rupted her.

"I do remember you. From Sweet Nothings, right?"

Emma could feel Liz's gaze on her, but she refused to
acknowledge it. "Yes. You have a good memory."

"You're not easily forgotten, ma'am." Walker tipped an
imaginary hat in Emma's direction.

"We were wondering if you could tell us what's going
on. I have a friend who lives here, and Liz's father"—she
indicated Liz with a nod of her head—"is downstairs in
assisted living."

"There's no cause for alarm. Don't worry."

"But what's happened?" Emma asked.

Walker ran his hands through his short, dark hair. "A resident took ill, and we're making sure the correct protocol is followed," Walker answered evasively.

Emma had to stop herself from snorting. Walker's response was so obviously designed to put them off. But she could tell by the look on his face that they weren't going to get any further.

"I do hope you ladies have a nice day. Mighty fine weather we're having." Walker seemed reluctant to leave.

Liz grabbed Emma by the arm and all but goose-stepped her toward the door. "Did you believe that?" she asked as they walked away.

Emma shook her head. "No, he's quoting the party line. Which makes me more suspicious that something *is* going on."

"Did you see the way he looked at you?" Liz glanced at Emma out of the corner of her eye.

Emma felt her face get hot.

"Don't go getting any ideas," Liz warned.

"What do you mean?"

"I saw Brian on Sunday after his date with you, and he was walking on air."

"What do you mean?" Emma stood stock-still in the middle of the hallway.

"I mean, he obviously had a fantastic time. I'm assuming you did, too?" She looked at Emma.

"Yes . . . yes, I did," Emma stammered. She remembered Brian's kiss and hoped the memory wasn't visible on her face.

"I don't want to see Brian getting his heart broken. He's finally happy again." Liz put her hands on Emma's shoulders. "You do like him, don't you?"

"Yes. Yes, of course, I do."

Liz ducked her head. "You probably think I'm being overprotective, but he was so hurt when he came back from Nashville, it almost broke my heart."

Emma felt as if her heart had escaped from her chest and was soaring high in the air. So their kiss had obviously meant as much to Brian as it had to her.

"Wait." Liz grabbed Emma's arm again. "Is that Crystal?" She pointed down the hall.

"It looks like her." Emma squinted as the figure retreated into the distance.

"Let's see if we can catch up with her and pry some information out of her."

They were about to go after Crystal when they heard the sound of a cough coming from behind them and Sylvia's friend Earl walked up to them.

"Good afternoon, ladies. You here for the circus?"

"Things appear to have calmed down," Emma noted.

Earl smoothed a finger over his handlebar mustache. "They have. That they have. Place was swarming with cops earlier, but they seem to have finished their business here."

"What happened? All we could find out was that a nursing resident had been taken to the hospital. I wouldn't think that that would warrant having the police out."

"You're right." Earl's watery blue eyes bugged slightly. "But there's more to it than that."

"How do you know?"

"My great-nephew just joined the force. He was at the station when the call came in. Of course, I had to pry it out of him." Earl laughed. "Applied the old thumb screws." And he laughed even louder.

Liz sighed somewhat impatiently and glanced at her watch.

"What *did* happen?" Emma prompted.

Earl smoothed his mustache again. "A nursing resident did take ill, like they've been telling us. Ambulance came and took her to the hospital. Nothing very exciting in that. Happens all the time. But then a couple of hours later the police arrived. No one would tell us what was going on, so I got Gordon on the phone, and he filled me in." He leaned closer to Emma and Liz. "I haven't told this to anyone else, so it's best if you keep it under your hats. Turns out they got the old gal to the hospital and began running their tests. She's unconscious—in some kind of coma. And what does the doctor discover?"

By now, Emma and Liz were tense with anticipation.

"The doctor discovers that someone tried to smother the poor old dear!"

Chapter 10

LIZ followed Emma back to Sweet Nothings, where they found the shop empty of customers and Arabella and Sylvia chatting with Bitsy over some banana cupcakes.

"Did you save some for us?" Emma said when she spied the white Sprinkles box.

"Of course." Bitsy opened the top and took out two cupcakes.

"Mmm." Emma licked a bit of frosting off her finger. "These are delicious. What kind of frosting is this?"

"Cream cheese."

"What is the news at Sunny Days?" Arabella leaned her elbows on the counter eagerly.

"Yeah, shoot." Sylvia eased onto the love seat, stuck out her legs and rotated her ankles.

Emma watched her with concern. Sometimes she worried that Sylvia was working too much—it was hard being on your feet all day. But she also knew that Sylvia would rather be working than sitting in her apartment.

"Did you talk to Crystal Davis?" Arabella popped the last bit of her cupcake in her mouth.

Emma shook her head.

"No, she was hiding in her office," Liz said.

Arabella tilted her head quizzically.

"We knocked on the office door, but she didn't answer. Later we saw her sneaking into the hall when she thought no one was looking. She practically ran the other way when she saw us coming," Emma explained.

Arabella laughed.

"That girl is less than useless," Sylvia complained.

"But we ran into your friend, Earl." Emma looked at Sylvia. "He called his nephew who is in the police department and got a few details at least."

"Well don't keep us in suspense," Sylvia grumbled.

Emma explained about the nursing resident being taken to the hospital and the doctor discovering that someone had attempted to smother her.

"This is too much." Arabella slumped against the counter. "First Jessica Scott and now this poor woman." She looked at Sylvia, then at Emma and Liz. "Do you think the two incidents are related?"

Emma shrugged. "I can't imagine how. Jessica was killed at our trunk show, so the person responsible must have been at the party." She shivered.

Liz finished the last bite of her cupcake. "Someone had to have substituted the poisonous flower for the one Bitsy originally put on the cupcake. I know I didn't pick any poisonous flowers by mistake."

"And I only used the ones Liz brought me," Bitsy said. Her expression darkened. "I've heard from some friends that the police have been around asking questions about me and Jessica when we were in college." Bitsy stifled a sob. "What if they find out what happened between us when we were rushing? They're bound to think I had something to do with her death."

"Oh, my dear, you needn't worry," Arabella said soothingly. "This new detective, what was his name?" She looked at Emma.

"Bradley Walker."

"Detective Walker. He seems much more on the ball than poor old Chuck Reilly. He's bound to discover the real culprit in due time."

"I hope you're right." Liz's face turned ashen. "I'm still the most logical suspect."

"No!" Emma declared. "Someone at that party is responsible, and it's not you, Liz, or you, Bitsy."

"But how did that foxglove flower get on the cupcake that Jessica ate?" Sylvia said from her perch on the love seat.

"We know neither Liz nor Bitsy had anything to do with it," Emma said firmly. "Therefore, someone else had to replace one of the harmless decorative flowers with the foxglove." Emma began to pace back and forth. She stopped, closed her eyes and rubbed her temples.

"I can't exactly imagine anyone carrying foxglove flowers around in their purse," Arabella said.

"No." Emma scrunched up her face. "But Deirdre has a garden. What if she has foxglove growing and someone noticed it? It would be easy enough to slip outside when no one is looking, pick one of the flowers and put it in place of one of the edible ones Bitsy used to decorate her cupcakes."

"Foxglove is a fairly showy plant, so it's possible a landscaper might have used it in the Porters' garden," Liz said. "We need to ask Deirdre."

Arabella cleared her throat. "That might sound as if we're accusing her." She frowned. "Deirdre's been a good customer. I would hate to offend her."

Emma and Liz looked at each other out of the corners of their eyes. "We could sneak in," they said almost in unison.

Sylvia gave a throaty chuckle. "What fun. I'm sorry I'd slow you down too much to come along."

"Same here," Arabella said wistfully. "Will you go along, Bitsy?"

"I'd love to. Hayley can mind the shop for me for a few hours. She's finally mastered making change and replacing the tape in the cash register." Bitsy rolled her eyes.

"When should we go?" Liz began to gather her things together.

"I wonder if Deirdre still takes riding lessons out at Skip Clark's farm?" Arabella brushed some crumbs off the countertop.

"I can find out." Emma peeked at the cupcakes remaining in Bitsy's box but then decided she really didn't need another one. "Mabel, the waitress at the Coffee Klatch, has a younger sister who works on Skip's farm. She might know."

EMMA was putting away the lovely camisoles and panties that had arrived from New York earlier, and which gave her such a pang of conscience, when she heard the front door of Sweet Nothings open. Even before she raised her head, a cloud of very expensive-smelling perfume wafted in her direction. Emma looked up to see Marjorie Porter standing in the middle of the shop. She was wearing a silk shirtwaist dress and had one of those handbags that cost thousands of dollars slung over her arm. As usual, her ash-blond French twist was perfect, without a hair out of place. It didn't matter how hard the wind blew; it knew better than to mess up Marjorie's hairdo.

Emma smiled. "Marjorie. So nice to see you." She edged out from behind the counter and advanced with her hand out.

Marjorie smiled briefly and barely touched Emma's hand. "Is Arabella around? I wanted to have a word."

"Of course." Emma moved back behind the counter and stuck her head into the stockroom.

"Aunt Arabella?"

Arabella emerged with a quizzical look on her face that quickly changed to a practiced smile. "Marjorie. How lovely to see you. What can we do for you today?"

Emma watched, barely suppressing a bubble of amusement. She knew Arabella couldn't stand Marjorie, but you would be hard-pressed to tell by the act she was putting on. Curious, Emma edged closer to the pair and kept her ears open.

"It's a shame that your lovely trunk show at my daughter-in-law's was ruined by that woman and her untimely death."

Emma listened as Arabella made the appropriately soothing noises.

"I was hoping," Marjorie said as she smiled coyly, swinging her imported bag from the crook of her elbow, "that you might consider putting on another trunk show. I know the members of my garden club would love it."

Arabella gasped and put both hands against her chest. "Really? We'd be honored, Marjorie."

Emma bit her lip and barely managed to stifle a chuckle. Arabella was really laying it on.

"But I'm thinking," Marjorie continued. "Most of the women in our group are . . ." She dropped her voice. ". . . middle-aged. Could you possibly do something on the new shape wear? I must confess, we're all curious about it," she said conspiratorially, patting her own slightly rounded tummy.

"Of course," Arabella said briskly. "That's a wonderful idea. There are so many options these days. Not like in our day," she said in a near whisper.

Marjorie stiffened. "I'm not so sure your day and mine are exactly the same."

Arabella nodded diplomatically as if to say *touché*. She gestured toward Emma. "Emma, Mrs. Porter has had the most brilliant idea."

Marjorie gave a tiny smile and preened like a peacock showing off its feathers.

"We're going to do a trunk show for her garden club," Arabella said in a lowered voice, as if the paparazzi were hovering on their doorstep.

Marjorie rolled her eyes heavenward. "I promise you"— she struck her chest with her open palm—"that there won't be another . . . incident . . . like the one that occurred at my poor, dear daughter-in-law's." She shook her head, and the very tip of her twist oscillated slightly. "I really do think that someone had it in for that poor woman."

Now Emma's ears really perked up. "Really?" she said innocently.

Marjorie gave a smug smile. "I could name a few. But," she said with an air of moral superiority, "mother always said, if you don't have anything nice to say about someone, then the less said the better."

"If you know something," Arabella said, "you really should share the information with the police, don't you think?"

"I'm sure the police aren't interested in gossip," Marjorie said tartly.

No, but we are, Emma thought, trying to telegraph the concept to Marjorie somehow.

Marjorie's expression softened slightly. "Of course everyone knows that Jessica treated that sniveling wretch Crystal Davis horribly. I can't imagine why she didn't sack her except that they're somehow related. But I can't imagine Crystal getting up the gumption to do anything about it." She paused, her lips pursed. "Then there's Lotte Fanning and that whole affair. She was at the trunk show, too."

"What about Lotte Fanning?" Arabella said.

Marjorie waved a hand. "Oh, nothing. I'm telling tales out of school. Very naughty of me." She glanced at the diamond-encrusted watch on her wrist. "I must be going. I'm so glad you're going to be doing a trunk show for us. Ta-ta."

"That woman is infuriating!" Arabella declared as soon as the door shut behind Marjorie.

"I know. Who is that Fanning woman she mentioned?"

"I don't know her well. She's part of Marjorie's crowd." Emma rubbed two fingers together.

"Exactly. Money. Although no one can quite keep up with Marjorie Porter in that department. Was that an Hermès bag she was carrying?"

Emma nodded.

"I suppose we should add Charlotte Fanning to our suspect list. Now for the fun part."

"What's that?"

"Finding out why she would have wanted to kill Jessica Scott." Arabella was quiet for a moment. "Blast Marjorie anyway for not telling us!"

Chapter 11

LATER that evening, Emma headed over to Arabella's for dinner. She loved visiting her aunt's old Victorian with its enormous wraparound porch. The house held many happy memories for Emma. As she pulled into the driveway, she could already hear Pierre beginning to bark. Emma looked through the pane of glass alongside Arabella's front door and watched with a smile as Pierre slid helter-skelter down the hallway in response to her ring. Arabella came along behind him, wiping her hands on her apron.

"Come on in." Arabella gave Emma a quick hug. "I've got some barbecued ribs in the oven. And ice-cold beer in the fridge if you've got a hankering for some."

"No, thanks." Emma hugged her aunt back. "I'd rather have a glass of wine if you have any."

"Of course. There's a sauvignon blanc chilling. I got the beer in case Brian wanted any."

Emma stopped dead where she was, on the oval foyer rug. "Brian's coming?"

"Oh! Didn't I say?" Arabella was all innocence. "I told him I was making some chess pie, and he begged to be invited."

Emma rolled her eyes. She knew Brian had probably done no such thing. Well, she wasn't sorry, that's for sure. She hadn't talked to him since Saturday, and as shy as she was feeling about seeing him after their kiss in the garden at the wedding, she knew she would have to face him sooner or later.

Arabella's old Victorian house was filled with relics from her carefree traveling days—statues of Buddha from the Far East, rugs from India, silks from Thailand—but her kitchen was pure Southern comfort. Emma perched on one of the stools that surrounded the butcher block–topped island in the center of the room. Steam rose from several pots hissing on the stove.

Arabella lifted one of the lids with the edge of her apron. "Almost done." She let the lid clatter back in place.

"What are you making?" Emma went over to peer into the various saucepans.

"Mashed potatoes and collard greens sautéed with bacon."

"Sounds delicious."

Emma resumed her perch on one of the stools. She realized her palms were sweating. It was absurd to be so nervous about seeing Brian, but in her mind, that kiss had created a seismic change in their relationship. She wondered if he felt the same way.

"Should we eat in here or in the dining room?" Arabella paused with a stack of plates in her hand.

"Let's eat in here. I love this room."

Emma took a pile of newspapers off the kitchen table and headed toward the mudroom with them. She knew Arabella had a recycling bin out there.

Arabella tilted her head in the direction of the pile of *Paris Post-Intelligencers* in Emma's hands. "I read that Wyatt Porter was picked up again on a suspected DUI."

Emma raised her eyebrows.

"Wyatt is the younger brother of Alfred, Marjorie's husband. He's been trouble practically from the time he was born. Not like Alfred who, if everyone is to be believed, has never set a foot wrong in his life." Arabella opened a drawer and began counting out silverware. "If it weren't for the Porter money, Wyatt might have spent more than a few nights in the local jail."

"Is he married?"

Arabella walked around the large, worn kitchen table setting out forks and knives. "No. But there was a scandal a while back that the Porters hushed up real quick. This woman from Memphis showed up here in Paris—and what a piece of work she was. Probably met him in a bar down there or something. Rumor has it she was claiming that Wyatt was the father of her child. Another gold digger."

"Maybe it was true?" Emma folded napkins and placed them next to the plates.

Arabella shook her head. "No, I don't think so. Everyone reckons Wyatt is a little light in the loafers if you know what I mean."

"Gay?"

"Yes. And the South still being the South, it's probably what drove him to some of those escapades of his. Of course he doesn't get any of the Porter money, least not a whole lot of it. The bulk of the estate always goes to the oldest male. Wyatt will get enough for a reasonably comfortable life, but nothing like what Alfred will inherit now that old man George Porter is gone."

"That doesn't seem fair."

Arabella shrugged. "You're right. But that's how the Porters have always done it. Of course Marjorie and Alfred already have the money from Marjorie's family, but I heard that they lost a bundle in the recent stock market crash, so this may have come just in time."

Emma was getting the salt and pepper shakers from the cupboard by the stove when the doorbell rang, sending Pierre into high gear. She followed him down the hall where he misjudged the distance and narrowly missed slamming into the front door.

Emma felt her heart going into overdrive. She wiped her palms quickly on her slacks and plastered a rather nervous smile on her face.

"Hey," Brian said as he pulled her into a quick hug. "It sure smells good in here." He bent down to scratch Pierre behind the ears.

Emma led Brian into the kitchen, where Arabella also gave him a hug.

"What's cooking?" Brian glanced at the stove.

Arabella gave him a rundown of what she was making.

"And chess pie. You promised me." Brian smiled at Arabella.

"Of course. How could I disappoint you?" Arabella opened the refrigerator. "Can I tempt you with a cold beer?"

"Absolutely." Brian slumped into one of the armchairs Arabella had pulled up to the fireplace on the far wall of the kitchen.

"You look tired. Rough day?" Emma sat down in the other chair but then immediately popped up again. "Aunt Arabella, can I help with anything?"

"Not right now, dear."

"Yes, I guess you could say it was pretty rough. We found some dry rot in the roof of a house we're renovating." He rubbed a hand across his face. "It's going to mean a lot more work than I anticipated, and we're a bit behind already because Jack, our carpenter, has been out sick."

"Sounds like you need this." Arabella handed him a frosty bottle of Killian's Irish Red and a tall, iced glass.

"You do spoil me, Arabella." Brian gave a tired smile.

"I'm sure everything will turn out all right in the end," Emma reassured him.

"You're probably right. It's just that . . ." Brian hesitated. "Never mind." He smiled at Emma.

Emma stayed quiet. Something was obviously on Brian's mind, but she couldn't force him to talk about it.

"Who's hungry?" Arabella pulled a baking dish from the oven, and the sweet and tangy aroma of barbecued ribs filled the air.

"Oh my, that sure does smell good. I think my day has suddenly taken a turn for the better." Brian put his beer down. "Here, let me carry that for you."

"Never you mind. I'm fine." Arabella slid the pan onto the counter. "But if you would go in that cupboard over there"—she indicated which one with her bent elbow—"and get down the big platter on the top shelf, I'd be very grateful."

Brian immediately hurried to perform his task. Emma got glasses from another cupboard and began filling them with ice water while Arabella spooned the collard greens into a serving dish.

Finally all the dishes were on the table, and Emma, Arabella and Brian were seated around it, their plates full. Arabella's ribs were superb, as Emma knew they would be. They were her favorite dish, and Arabella used to make them for Emma's birthday every year.

By the time Arabella brought the chess pie to the table, Brian was looking much more relaxed. He leaned back in his chair and drained the last of his beer. "I swear, Arabella, I'm going to have to loosen my belt a notch after this feast."

Arabella smiled at him. "And there's still pie. It's hard to imagine how sugar, eggs and butter can come together and transform into something so delicious."

"There's chess pie, and then there's your chess pie, Arabella. Yours is the best I've ever had."

Arabella's face turned pink with pleasure as she handed around the dessert.

They ate in silence for a moment, and then Arabella addressed Brian, her voice soft with fondness. "I think something is bothering you today, Brian. Do you want to tell us about it?"

Brian looked down at his nearly empty plate. "It's nothing, really. Nothing important. I've moved on. It's just . . ."

"Just what?" Arabella said softly.

Brian closed his eyes briefly. "It's just that I heard that Amy—she's my ex-fiancée—is getting married next month."

"I can see how that would be . . . disturbing," Arabella said.

Emma was quiet. So that's what was bothering Brian. She could understand how he must feel—not only had Amy rejected him, she had now chosen someone else.

They took their coffee into the living room, and by the time Brian had finished his, he looked considerably more cheerful. More than once his laugh rang out as Arabella recounted one of her foreign escapades.

And when Emma walked Brian to the door later, the

warm hug he gave her definitely indicated that Amy and her news had been forgotten, at least for the moment.

EMMA wasn't at all hungry when she woke up on Wednesday morning, but she needed to talk to Mabel at the Coffee Klatch to find out whether Deirdre was still taking riding lessons, and if so, on which days.

Half an hour later, Emma arrived at Sweet Nothings with a cup of green tea and the knowledge that Deirdre spent Wednesday afternoons at Skip Clark's farm going riding. She pulled her cell phone from her purse and called Liz and Bitsy. Sylvia would be in the shop doing bra fittings that afternoon, and between her and Arabella, they ought to be able to manage for an hour or two on their own.

Liz and Bitsy agreed to meet Emma at Sweet Nothings at two o'clock. Meanwhile, Emma got to work cleaning the counters and changing the window display. Paris was still a fairly conservative town, and she had to be careful what she put on display. She chose a demure mint green peignoir set with a high collar edged in lace and short, puffed sleeves.

By the time Arabella arrived an hour later, Emma had finished the window and was doing some research on shape wear for their trunk show at Marjorie Porter's. She would have to order in some new things. Emma bit her lip. She hoped there was enough left in their credit line at the bank. And she hoped Marjorie's garden club would buy.

The rest of the day went quickly, and Emma was finishing a hasty ham and pickle sandwich when Liz and Bitsy arrived. They bid Arabella and Sylvia good-bye and piled into Liz's station wagon for the drive to Deirdre Porter's house.

The wrought-iron black gates that segregated the Kingsvale Estates from the rest of the world were locked, but Emma remembered the code from the last time they were at Deirdre's. She recited the numbers to Liz, and Liz punched them in. Seconds later the gates magically opened, allowing them entrée into the exclusive community.

The tree-lined streets were immaculate, the lawns and gardens perfectly manicured, and all the windows gleamed in the afternoon sun. A hush hovered over the neighborhood, with no sound of distant traffic audible.

Liz drove past Deirdre's house, first checking the driveway to be sure it was empty. No cars were sitting outside the enormous three-stall garage, so Liz turned around at the end of the cul-de-sac and headed back. This time she drove past Deirdre's house in the opposite direction. They didn't want to arouse any suspicion by pulling into the driveway, so Liz parked at the curb, several houses away.

They tried to be as quiet as possible as they walked down the street, back toward Deirdre's impressive, Georgian-style home. Emma felt as if eyes were staring from behind every pair of curtains, and she swore she saw a few of them twitch, but no one came out to challenge them. They stopped and stood in front of the Porter house.

"Okay, what now?" Bitsy nibbled on her thumbnail nervously.

Emma looked all around, but no one was in the area. "I think we can get to the backyard through that gate over there." She pointed toward an ornamental wrought-iron fence.

"I don't know why, but I have the strangest feeling someone is watching us," Bitsy said as they made their way through the gate and into the back gardens.

"It's nerves," Liz reassured her. She pulled a piece of

folded paper from her pocket. "This is what we're looking for." She held out a photograph of the flower for them to see. "Foxglove comes in a number of colors—from various shades of purple to pink, white or yellow. The flowers are bell shaped and grow on tall, slender stalks."

"It looks so pretty," Bitsy commented.

"Yes, but it can be deadly," Liz replied. "That's why I wouldn't grow any in our garden. It's not just because of the children. It's poisonous to pets and livestock as well."

Bitsy shivered. "I don't know why anyone would plant it then."

"It's a very pretty biennial, and it grows quite tall so it's often used in the back row of a garden."

Emma glanced around the large, beautifully landscaped yard. French doors from the back of the house led to a circular terraced brick patio where expensive-looking lawn furniture was hidden under canvas covers. The patio was ringed with flower boxes, but the plants were all low to the ground, so Emma doubted they would find any foxglove there.

They spread out around the garden. Emma tried to carry a mental image of the conical-shaped flower in her head. She wasn't much of a gardener and couldn't easily identify anything beyond roses, tulips, pansies and petunias. The yard was banked toward the sides, and Emma noticed some taller plants growing behind some lower ground cover. As she moved closer, she began to get excited. The flowers, at least from a distance, looked an awful lot like the ones in Liz's picture.

Emma stepped as delicately as possible into the flower bed and reached for one of the taller stalks growing behind. She pulled it closer. The flowers were bell shaped and a vivid purple.

"Liz!" she called excitedly. "I think I've found some."

Bitsy and Liz both arrived at a trot.

"Where?" Liz was slightly breathless.

Emma grabbed the stalk again and pulled it toward them.

"Yes. That's definitely foxglove." Liz's expression was serious. She turned toward Emma and Bitsy. "It's definitely possible someone came out here, picked a flower from this plant and replaced one of the edible ones on Bitsy's cupcake." She put a hand up to shield her eyes from the sun and looked toward the house. "It's close enough to the French doors that lead to the kitchen, too."

Both Emma and Bitsy turned to follow her gaze.

"And everyone was busy in the dining room and living room and not likely to notice someone stepping outside."

"I imagine any footprints would be gone by now," Bitsy said, looking at the ground around her.

"We had that rain the other night. I'm sure that wiped out any evidence." Emma sighed.

Liz edged her way into the garden, closer to the foxglove plant. "See this?" She pointed at a truncated stalk. "Someone broke a piece off here. I definitely think this is where that flower came from."

Emma's feeling of triumph was short-lived.

"Hello!" someone called across the lawn to them.

They all jumped.

"Hello? What are you doing in Miss Deirdre's garden?" The woman brandished a cell phone. "I'm going to call the police right this minute."

Emma, Liz and Bitsy hurried toward the woman. She was wearing a pair of denim capri pants and a red T-shirt with *Patriots Wrestling* on the front. She had her phone in one hand and a sponge in the other.

"Please." Emma held up a hand. "We're friends of Deir-dre's. We stopped by to see her garden."

The woman lowered the phone from her ear, but the suspicious look on her face only intensified.

"How come Miss Deirdre didn't tell me anything about you ladies coming around this afternoon? I've been cleaning for Miss Deirdre for two years now, and there ain't ever been no surprises."

Up close, Emma judged the woman to be in her early forties with tired lines around her sharp blue eyes.

"I'm sorry." Emma held a hand out. "We should have called first. I apologize. My friend here," she gestured toward Liz, "is a gardener and wanted to get some ideas for her own garden. Deirdre suggested we come over to see what her landscapers have done." Emma crossed her fingers behind her back.

The woman looked far from convinced, but at least she no longer had the police on speed dial.

"We're really sorry to have bothered you," Bitsy said in the most honeyed tones. "We'll be going now."

Emma started to move toward the street with them but then had an idea.

"You've been cleaning for Mrs. Porter for a while?" She tried to achieve a friendly look, but it was difficult in the face of the woman's suspicious glare.

The woman nodded. "I come every week except if she needs me for something special, then I come more often."

"Special?"

"Like if she and Mr. Porter entertain, or it's the holidays."

"I imagine after that party last week . . ."

"Oh yes. The place was a mess. I gave the kitchen a good

scrub. Had to do the floors, too, even though I'd just done them. Someone tracked mud from the garden clear across the floor."

"Mud?"

The woman nodded. "Straight from the doors to the patio"—she gestured behind her toward the back of the house—"and right to the kitchen table."

Chapter 12

"DO you think she'll say anything to Deirdre?" Emma asked as Liz gunned the engine and the car shot away from the curb.

"Probably. But will she know it was us? We didn't give our names," Bitsy said.

"I don't think it would be that hard for Deirdre to figure it out." Liz slowed as the gates to the community fanned open.

"Do you think Deirdre will be mad?" Bitsy leaned forward with her elbows on the back of Emma's seat.

"I hope not. Aunt Arabella doesn't want to lose her as a customer."

"None of us does." Bitsy stuck out her lower lip. "She must order several dozen cupcakes a month from Sprinkles."

"The goodwill of the Porters alone is worth money in

this town." Liz turned onto Washington Street. "But at least our trip wasn't in vain. We found where that foxglove flower came from."

"Yes," Emma added, "and we also have confirmation that someone went out into the garden during the trunk show."

"I wish we knew who," Bitsy mused.

"That makes two of us," Emma said.

Liz drove around the corner and stopped in front of Sprinkles. They could see Hayley's two-toned black and fuchsia hair through the window. Bitsy got out and Emma turned to Liz.

"Did you know that Brian's ex is getting married next month?"

Liz glanced at Emma. "He told you?"

"Yes. He seemed a bit . . . upset."

"Not upset exactly." Liz reached over and patted Emma's hand. "It means that chapter really is over. I think ultimately it will give him a much-needed sense of closure." She smiled at Emma. "And then he'll be ready to move on. You just need to bide your time a little longer."

Bide my time. What a strange thought, Emma realized, since she'd been in love with Brian since she was a young girl. If the kiss he'd given her at the wedding was any indication, she wouldn't have to wait much longer.

EMMA finished out the afternoon, said good night to Arabella and walked around the corner of the building to the stairs to her apartment. Tonight she would be more than happy to have a quiet evening with a microwavable dinner and some time spent on her laptop exploring shape wear for their upcoming trunk show at Marjorie Porter's. She trudged up the stairs and opened the door to the space Arabella had given her above Sweet Nothings. Emma always felt a sense of peace as soon as she walked through the door, and tonight was no different.

She kicked off her shoes, poured herself a glass of sweet tea and plopped down on the sofa with her laptop. Emma clicked on the web site for a company known for its lingerie and scrolled through the pages. She wasn't completely unfamiliar with the garments women used to remake their figures—she'd used a few of those tricks herself. But the number of possibilities available was mind-boggling—from capris to full slips to camis to bicycle shorts. It was possible to compress any part of the body—or the entire body itself—into a size considerably smaller than normal. Emma was convinced that Marjorie's garden club would be keen to buy when they saw what these undergarments could do.

She jotted down a list of the things she wanted to order and the company's phone number. She took a sip of her tea, nibbled the end of her pencil and looked at her list again. Did she dare order so many things? Would they sell? She scratched a few items off her list and crossed her fingers.

Emma closed her laptop and went out to the kitchen. She opened the freezer and stared at the contents. She had a couple of frozen meals she kept for nights when she didn't feel like cooking. She sorted through them and decided on a Thai chicken dish that was usually fairly decent.

While it was in the microwave, she thought about the events of the afternoon. It appeared obvious now that someone went out to Deirdre's garden, picked a foxglove flower and slipped it onto one of Bitsy's cupcakes. She would go to Detective Walker tomorrow and let him know what she'd discovered. Perhaps the police had some way of recovering any footprints that might have been left in the garden. She rather doubted it, but at least Walker would know what to do.

She thought about Arabella's and her conversation with Marjorie Porter. Apparently this Lotte Fanning woman had it in for Jessica, too, for some reason. Unfortunately neither Emma nor Arabella was acquainted with her. The microwave pinged, and Emma removed her cardboard dinner and took it to the small table in the dining area of the living room.

As she passed the small mirror on the wall by the bookcase, she noticed that her hair was getting a little on the raggedy side. She'd cut it short just before returning home to Paris, and during the summer heat, she was very glad to have it off her neck. She'd thought about growing it back, but she liked it the way it was. Although at the moment, it was in desperate need of some shaping. She'd call Angel Cuts in the morning and make an appointment.

Emma started to sit down when a thought struck her. Almost everyone in Paris went to Angel Cuts. Angel Roy offered the shopkeepers a discount, and her prices were very reasonable. Most people preferred to go to someone local rather than one of the chains out at the mall. All of which meant it was quite possible that Lotte Fanning was a client. And if she was, then perhaps Angel would know why Marjorie Porter thought that Lotte might have wanted Jessica Scott dead.

Emma grabbed her cell phone, entered a note to remind herself to make an appointment at Angel Cuts in the morning, then went back to eating her microwaved chicken dish with more gusto than before.

EMMA called Angel Cuts first thing and managed to get an appointment for noon that same day. She crossed her fingers that she would come away with more than just a haircut. Then she called Arabella to see if she could open Sweet Nothings. Emma was bound and determined to have a chat with Detective Walker before the sun got any higher in the sky.

Arabella was already up and dressed and more than happy to head to the shop immediately. Emma dabbed on some lipstick and pulled a comb through her hair. Too bad she couldn't have gotten her haircut before going to see Walker. The thought brought her to a standstill. She had no interest in Walker, so what difference did it make? She managed to convince herself, as she walked toward the Bug, that it was just that she prided herself on always trying to look her best. Walker had nothing to do with it.

Emma put the Bug in gear and headed toward Caldwell Street and the police department. For a moment she wondered if she ought to have called first, and she crossed her fingers that Walker would be in.

She kept them crossed as she approached the reception desk in the lobby of the brick building that housed the Paris Police Department.

"I'd like to see Detective Walker, please."

The harassed-looking older woman who greeted her jerked a thumb toward the front door.

"Walker's gone into town to get a bite to eat."

Darn! "Do you happen to know where?"

"The Coffee Klatch, where else?" she said as if that settled that. "Being a bachelor he don't like to cook for himself. Probably don't know how anyways, so he starts every day with a big old farmer's breakfast."

Emma thought about what that would do to her waistline, although it obviously hadn't hurt Walker's. He was as trim as an athlete.

"Course he always works straight through lunch, nibbling

on one of them granola bars." She shook her finger at Emma. "I told him more than once he needs to get himself a wife. Then he'd be going home to a hot meal and not one of them microwavable dinners."

The woman began to eye Emma appraisingly. Was she considering her as a possible candidate for the unmarried Detective Walker? Emma decided not to find out, but quickly said good-bye and headed back to her car.

She hated barging in on Detective Walker's morning meal, but she didn't want to wait until later in the day when the store would get busy and she might not be able to get away.

She left the Bug in the parking lot behind Sweet Nothings and walked down to the Coffee Klatch. It wasn't crowded, and Emma quickly picked out Walker sitting by himself at a table near the kitchen.

As soon as the hostess saw Emma, she grabbed a menu and headed her way.

"Thanks." Emma waved her away. "I'm meeting someone." She pointed in Walker's direction.

The hostess brandished the menu at Emma, but Emma shook her head and strode resolutely toward Walker's table.

He looked up, startled, when she came abreast of him. He put down his fork and immediately jumped to his feet.

"Please, don't let me interrupt you." Emma gripped the edge of the vacant chair tightly.

"I can't sit while a pretty lady stands. I'm too much of a Southerner for that."

Emma smiled. "Well then I guess I'll have to sit."

"I guess you will." Walker sank into his seat as Emma pulled out the empty chair.

"Please don't let me interrupt your breakfast." Emma

indicated Walker's half-full plate of scrambled eggs, ham and buttered grits.

Walker gave a slow smile that deepened the dimple in his right cheek. "Now you know that no true-blue Southern gentleman is going to lift his fork while a pretty lady is sitting opposite him still waiting for her food."

His smile was contagious, and Emma found herself grinning back. "Well, this Southern lady has already had breakfast, so how do we handle that?" She leaned over the table slightly toward Walker.

Walker furrowed his brow in mock seriousness. "Now that is something of a puzzle."

"How about if I order a cup of tea? Will that do?"

"Brilliant idea, ma'am." Walker grinned and gestured toward the waitress.

Mabel headed toward their table with the purposefulness of an ocean liner heading out to sea. She gave Emma a strange look when she saw her. Of course Mabel was used to seeing Emma coming in with Brian. Suddenly Emma wondered what everyone else might be thinking? She gave a quick look around, but there was no one she knew. She relaxed slightly and ordered a cup of green tea.

"Green tea?" Walker said as soon as Mabel headed toward the kitchen.

"It's not unlike regular tea," Emma explained. "But green tea undergoes minimal processing and isn't fermented like black tea. It's supposed to be full of antioxidants."

"I take it that's a good thing."

"A very good thing," Emma agreed.

Mabel slid a cup in front of Emma, and the liquid sloshed over the side onto the saucer. Emma lifted it to her lips and was relieved to see Walker pick up his fork.

"While I wish you'd come here just to see me, I'm going to guess that's not the case." Walker looked at Emma inquiringly.

She put her cup down a bit too abruptly, and it clanked against the saucer.

"No, I'm afraid not."

"I'd even venture to guess that it's about the case I'm working on. The death of that young lady, Jessica Scott." Walker swiped his napkin across his lips.

"Yes." Emma began shredding the paper napkin in her lap. "I thought you ought to know that my friends and I discovered foxglove growing in Deirdre Porter's garden. And the cleaning lady said that after the party, she found muddy footprints leading from the garden right to the kitchen table. I mean, we did hear it was foxglove that was the cause of death." Emma fiddled with the remnants of her napkin.

"Did she now. That's very interesting." Walker forked up the last of his hash browns. "We'll definitely look into that."

Emma was relieved that he hadn't blown her off. Of course it might be that he was just being polite, and he would forget about it the minute she turned around.

"Now that we have that out of the way . . ." Walker grinned at Emma across the table.

The conversation was taking a turn that suddenly made Emma nervous. "I've . . . I've got to be going." She reached for her purse.

Walker shot out of his seat as soon as Emma began to stand up.

"Will you . . . will you let me know what you find?"

Walker sketched a salute. "I certainly will. Anything that gives me another chance to talk to you."

Emma all but bolted from her seat. She turned around to

see Liz staring at her with a strange expression on her face. Before Emma could reach her friend, Liz had blasted through the front door of the Coffee Klatch and was on her way down the street.

THE look Emma had seen on Liz's face worried her all afternoon. Several times she tried calling her friend, but there was no answer either at the Bannings' house or on Liz's cell. Emma couldn't imagine what had come over Liz. Had she jumped to the wrong conclusion when she saw Emma sitting with Walker?

Emma tried her one last time, but then it was time to leave Sweet Nothings for her hair appointment. She was getting her purse when a symphony of blaring horns came from outside on the street. Emma ran to the window in time to see Sylvia's ancient Cadillac turn left onto Washington Street from the right lane. The horns reached a crescendo and then tapered off as Sylvia sailed down the street, seemingly oblivious to the red faces of the wildly gesturing drivers around her.

"Sylvia's here," Emma announced.

"I suspected that," Arabella said dryly. "You might as well run along to Angel's then. I'll keep my fingers crossed that you have some luck."

"Thanks." Emma paused in front of one of the mirrors and finger combed her hair, succeeding only in making it look even messier. No matter. Angel would soon set it right.

The breeze had a hint of coolness to it that was barely noticeable, the warmth of the sun easily counteracting it. Emma strolled down Washington Street, stopping to wave to Willie behind the window of the Meat Mart. She glanced toward the Toggery, Paris's oldest remaining store, and thought she saw Les in the window. She raised a hand in salute.

Emma was passing Let Us Cater to You, when the door opened and Lucy popped her teased, white head out.

"Emma!" She gave Emma a big hug. "How are things down at Sweet Nothings?" The sun glinted off the enormous cubic zirconia solitaire she wore on her left hand. She'd bought it for herself to fool everyone into thinking that her latest husband, Harry, was a wealthy man. She hoped it would forestall any questions about the prudence of her making a fifth match.

"Fine. Just fine." Emma returned the embrace.

"I saw the story in the *Post* this morning about that poor woman, Jessica Scott." Lucy waved a hand and her ring flashed in the sunlight.

A sense of dread settled over Emma like a cloud. Would this article have mentioned Liz? She hoped not.

"What did it say?"

The phone rang inside Lucy's shop, but she ignored it. "It said something about how she died on account of eating some kind of poisonous flower on one of the cupcakes that were served. Said they came from Sprinkles." She shuddered. "Not sure I want to eat any more of those. Although the devil's food ones are to die for."

"It won't happen again," Emma reassured her. What would happen to Bitsy's business if everyone felt that way? "It's beginning to look as if someone swapped out the edible flower for the poisonous one."

"Oh my heavens." Lucy put a hand over her mouth. "As in . . ."

Emma nodded. "Yes. Murder."

"What are things coming to?" Lucy asked, looking skyward.

Emma gave Lucy another quick hug and hurried down the street toward Angel Cuts. She wondered how the newspaper had gotten hold of the story about Jessica. She was surprised they hadn't run something earlier but suspected that the Porters had managed to squash any reports. Marjorie probably didn't want the world knowing that someone had been murdered at her daughter-in-law's party.

Emma pushed open the door of Angel Cuts. Warm air redolent with the scent of hair spray and shampoo and overlaid with undertones of chemicals hit her in the face.

The shop was humming as always. Angel did a brisk business and was even considering expanding. The girl at the reception desk had the telephone receiver sandwiched between her shoulder and her ear, and was talking to two other women who were standing by the desk. Emma waited patiently until the woman had dealt with everyone else, then gave her name and found a seat in the reception area.

She thumbed halfheartedly through some dog-eared magazines, listening to the chatter around her. The monotonous hum of the dryers made her feel sleepy, and she let her head fall back against the chair cushion. The spot was warm from the sun coming in the window, and she was soon dozing off.

"Emma? Emma, wake up."

Emma woke to find Angel gently shaking her arm.

"You must be tired, girl."

Emma yawned. "I am. We've been going nonstop since Sweet Nothings opened."

"You need a spa day." Angel led Emma to the washbasins at the back of the shop. She wrapped a strip of paper around Emma's neck then swirled a plastic cape over her. "We're going to start doing spa days next week—hot stone massage, mani, pedi, facial and a wash and blow-dry. You should book one for yourself."

"It sounds heavenly," Emma said as Angel ran warm water over her hair. "You must be doing well."

Angel shrugged and snapped her gum. "Can't complain. Customer service is what people want, I always say. And that's what I give 'em. Not like the big chains where you're no more than a number." She poured some shampoo into her hand and began to scrub Emma's head. "I know my customers. I know their names, their husband's names, their kids' names. Heck, more often than not I even know their pets' names. You can't tell me the operators at that swanky place over at the mall can say the same thing."

Emma mumbled something. She was feeling sleepy again thanks to the warm water and Angel's gentle massaging of her scalp. She was almost dozing off when she remembered her true mission.

Angel wrapped Emma's head in a towel and led her over to her station. All sorts of cards and mementos were stuck in the frame of her mirror. Emma noticed some snapshots of two blond children—a boy and a girl. They weren't Angel's; she knew that. Perhaps they were a niece and nephew. There was a ticket to the Paris Fish Fry—billed as the biggest in the world—and a prayer card from someone's funeral, though Emma couldn't quite read the name on it.

"Just a trim today?" Angel swung Emma around to face the mirror.

Emma nodded. "How's Tom?"

"Tom? Ancient history." Angel pointed at the snapshot of a man in a baseball cap tucked into her mirror. "Tyler. Tyler Johnson. Tom never did understand what I was trying to do with the business. Tyler gets it, though."

Emma smiled. "Nice-looking guy."

"Smart, too." Angel combed Emma's hair forward and began snipping her bangs.

"Is Lotte Fanning possibly a client of yours?" Emma asked, as Angel pushed her head forward and began trimming the hair at the nape of her neck.

"Lotte Fanning? Oh, I imagine you mean Charlotte Fanning. At least that's what she calls herself when she comes here. She's so very la-di-da, it just about makes your teeth ache, but she's a good tipper and always has a little something for the girls at Christmastime."

"Someone told me that she really had it in for Jessica Scott, the girl who died at our trunk show. I don't know if you've heard about it."

"I saw a piece on it in the paper this morning. Said there was something wrong with the cupcakes?"

"Not the cupcakes, no. They were fine," Emma said emphatically. "It was the flower on the cupcake. Bitsy uses edible flowers for decoration, and someone swapped one of those for a poisonous foxglove flower."

"Oh my!" Angel stopped with her scissors in midair. "Who would ever do such a thing?"

"I have no idea," Emma admitted. "But Charlotte Fanning was at the party, and someone said she didn't at all like Jessica, the murdered woman."

"Really?"

"Yes. The thing is, we can't imagine why. We were hoping you might have some information."

Angel shook her head emphatically. "Don't tell me you're up to your snooping again. Didn't it almost get you killed last time?"

Emma hung her head sheepishly. "It's just that people might blame Bitsy because of her cupcakes, and I can't stand by and let that happen."

"I'm afraid I don't know much of anything about Mrs. Fanning." Angel smoothed some product through Emma's hair. "But Flora always did her nails. Perhaps she knows something."

"Can I get an appointment with her?" Emma examined her nails and came to the conclusion that she needed a manicure.

"Check with Janellyn at the desk. Perhaps she can fit you in."

Emma tried to relax through the rest of her appointment, but her entire focus was on Flora, and what she might know about Lotte Fanning. As soon as Angel finished blow-drying her hair, she hotfooted it to the reception desk.

Janellyn ran her finger down a long column of appointments while Emma held her breath. She could always come back, of course, but like a child, she wanted the answer right now.

Finally, Janellyn looked up. "If all you want is a plain manicure, nothing fancy, no tips or acrylics, Flora should be able to fit you in." She pointed toward a rack of nail polish. "Why don't you pick out your color while I go see if she's ready."

Emma stared at the rows and rows of nail polish hues until they all blurred together. She finally grabbed a bottle off the shelf when she saw Janellyn gesturing to her.

Flora smiled at Emma and stuck her right hand in a dish of soapy water, all without saying anything.

"Nice day today, isn't it?" Emma said to break the ice.

Flora nodded.

"Have you worked here long?"

"Yes."

Emma barely restrained from rolling her eyes, although Flora probably wouldn't have noticed since she was bent over Emma's left hand and going at her nails with an emery board. Emma felt slightly chagrined. She had been neglecting her hands lately. Not like when she worked in New York and would skip lunch in order to be able to afford a manicure.

"Do you know Charlotte Fanning?" Emma asked but then continued without waiting for an answer. "Angel thought she was a client of yours. I saw her at a party the other day, and she was going on and on about what a wonderful manicurist she had."

Flora looked up and slowly smiled. "That would be me." A flush rose from the neck of her plain white blouse to the roots of her light brown hair.

Emma smiled back at her. "Mrs. Fanning was so complimentary about your work. Said she wouldn't have anyone else." Emma crossed her fingers behind her back.

"She always chooses debutante pink for her nails. Says it's the only appropriate color for a lady."

Emma glanced at the bottle of midnight blue polish she'd randomly grabbed off the shelf and cringed.

"I imagine you're a wonderful confidante to Mrs. Fanning as well." Emma threw the idea out much like a fisherman testing a new lure.

The expression on Flora's face was one of confusion.

Emma was equally confused but then realized that Flora might have been stumped by the word *confidante*.

"I imagine Mrs. Fanning confided in you a lot . . . told you everything," Emma added when Flora still looked confused.

Flora's face cleared, and she shook her head. "Yes, she talked about her daughter all the time. Missy, her name is. Not sure if that's short for something or not."

"I imagine she's very proud of her daughter." Emma was digging, but she didn't know what else to do.

"Oh yes. She graduated UT with all A's. She was supposed

to go work at that place for seniors, Sunny Days, but something happened. Mrs. Fanning was that upset about it."

Flora fell silent, and Emma realized she had probably gleaned all the information she was going to. She stared at her newly painted midnight blue nails thoughtfully. If Jessica had stood in the way of this Missy getting the job she anticipated having at Sunny Days, would that have been enough to drive Lotte Fanning to murder?

Chapter 13

ARABELLA arrived at Sweet Nothings the next morning looking even more cheerful than usual. "Good morning," she sang out as she unclipped Pierre's leash and stowed it behind the counter. "Isn't it positively gorgeous out?" She had her long silver hair piled on top of her head in an updo and was wearing a top Emma hadn't seen before.

"New top?"

Arabella circled in front of Emma. "Like it?"

"Yes." Emma admired the oversized white linen blouse with the embroidery on the front. "What's the occasion?"

Arabella's cheeks turned a becoming pink. "Francis is coming for dinner."

"Aha," Emma said.

"Maybe later you can run down to Sprinkles and get me some cupcakes, okay?" Arabella said.

"You're not making your famous chess pie?"

Arabella shook her head. "As much as Francis loves it, I thought it was time for something different. Besides, I'm trying my hand at a *bastilla*—I had it several times when I was in Morocco. Of course I'm not going to make it with pigeon, which is traditional. A nice chicken from the Meat Mart will have to do. It's a huge undertaking, so dessert will have to be store-bought."

"What else goes into it?"

Arabella thought for a moment. "If I had to describe it, I would say it's a sort of chicken pot pie but with a phyllo dough crust that is dusted with powdered sugar, cinnamon and ground almonds. It has all sorts of exotic ingredients like orange water, but I'll have to do the best I can with what I can find."

"It sounds more like a dessert than a main course."

Arabella laughed. "Oh, I must tell you about the dinner party I attended in New York one time. I was invited by the Moroccan ambassador, and I was so naïve!" Arabella put both hands against her cheeks. "Dinner was served—a *bastilla*— and I was positive that the cook had made a terrible mistake and had served the dessert instead of the main course. Fortunately I didn't say anything, because I soon learned that this pigeon pie, despite its powdered sugar and cinnamon, is dinner for many people from that part of the world."

"I'd be glad to run and get some of Bitsy's cupcakes for you and Francis. But promise to save me a piece of this . . . What did you call it?"

"*Bastilla*. I certainly will. I think you'll like it."

LATER that afternoon when there was a lull in customers, Emma grabbed her purse from behind the counter. "I'll head over to Sprinkles now," she called to Arabella who was sitting at the desk in the stockroom working on the invitations to the trunk show at Marjorie Porter's. "What flavors do you want?" Arabella looked up. "You decide, dear. All Bitsy's things are so delicious."

The wind had picked up, and a tsunami of dust and leaves was blowing down Washington Street. Emma lowered her head and narrowed her eyes against the debris. She turned the corner onto Market Street and was grateful that the turn put the wind at her back. A splash of red in the Gallery caught Emma's eye—a pile of pretty silk pillows mounded on a neutral-colored sofa. One of them would look great on Emma's couch. She was about to go in, but then decided she didn't want to leave Arabella alone too long in the shop. She could come back another day.

Emma pushed open the door to Sprinkles and was taken aback to find it empty. It must be a momentary lull, she thought. Usually people were three and four deep at the counter all day long. She glanced into the glass cabinet where cupcakes marched in unbroken rows. Emma was surprised to note that none of them had been embellished with Bitsy's signature edible flowers.

The curtain to the back room swished open, and Bitsy emerged. Emma was shocked to see that her eyes were all red and swollen. She must have been crying.

"What's wrong?" Emma said in alarm.

Bitsy sniffed and pulled a tissue from her sleeve. She dabbed at her eyes. "Oh, Emma, I don't know what to do." She glanced toward the display cases crammed with cupcakes of every flavor.

"What's wrong?" Emma asked again.

Bitsy opened her mouth but all that came out was a sob.

Emma put her arms around her friend. "Whatever it is, it can't be that bad."

Bitsy gave a loud sniff that turned into a hiccup.

"Is it something to do with the shop?"

Bitsy nodded. "No one has been in all morning."

"Maybe it's an off day?" Emma tried to think of a reason why fewer people would be buying cupcakes on that particular Friday.

"No. You don't understand. Not a single person has come in today. Not even one."

"But why—"

"It's because of that article in the *Post-Intelligencer* yesterday." Bitsy finished with a sob quickly followed by another hiccup. "I'm ruined. I've put everything I have into this shop. I don't know what I'll do."

"Now, now, it's probably not as dire as all that," Emma said, although her heart was sinking.

"I've stopped using the edible flowers on my cupcakes." Bitsy gave a loud sniff and rubbed her nose with the tissue. "I feel terrible doing that to Liz, but I can't take any chances. Then today, people suddenly stopped coming in. Normally by now I'd have sold most of my inventory." She waved a hand toward the still full display cases.

"I wonder . . ."

"What?" Bitsy looked up, her large eyes filled with tears.

"I wonder if someone planted that story in the *Post*. There's been nothing in the paper up till now."

"That's true." Bitsy wiped her eyes and nose with the tissue, took a deep breath and straightened her blouse.

"The timing seems odd." Emma wandered around Sprinkles staring, unseeingly, at the rows and rows of delicious cupcakes. She picked up the copy of the *Post-Intelligencer* that Bitsy had lying out on the counter. "First— nothing. Frankly, I can easily imagine Marjorie Porter forbidding the paper to run any stories on Jessica's death. She wouldn't want her daughter-in-law's name in the paper."

Bitsy gave a short laugh. "That's for sure. The only time a true Southern gentlewoman is supposed to have her name in the paper is when she's born, when she's married and when she dies."

Emma nodded. "So Marjorie kills any mention of the trunk show and how Jessica died at Deirdre's."

"But why would they print something now?"

"What if Marjorie changed her mind and gave them the go-ahead?"

"Why on earth would she do that?"

"Maybe Deirdre's cleaning lady told Deirdre about our visit to the Porter garden. And maybe that ticked Deirdre off enough to mention it to Mama Porter. Mama Porter decided we had to be made to pay so she called the paper."

Bitsy was slowly nodding. "I think you could be right."

"Everyone reads the story in the *Post*." Emma picked up the paper and scanned the article. She pointed to one of the paragraphs with her index finger. "It says right here, 'The foxglove flower that killed Jessica Scott was believed to have come from one of the cupcakes provided by Sprinkles on Market Street.'"

Bitsy slumped against one of the display cases. "I'm ruined."

Words of sympathy rose to Emma's lips but were stilled by a sudden thought. What if Sweet Nothings was next? What was to stop Marjorie from taking some action against them? Bitsy hadn't been the only one sneaking into Deirdre's garden—Emma and Liz had been there, too.

EMMA was looking forward to hearing about Arabella's evening with Francis. She was also looking forward to sampling a piece of Arabella's *bastilla*. She hoped that Francis was appropriately appreciative of all the work Arabella had gone to.

Arabella's expression was less than rosy when she arrived at Sweet Nothings on Saturday morning.

"What's the matter?" Emma asked as soon as Arabella had fixed herself a cup of coffee.

"Nothing's the matter. What makes you think something is the matter?" Arabella said rather more sharply than usual.

Emma's stomach clenched. Had Arabella found out about the extra money she'd spent on the lingerie from Monique Berthole? It didn't seem likely. Besides, Arabella was the sort to tackle things head-on. It was one of the traits Emma treasured about her.

Emma watched as Arabella absentmindedly stirred three spoons of sugar into her coffee.

"Something's wrong. I know it."

Arabella took a sip of her coffee and grimaced. "Good heavens, what on earth did I put in here?"

"A lot of sugar."

"You can say that again." Arabella put the cup down decisively.

"I wish you'd tell me what's bothering you."

Arabella frowned and rubbed a hand across her forehead. "It's rather silly, to be honest with you. It's not as if I didn't know that Francis was a police officer."

"This has something to do with his job?"

Arabella nodded. "He's been put on a new assignment. He swears it isn't dangerous, but I don't believe him for a minute. Why can't he retire and enjoy life on his pension? He's old enough. There's no need for him to be risking life and limb at his age. Leave that for the younger men."

"But isn't that part of what you like about him?"

Arabella looked sheepish. "I suppose you're right. That sense of danger is . . ."

"Sexy?"

"I prefer the word *alluring*."

Emma filled a mug with water and put it in the microwave. "How dangerous is this assignment of his?"

"He insists it's nothing, but it sounds quite perilous to me. It seems he's going to be working undercover. Apparently there has been a string of bank robberies around Henry County. Not the usual bumbling sort of affair where the thieves make off with less than a thousand dollars' worth of marked bills. These thieves are emptying safe-deposit boxes."

"What is Francis going to do?" Emma retrieved a tea bag from the counter over the small sink and dunked it into her mug.

"He's going to pretend to be the night watchman at one of the banks they expect the thieves to target next." Arabella's face clouded over.

"What's wrong?"

"During the last two robberies, the night watchman was shot. One of them died," Arabella added in a very small voice.

Emma tried to hide her dismay. This venture of Francis's did sound very dangerous indeed.

"I wonder how Bitsy is today. I do hope yesterday was a fluke and that business picks up for her today," Arabella said, adroitly changing the subject.

Just then the door banged open and Sylvia entered. She stopped on the threshold for a prolonged fit of coughing.

"Can I get you some water?"

Sylvia shook her head. "I'll be fine in a minute." Her coughing slowly subsided. "I think I'm going to have to give up smoking. We're not allowed to light up at Sunny Days at all, not even in our own rooms, and it's becoming a nuisance sneaking out to the parking lot."

"Good idea," Arabella said.

"I heard that woman they took to the hospital the other day is coming back soon. She's still in a coma, but there's nothing more the hospital can do for her."

"Is there any chance she'll regain consciousness?" Arabella smoothed the front of her skirt.

Sylvia shrugged. "Who knows. Miracles do happen."

Something thudded against the front door and was swiftly followed by a sharp knock.

"Coming," Sylvia yelled as she made her way to the door.

Two large boxes and a burly UPS deliveryman in brown shorts stood on the doorstep.

"Is this . . ." He glanced at his clipboard. "Sweet Nothings?"

"Yes," the three of them chorused at once.

He held out the clipboard. "Delivery. Someone want to sign for me, please?"

Sylvia grabbed the proffered pen and paper and scrawled her signature on the dotted line.

"Where do you ladies want me to put these?" The deliveryman tapped the nearest box with his toe.

"Over by the counter is fine," Emma said, peering at the label on the nearest box.

"What is it? Christmas?" Sylvia joked.

"No. It's the shape wear I ordered for our trunk show at Marjorie Porter's."

"Let's hope this one goes better than the last," Sylvia grumbled.

"Why?" Arabella raised her brows. "I thought we did rather well at the last one."

"Sure." Sylvia shrugged. "As long as you consider some-one dropping dead a success."

Chapter 14

SATURDAY turned out to be very busy at Sweet Nothings. Four women drove over from Nashville, having heard about the shop from a friend. Arabella sold the tall brunette a pair of peach silk 1930s pajamas embellished with ecru lace for a handsome sum. The petite blonde snapped up a baby blue World War Two–era Carol Brent bed jacket for her daughter to wear in the hospital after her baby was born.

Sylvia fitted the other two women for bras, and one of them also walked out with a shopping bag filled with an array of panties and camisoles from the Monique Berthole collection. When Emma saw the numbers adding up on the register, she began to feel hopeful that they might pull out of their financial hole sooner rather than later.

A busy day means a tiring one, though, and Emma nearly crawled up the stairs to her apartment after flipping the *open* sign to *closed*, straightening the stock and turning out the lights.

She was about to stretch out on the window seat with a glass of cold lemonade when she noticed that her plants needed watering. She was growing a selection of herbs on the windowsill—basil, chives, rosemary and some arugula to add to salads. The basil, in particular, was looking rather limp. She filled a pitcher with water and poured some in each of the pots.

She was hungry, but when she looked in her refrigerator she was dismayed to see the sparse contents—a few containers of yogurt, a piece of cheese, some bread and a few spoonfuls of leftover tuna salad. She was reaching for her cell phone to order a pizza when it rang.

"Hello?"

"Emma?"

It was Brian. "Yes?"

"I'm so glad you're home. I was afraid you might be . . . out."

Emma realized it *was* Saturday night. A night when many single women had a date.

"I was hoping to be done early enough to take you to dinner, but after closing up the hardware store, I had to check on a renovation job. We're on a tight deadline, so my crew is working six days a week. Have you eaten yet?"

Emma felt her stomach grumble and thought of the contents of her refrigerator. "No, I haven't."

"Do you like Chinese food? I could swing by the Golden Dragon and pick up a few things if you like."

"Sounds great."

"I really want to talk to you about Liz."

Emma jerked and nearly dropped the telephone. Had Liz said something to Brian about seeing her with Detective Walker? The situation was easily explained. Most likely it was something else. It sounded as if Brian was worried about his sister. Emma had started to worry, too.

"I'll see you in a few then."

Emma hung up the phone, tossed it on the sofa and dashed into the bathroom. She knew she could wash her face and redo some minimal makeup in under five minutes. Once again, she was glad she'd cut her hair short. A little product, a little scrunching, and it would look as fresh as ever.

Fortunately the apartment was already reasonably tidy. Emma removed two glasses from the sink and transferred them to the dishwasher and added the newspaper to the recycle bin. By the time Brian arrived, she was sitting on the sofa flipping through a magazine trying to feel as calm and collected as she hoped she looked.

Brian came in with a brown paper grocery bag in each arm. Delicious smells redolent of soy, garlic, ginger and other exotic ingredients emanated from within. He put the bags down on the table and pulled a bottle of white wine from one of them.

"I got us a nice pinot grigio. At least the clerk in the store said it's good. It's already slightly chilled, but if you have a bucket and some ice, that would be good."

Emma was glad to have something to do. Brian seemed larger than ever in her tiny apartment, and they kept accidentally touching as they moved about the small space.

Brian poured them each a glass of wine then pulled several white containers from the bags. "I've got beef with broccoli, General Tsao's chicken and some shrimp fried rice. Hope that's okay."

"Sounds delicious." Emma put out plates, napkins and forks.

"Do you want one of these?" Brian held up two paper-wrapped bundles of chopsticks.

"Sure."

"I never could get the hang of them," he said as he opened the containers and motioned for Emma to go ahead.

She helped herself to a spoonful of each dish, then unwrapped the set of chopsticks Brian handed her.

"You're really good with those." Brian watched as Emma lifted a piece of chicken to her mouth.

Brian had unwrapped the other set and was trying to imitate the way Emma was holding them.

"No, like this." She leaned toward Brian and positioned his hand on the chopsticks. Touching him felt so good, and she hated to move her hand away.

Brian tried levering a piece of broccoli toward his mouth, but he dropped it, and it slithered down his shirt, leaving a greasy stain.

"I guess this is going to take some practice." He rubbed at the spot on his shirt. "Someday I'd love to travel and see a bit more of the world and learn to do things like eat with chopsticks." He picked up his fork.

Emma had a sudden vision of her and Brian traveling to Hong Kong, India, Malaysia and other exotic places that Aunt Arabella had described to her. Much as she wanted to eventually settle down, it would be fun to see a bit of the world first.

Brian reached for the fried rice and spooned more onto his plate. "I wanted to talk to you, because I've been really worried about Liz."

Emma raised her brows questioningly.

"This whole situation is getting to her. I know she's blaming herself for that woman's death, which is absurd."

"It is absurd. Especially since we found the same plant

growing in Deirdre Porter's garden. It's obvious someone simply switched the flowers."

"I know, but Liz refuses to believe that for some reason. I think the stress of her and Matt's situation is getting to her. She's been looking for more freelance work, but it's hard when you have two little kids to take care of. Matt has a lead on a really good contract, but they won't know for a few more weeks if he's got it or not. I know Liz is terrified that they might lose the house. They took out a second mortgage to finance all the renovations they did."

"Oh no. Surely it can't be as bad as all that?"

"Probably not. But when you get into one of those downward spirals, everything seems bleaker than it is." Brian looked down at his hands as if he were studying them. "I had this idea, and I was wondering what you thought." He hesitated briefly. "I could really use some help with the bookkeeping for my renovation business. Liz has always been good with numbers . . . Do you think she'd be offended if I offered her a part-time job? I can't pay all that much, but it might help."

"I think that's a great idea."

"You don't think she'd view it as a handout? I thought of offering to loan them some money—I've managed to save a bit here and there—but knowing Liz she wouldn't go for it."

"You're right. I can't imagine Liz accepting a loan. But a job is different."

"You really think so?"

"Yes. I think you should do it."

"There's another benefit to bringing Liz on board, you know. It'll free up some of the time I've been spending tracking expenses and balancing the books. I'll be able to take you on proper dates." He swept a hand toward the empty Chinese food containers. "I mean, this is fun, but I really want us to be able to spend more time together." He looked down again. "Assuming you want to, that is."

Emma hoped the grin she could feel spreading across her face would be answer enough.

Brian pushed his plate away and reached into the bag from Golden Dragon. "Let's not forget our fortune cookies."

He handed one to Emma.

She cracked it open and pulled out the slip of paper inside. "What does yours say?" She looked at Brian.

"You first."

"Mine says, *Everything will now go your way.*"

"Wow, wouldn't that be nice."

"What about yours?"

Brian squinted at the tiny piece of paper. "*You must work long and hard to achieve your goals.*" He sighed. "That's certainly true."

Emma began to gather the empty containers, and Brian carried their dishes over to the sink. He rinsed while Emma stacked them in the dishwasher.

They finished the dishes, and Brian brought their wine to the sofa. He sat down, his long legs stretching halfway to the kitchen in the tiny living room.

He looked at Emma. "I feel a lot better now having talked to you. I'm going to call Liz first thing in the morning." He put out a hand and smoothed a curl of hair away from Emma's eye with his finger. "I'm really glad you came back to Paris, you know."

Emma felt heat suffuse not just her face, but her whole body. She didn't blink; she didn't even dare breathe.

Brian leaned closer and suddenly he was kissing her—a

long, passionate, satisfying kiss that made Emma forget everything but the moment.

THE shape wear trunk show at Marjorie Porter's was scheduled for Tuesday evening. It was the garden club's regular night to meet for tea at Marjorie's house. Marjorie had called everyone to let them know they were in for a special treat. Emma was praying for a good number of sales.

Promptly at five o'clock, Emma hung the *closed* sign on Sweet Nothings' door and began to load the trunk of her car, Arabella's Mini and Sylvia's Cadillac with boxes.

"Think we got it all?" Sylvia asked as she eased behind the wheel of her ancient vehicle.

"I think so." Emma consulted her clipboard. "I've checked everything off."

"We're good to go then." Sylvia started her car and tooted the horn as she pulled out of the parking lot.

Emma and Arabella followed her to the extremely exclusive area where Marjorie Porter lived. The Porters had purchased an enormous piece of land, and an architect from Memphis had created an exclusive design for their ten thousand square foot brick house. There were two pools—one indoors, one out—a tennis court, a putting green and enough lawn to accommodate a polo match.

The Sweet Nothings convoy pulled into the circular drive and stopped at the massive front door.

"Well, don't let's just stand here," Sylvia said when they all exited their cars. "Someone go ring the bell."

Emma strode up the slate path and pushed the ornate, wrought-iron doorbell.

A minute later the door was flung open, and Marjorie stood there openmouthed. "What are you doing here?"

"We're . . . We're here for the trunk show?" Emma stuttered, ending the sentence on an up note so that it turned out sounding like a question.

"Good heavens!" Marjorie shrieked. "You need to go around to the back door immediately." She pointed around toward the side of the house. "This entrance is for guests only."

"Sheesh," Sylvia grumbled. "The servants' entrance, no less! I never would have thought."

"It's probably easier for us to unload if we go around back," Arabella said soothingly. "I'm sure Marjorie didn't mean anything by it. Did you see all that white carpeting? She's probably afraid of dirt."

Sylvia continued to mumble, but she got back into her Caddy and followed the drive around toward the back of the house, Arabella and Emma right behind her. They pulled into an area the size of a small parking lot and popped open their trunks.

Sylvia and Arabella weren't much use when it came to carrying boxes, so Emma struggled with them as best she could. A woman in a maid's uniform held the door open for her. It led to what Emma thought was generally termed a mudroom, although there wasn't a single speck of dirt or mud to be seen. She dropped the first load of boxes and went out to the car for the rest.

"Let me help with something, please," Arabella begged.

Emma shook her head. "Almost done. Why don't you go inside and see where Marjorie wants us to set up."

Emma hustled the last few boxes into the house and stood for a moment to catch her breath. The mudroom led to a restaurant-sized kitchen complete with restaurant-grade appliances. No expense had been spared—from granite on the countertops to Brazilian wood on the floors. The funny thing was, Emma had the sneaking suspicion that Marjorie never set foot in the room unless she was after a midnight snack.

Finally they got everything unloaded. Emma had decided against mannequins. Shape wear didn't look very pretty—it was the effect it created when you were dressed that counted.

Emma, Arabella and Sylvia edged into the living room where a few women were already talking, punch glasses in hand. The doorbell rang repeatedly, and more and more guests arrived until the room was full. Emma recognized Charlotte Fanning and wondered how she might approach her? Deirdre was there as well, of course, and several of the women Emma remembered from their trunk show at Deirdre's house.

Emma had never had any ambition to be on the stage, and she was quite nervous about getting up in front of the crowd. But she'd done her homework and knew her stuff. The women were definitely very interested, and the whole presentation went quite smoothly.

Emma was packing up some of the merchandise when a young woman came up to her. She had blond hair, carefully coiffed, blue eyes expertly ringed with liner and lush lips painted pink.

"This has been wonderful," she said to Emma in honeyed tones. "I'm getting a pair of those capris for myself. I bought a pair of skinny jeans for the fall, and I need something to smooth everything out."

Emma looked her up and down and failed to find a single inch that needed smoothing, but she wasn't about to turn down a sale.

The girl stuck out her hand. "I'm Missy Fanning, by the way."

Emma shook Missy's perfectly manicured hand and

introduced herself. Here she was being presented with the perfect opportunity to learn more about Lotte Fanning, her daughter and their connection to Jessica Scott and possibly her murder, and her mind was going blank. She nearly broke a sweat racking her brain for a way to introduce Jessica into the conversation.

"Your friend," Missy pointed at Sylvia, "lives at Sunny Days, doesn't she?"

Emma nodded.

Missy pursed her plump pink lips into a perfect pout. "I should have had that administrator's job there." Her lips turned farther downward. "I had the best credentials, but that woman, the one who was killed?"

Emma nodded silently, not wanting to stem the flow of information. "She's the niece of the chairman of the board. Isn't that what they call nepotism?"

"Ah . . . yes . . . I think so," Emma stammered.

"My mother was absolutely furious when she found out. She does know someone on the board, but I guess the chairman trumps all. But . . ." She examined her blush pink nails closely. "Now that that woman is dead, I'm a shoo-in for the job. As a matter of fact, I have an interview next week."

Emma looked at Missy. Did she not realize that she had handed her mother the perfect motive for murder?

Before Emma could think any more about it, Marjorie was announcing dessert and coffee in her loud, overbearing tones, and everyone began the exodus toward the dining room.

The room was enormous, and Marjorie smugly announced that the dining table, the size of a football field to Emma's eyes, had been custom-made for the space. The chandelier hanging above it would not have looked out of place at Lincoln Center and boasted hundreds of sparkling crystals.

The table was spread with a delectable array of sweets from miniature pies that Emma recognized as coming from Let Us Cater to You to fancy French pastries Marjorie must have ordered from Nashville or Memphis. An enormous silver tea set dominated one end of the table and an equally large silver coffee urn the other.

"Please help yourselves," Marjorie ordered everyone. "And don't be afraid. There are no cupcakes from that place that managed to poison poor Jessica Scott."

Emma stifled a gasp. Had that announcement really been necessary? Poor Bitsy. Would Sprinkles ever recover?

Chatter broke out as everyone grabbed plates and helped themselves to refreshments. Emma noticed a pale young woman with limp, curly red hair hovering around the food. She was wearing a pale pink uniform and had an apron around her waist. She'd been at Deirdre's as well, helping in the kitchen.

She looked up, noticed Emma and began making her way in Emma's direction.

"That girl was a friend of yours, wasn't she?" she said in hushed tones. "The one who brought the cupcakes to Mrs. Porter's party?"

"Yes."

"I don't think it's fair, her being blamed when it wasn't her fault."

Emma wondered what the girl was getting at. "What's your name?"

"Gladys. Gladys Smit. Named after my grandmother. On my mother's side; we don't have much to do with Pa's family." She looked into Emma's face searchingly. "Can I tell you something?"

"Of course."

"I honestly don't know what to do." She began to pleat

her apron, running the fabric through her fingers again and again. "I didn't tell the police about it because I didn't want to cause trouble. You know what I mean?"

Emma nodded silently.

"Because honestly, I'm sure she had a perfect reason to be out there, and it didn't have anything to do with, you know, what happened."

"What do you mean, what happened?"

"With that girl dying and all."

"Oh, of course." Emma frowned. "Do you mean you saw someone go outside to the garden that afternoon?"

"Yes. And I thought I'd talk to her and get her advice. You know, kind of figuring she'd laugh and say to go ahead, tell the police, she had nothing to hide. But she didn't."

"Who was this?" Emma asked.

The girl gave a laugh that ended in a stifled sob. "She said I ought not to tell anyone *ever* what I saw because it would cause needless trouble and that I was selfish and inconsiderate for only thinking about myself at a time like that."

"Who was this?" Emma asked again.

Before Gladys could answer, Marjorie came sailing up to them. "Gladys, the teapot needs filling. Please see to it immediately."

Gladys took off at a trot toward the kitchen.

Emma spent the rest of the evening trying to catch up with Gladys again but never did manage it. Finally it was time to leave, and she stuck her head into the kitchen one more time.

"Are you looking for something?" Marjorie asked, coming up behind Emma and making her jump.

"Is Gladys still here?"

"Gladys? Whatever do you want with her?" Marjorie sniffed.

"I wanted to ask her something."

"I'm afraid you're too late. She's already gone."

As Emma gathered together the rest of her things, she wondered who Gladys had been talking about. Had someone merely gone out to the garden for a completely innocent purpose, or had it been the killer picking the deadly foxglove flower?

Chapter 15

EMMA was behind the counter of Sweet Nothings the next morning when the door flew open and nearly ricocheted off the hinges.

"Emma, you've got to come help!" Arabella was red-faced and panting.

"What's happened?" Emma dropped the nightgown she was folding.

"It's Pierre. He pulled the leash right out of my hand and bolted." Arabella's voice quivered as if she were going to cry.

Emma knew how much Pierre meant to Arabella. She made him special meals and even allowed him to sleep on the bed with her, although he had a second duplicate toile dog bed at home right next to Arabella's antique four-poster.

"You sit down, and I'll see what I can do."

Arabella collapsed onto the love seat and Emma dashed out the door. The street was quiet and empty. None of the shops were open yet. Emma looked right and left, but there was no sign of Pierre.

She heard a loud voice coming from across the street. Someone inside the Gallery was shouting. The shouts were followed quickly by several sharp barks that Emma thought sounded an awful lot like Pierre.

Arabella came out of Sweet Nothings to join Emma on the sidewalk.

"That sounded like Pierre, didn't it?" she asked hopefully. "He must have gone after that dreadful Bertha again."

"Yes, it sounded like it was coming from the Gallery." Emma pointed across the street.

She took Arabella's arm, and together they crossed the street. The door to the Gallery wasn't locked, so they pushed it open and Emma peeked in. The bark had been Pierre's alright.

Emma pushed the door open farther and she and Arabella walked in. Zimmerman had Pierre by the scruff of the neck and was berating him loudly. Pierre was ignoring him in favor of sniffing Bertha, Zimmerman's dachshund. Bertha was obviously relishing Pierre's affections, and no one was paying any attention at all to Zimmerman's blustering.

He looked up when he heard Emma and Arabella enter.

"This dog of yours is a nuisance." He gave Pierre an extra shake.

Arabella raised her chin and drew herself up. "Well!"

"Well, indeed. This cur here"—Zimmerman gave Pierre another shake—"barged in and began, ahem," he cleared his throat, "bothering my poor Bertha. And not for the first time, either!"

"That cur, I'll have you know, is a purebred French bull-dog. His father took Best in Show at Westminster."

Zimmerman looked anything but impressed. "It makes

no never mind to me. I won't have him messing with my Bertha."

"He was hardly *messing* with her." Arabella took Pierre's leash from Zimmerman and wound it tightly around her hand. "Bertha would be a most unsuitable match for my Pierre Louis Auguste, I assure you."

And with that she turned on her heel and dragged Pierre out of the Gallery. Emma had no choice but to follow behind.

EMMA made herself a cup of green tea and poured Arabella her favorite coffee brew—a Sumatran blend that she sent away to New York for. Pierre had slunk off to his dog bed, trying to look as if he'd been there all along and none of this had actually happened. Finally, Emma's heartbeat returned to normal, and she could see that Arabella's hands had stopped shaking.

"Testy old fellow," was all Arabella said further on the subject.

"Shouldn't Sylvia be here by now? It's her day for bra fittings, isn't it?" Emma consulted an appointment book she kept under the counter.

"I think so. I suspect she'll be along any moment now."

Just then the door swung open, and Sylvia entered, brutally yanking her oxygen tank over the threshold.

Both Emma and Arabella looked up. Sylvia's face was puckered into a scowl worthy of a Halloween mask, and one of her hoop earrings was missing.

"Good heavens, what's wrong?" Arabella half rose to her feet.

"That Decker woman"—Sylvia stabbed the air with a nicotine-stained finger—"has renewed her campaign against me. She's insisting that I'm responsible for the things going missing at Sunny Days, and she tells everyone who will listen."

"Today is beginning to feel more like a Monday than a Wednesday," Arabella muttered.

"I'm going to move out of that place. Angel's still got that apartment over the shop for rent."

"Won't that upset your children? I really do think it's best you stay. You've been enjoying yourself, haven't you?"

"What about Earl?" Emma added. "He'd miss your company and your card playing."

Sylvia looked sheepish. "I might not have any choice."

"What do you mean?" Arabella asked sharply.

"I kind of had a bit of a dustup with that Decker woman."

"Dustup?" An extremely wary expression came over Arabella's face.

"Yeah. I couldn't take it anymore. If there's one thing I can't stand it's being unjustly accused. Aren't we supposed to be innocent until proven guilty?"

Sylvia glared at Arabella, her one earring quivering with indignation as if in sympathy with its owner.

"Exactly what did you do?" Arabella looked at Emma in alarm.

"I just sort of cuffed her on the ear. I didn't draw blood or anything. The way she carried on you'd think I'd sliced her open with a knife."

Arabella shuddered at the graphic image.

"What happened then?"

"That fool Crystal Davis came running and insisted on having the nurse, then the doctor. And now they're saying they want to have me tested for dementia. Me!" She pointed at her chest. "That Decker woman is the one with dementia, if you ask me."

"Oh dear," was all Arabella said.

"We've got to find out what's really going on," Emma said. "I'm volunteering there tonight. Another ice cream social. Hopefully I can get away and do some digging." She put her arm around Sylvia. "We'll get to the bottom of this. Don't worry."

EMMA pulled into the parking lot at Sunny Days and sat for a moment. She tried Liz on her cell again—she'd called her several times earlier as well—but there was no answer. She had the feeling that Liz was ducking her calls. Could she really have misunderstood Emma's meeting with Walker at the Coffee Klatch?

Emma sighed. She was tired, but she'd promised to help dish out ice cream, and she really had to look into what was going on with Sylvia.

Everyone was gathered in the activity room when Emma arrived. She spotted Catherine Decker immediately and was relieved to see that she didn't bear any bruises, cuts or scrapes from her confrontation with Sylvia. It couldn't have been that bad after all. Catherine was surrounded by a group of extremely solicitous-looking residents who kept shooting glances across the room to where Sylvia and her friend Earl stood all by themselves. It was pretty obvious whose side the residents had taken.

Emma skirted the crowd and went up to Sylvia.

"Now I know what it feels like to be a pariah or one of the untouchables." Sylvia gave a harsh laugh, but Emma could see the hurt in her eyes.

"Never mind, my dear. We'll show them all." Earl tapped the floor with his cane for emphasis.

A table was set up with a row of ice cream cartons, and someone stood behind each of them save for one. Emma grabbed an apron from the utility closet and took up her station behind a giant container of butter pecan ice cream. She smiled as she dished out generous scoops, but her mind was elsewhere. She felt terrible for Sylvia and was glad that she had Earl on her side.

Finally all the ice cream had been dished out, and the residents were seated at the tables, many with their napkins tucked under their chins. Emma tossed her apron in the laundry cart and edged out of the room.

The hallway was empty. Ice cream socials were hugely popular, and only illness or death kept the residents from attending. Emma walked down the hall, not quite certain what to do. Most of the doors were closed, and after twisting one or two knobs, she realized that most were locked as well. If someone was stealing from the residents, they had to be doing it while the resident was in the room. How on earth would they get in otherwise? Emma couldn't imagine any of the septuagenarians or octogenarians that lived at Sunny Days picking a lock or scaling the front of the building and going in through the window.

She was about to turn around and go back when she noticed one of the doors opening. That was odd. She would have bet that everyone was already in the activity room. The door opened extremely slowly, and someone peeked a head around the edge.

It was Crystal Davis.

What was she doing coming out of one of the residents' rooms? She had something in her hand, and when she saw Emma, she tried to hide it.

"What are you doing here?" Crystal demanded.

I could ask you the same thing, Emma thought.

"Volunteering." Emma had learned over time that sometimes the best answer was the shortest one.

Crystal looked doubtful but didn't say anything. Emma was trying to get a glimpse of whatever it was she had so swiftly tucked out of sight. Crystal nodded and began to edge past Emma, transferring the object in front of her as she went past, but Emma was able to get a glimpse of a fairly new-looking digital camera.

Why was Crystal hiding it? *Unless it wasn't hers . . .* Emma had to stop herself from exclaiming it out loud. Was Crystal the one stealing items from the residents' rooms? She had a passkey and easy access. Crystal continued down the hall, and Emma decided to follow her.

Emma followed behind Crystal until they came out to the reception area, at which point Crystal went into her office and closed the door. Emma loitered behind a potted palm for as long as she dared and was rewarded when Crystal emerged ten minutes later, leaving the door ajar.

Emma didn't hesitate. As soon as Crystal was out of sight, she slipped through the partially opened door and into Crystal's office. It was a small, windowless room with a desk in the corner and filing cabinets lining the other walls. Crystal had done little to make it comfortable beyond an old, fraying postcard from Florida taped to her computer monitor. A door at the back of the room led to a much larger office with a big picture window. Emma supposed that was where Jessica Scott had worked.

There was no sign of the camera, and it hadn't looked as if Crystal was carrying anything with her when she left. A metal cabinet stood in the far right corner—the kind used for hanging up coats and stashing umbrellas. Emma turned the lever and eased open the door.

A sound outside the room made her jump, and she stopped and held her breath. A shadow went by the open door, but no one looked in. She was safe. She eased the cabinet door open the rest of the way, and gasped when she saw the contents.

The cupboard was crammed with items—radios, CD players, several MP3 players, a couple of hearing aids, umbrellas, silver picture frames and what looked to be Mr. Mason's missing Korean War medals. Some of the items were valuable, and some had no value at all except perhaps to the owner. Why on earth had Crystal stolen them? Was it some strange compulsion—like a magpie collecting shiny objects that catch its eye?

Emma was closing the cabinet door when Crystal burst into the room.

"What are you doing?" she demanded.

"I could ask you the same thing! You've stolen these things from the residents, haven't you?"

"I . . . I . . ." Crystal stammered.

"Haven't you?" Emma could feel her face burn with fury. All along Crystal had been letting Sylvia, and goodness knows who else, take the blame for her thievery. "Why? Why take these things? Some of them are completely useless to you."

Crystal began to whimper. "I can't help it. It's like some strange addiction. Afterward I feel . . . calm . . . and at peace." She was crying openly now.

"Did Jessica know about this?"

Crystal nodded and wiped her nose with her sleeve. "She said if I ever quit this job, she'd tell everyone about my . . . taking things. I'd never get another job. Ever."

"So that's why you stayed even though she treated you so badly."

Crystal nodded mutely. "I didn't have any choice."

No, Emma could see she didn't have any choice except maybe one—to murder Jessica Scott.

Chapter 16

EMMA crawled behind the wheel of the Bug and looked at the clock. She was surprised to see it was barely past seven thirty. She felt as if a lifetime had passed since she'd arrived at Sunny Days to help serve the residents their post-dinner ice cream treat.

Crystal had eventually dissolved into a puddle of tears, and Emma had been forced to try to calm her down and soothe her enough to get her to talk. They'd agreed that Crystal would leave her job at Sunny Days. As soon as she was gone, the cabinet would be opened and all the stolen goods would be revealed. If the residents got their precious items returned, perhaps no one would insist on calling the police.

Emma, on the other hand, had ideas of her own. She was going to call Gladys Smit and see if the woman she saw go into the garden at the trunk show at Deirdre's had been

Crystal. Emma was quite positive that it had to have been. Desperate to get out from under Jessica's iron rule, Crystal had killed her persecutor. Now it was up to Emma to prove it.

Emma was about to pull out of the parking lot when she thought she might as well tie everything up tonight. She pulled her cell phone from her purse, called information and got Gladys Smit's number.

Unfortunately the phone rang and rang and rang without anyone answering it. Disappointed, Emma dropped her cell into her purse and headed back to her apartment over Sweet Nothings.

Emma's phone rang as she was opening her apartment door. Arabella was anxious to know how the evening had gone. Emma filled her in on the details. Tomorrow she would track down Gladys and try to confirm things.

Tonight, however, she made herself some tea and toast and crawled into bed with a book.

THURSDAY wasn't Sylvia's day at Sweet Nothings, but Arabella was certain she could handle the shop alone and urged Emma to visit Gladys Smit as soon as possible. Emma headed out the door just before lunch, when they were least likely to be busy. She'd found Gladys's address easily enough via whitepages.com—small garden apartments about ten minutes away. The place was quite run-down, with peeling paint and no gardens to speak of. One of the units had a wreath of fading pastel Easter eggs on the front door. It turned out to be Gladys's apartment.

The two parking spaces in front of the unit were empty, which most likely meant that Gladys was out. Emma rang the bell anyway and waited hopefully. She thought she saw the curtain in the window twitch, but no one came to answer the door. She was turning away when the neighbor next door stuck her head out the window.

"Looking for Gladys?" She had jet-black hair permed into impossible curls that were at odds with the hard lines around her eyes and mouth.

"Yes."

"Today's her day for the Rowlands. She does for them every Tuesday and Thursday." She shook her head, but her well-shellacked curls didn't move. "I haven't seen her around today. And not yesterday, either, come to think of it. But she didn't say nothing about going away. Besides, where would she go?"

Emma assumed that was a rhetorical question. "You don't happen to know where these people live, do you? The Rowlands?"

The woman stuck her arm out the window and gestured vaguely toward the north. "You know that new development they just finished building over that way? With all those big houses?"

Emma had a vague idea, but she figured she could always look up the Rowlands' address the way she had Gladys's.

She thanked the woman and turned away, digging her cell from her purse as she walked toward her car. She slid into the front seat and brought up the Internet on her phone. In a few minutes she had the Rowlands' address and was heading in that direction.

The woman was right about the development—it was brand-new and all the houses were enormous. She found the right house easily enough. Landscapers were rolling sod across the barren front yard while another crew was planting a birch tree along the walk leading to the back of the house.

Emma skirted the workers carefully and went up to the front door. Her knock was answered almost immediately by a harassed-looking woman in her forties. She was wearing a tennis outfit, and a racket was propped against the chest in the foyer.

"I thought you were Gladys," she said when she saw Emma. "Although why she would come to the front door, I can't imagine."

Somewhere inside Emma could hear a toddler yelling for juice.

"Keep your shirt on. I'll be right there," the woman called over her shoulder. "I can't imagine what's happened. Gladys should have been here by now. She always watches Hannah for me when I have my lesson." She gestured toward the racket, then turned back and stared at Emma. "What do you want?"

"I'm sorry. I was actually hoping to catch Gladys. Her neighbor said she would be here."

"She should be. I have no idea where she's gotten to. She hasn't called, either."

"I'm sorry to have disturbed you." Emma started backing away.

The woman slammed the door shut without another word.

What now? Emma thought as she drove back toward the shop. She hoped nothing had happened to Gladys. The thought gave her a chill, and she rolled her window up.

Arabella looked up expectantly when Emma got back to Sweet Nothings. Emma shook her head. "Gladys wasn't home. I managed to find out where she works on Thursdays, but she didn't show up today. No one seems to know where she is. Her neighbor hadn't seen her all day today or yesterday."

"That's odd." Arabella shrugged. "Perhaps she's gone away for some reason."

Emma was about to answer when the door opened.

"Hey y'all," Angel Roy called out. "I'm here to do me some shopping. I've got a new squeeze and I need something to impress him with." She smiled coyly. "Other than the usual." She wiggled her rear end suggestively. "Men do like their presents gift wrapped."

"You're absolutely right." Arabella hesitated with her hand on a drawer. "Are you thinking of something vintage or contemporary?"

"This boy's the contemporary type."

"Color?"

"Something pastel and pretty."

"I have just the thing." Arabella opened the drawer, took out several items and displayed them on the counter.

"Oooh," Angel squealed. "Those sure are pretty." She picked up a pair of the bikini panties. "Tyler'll like these for sure."

"What does Tyler do?" Emma asked.

"He works over at the car wash on Market Street."

Emma wondered when Angel was going to find someone as ambitious as she was. This Tyler didn't sound like that sort.

"Oh, did I mention Tyler happens to *own* the car wash? And he's thinking about opening another on the other side of town. Tyler and me are of like minds, that's for sure."

"What about Tom Mulligan? You dated for quite awhile," Arabella asked as Emma pulled a few items from the display case and placed them on the counter along with the things Arabella had chosen.

"Oh, we're still friends. No hard feelings. As a matter of fact, I ran into him at that bar out on Route 69 last night, and he couldn't have been nicer. Oh!" Angel squealed as she held a lacy bustier up to herself and admired the effect in the mirror. "Get this. Tom told me that the police were around his shop yesterday asking all kinds of questions."

"Is Tom in trouble?" Emma asked.

"No, not at all. They were wondering if anyone had brought in a car for some bodywork. Seems like there was a hit-and-run accident Tuesday night."

"Really." Emma put down the garment she was holding.

"That's terrible." Arabella tut-tutted. "I don't understand how someone could do that."

"Neither do I." Angel gathered up some of the things she wanted to try on. "The poor woman was on a bicycle, and this car hit her and then boom"—she snapped her fingers—"it took off like that."

"Is she okay?" Emma's heart had started to beat hard.

Angel shook her head. "No, she's dead. Didn't even make it to the hospital, poor thing."

"You don't happen to know—" Emma began.

"She did work for the Porters on occasion. Both the old lady and the daughter-in-law. As a matter of fact, she was helping serve at some shindig Mrs. Porter was having that night."

"Is there any chance the police mentioned her name?"

Angel shook her head. "No, but the main squeeze of a friend of mine works in the police department. Animal control, but he keeps his ear to the ground. Said her name was Gladys Smit."

Chapter 17

BY the time Angel left, the coffers of Sweet Nothings were considerably richer. Obviously Angel spared no expense when reeling in a new beau. She carried off two bags full of beautiful lacy pastel undergarments to tempt her latest conquest.

Emma looked at the figures on the register. "Angel's salon must be doing very well if she can spend money like that."

A shadow crossed over Arabella's face.

"What's wrong?"

"Nothing, really. It's just that I feel guilty for keeping you here with me. You've given up your job in New York where I'm sure you made much more money and had lots more fun."

Emma threw her arms around her aunt. "I wouldn't trade this experience for anything in the world."

Arabella squeezed her back. "Just so you're sure."

Emma thought of Brian. "I'm positive."

"What do you make of that hit-and-run?" Arabella turned to Emma.

"I can't believe it. Do you think it really was an accident?" She looked at Arabella.

"I don't know, dear. It seems awfully coincidental, don't you think? Here's Gladys about to tell you who she saw going out into the garden, and the next minute she's being run off her bicycle. Of course, coincidences do happen. All the time, I'm afraid."

"Or, maybe someone else had it in for Gladys. Although she hardly seemed the type to rack up enemies like notches in a belt."

"I thought she was even blander than vanilla ice cream. But you know that saying—still waters run deep. Is there any merit in checking with her neighbors? Perhaps an old beau had it in for her or she got herself mixed up with the wrong people somehow?"

"I can certainly try. Do you think Francis would be able to get any information through the Bureau?"

"Possibly. I can always ask him."

"How is his undercover work going, by the way?"

Arabella's face brightened. "He said that so far it has been nothing but boredom and sore feet from making rounds night after night. I'm so relieved. I was quite terrified when he told me about it."

EMMA and Arabella were about to close up shop when the telephone rang. Arabella grabbed the receiver. She listened for several seconds, then put her hand over the mouthpiece.

"Sylvia's calling to see if we can come over for a drink."

"Sure."

Arabella spoke briefly with Sylvia and hung up the phone. "Do you mind if I drive? It will give me an excuse to refuse that incendiary vodka Sylvia always offers us."

Ten minutes later, they'd finished closing Sweet Nothings for the night and were headed toward Sunny Days in Arabella's car.

Sylvia answered their knock immediately. Emma suspected that she had been standing by the door waiting.

"Come in, come in." The string of gold bangles on her wrists jingled melodically as Sylvia waved her arms at them.

Emma and Arabella were somewhat surprised to see Earl sitting in an easy chair, looking as if he quite belonged, his long legs stretched out in front of him, a small glass in his hand and his cane leaning within easy reach against an end table.

"Pardon me if I don't get up." He smiled apologetically. "It's getting harder and harder to get out of chairs these days."

"You need one of those chairs where the seat pops up and pushes you to your feet." Sylvia reached for the iced vodka bottle on the coffee table.

"I'm not quite ready for that yet."

"You mean you're not ready to admit you're ready for that yet," Sylvia corrected.

Earl laughed. "You're probably right." He gestured toward the bottle in Sylvia's hand. "Enough of that. We're ignoring our guests."

Emma's ears perked up at the word *we*.

"None for me, thanks. I'm driving." Arabella held up her hand.

"Only a sip for me," Emma said. "I have to get some work done later tonight."

Sylvia filled a tiny glass for Emma and refilled Earl's. "What can I get you?" She looked at Arabella.

"I'm fine for now. I'm excited to hear what your news is."

Emma looked at Earl, comfortably ensconced in his chair, and noticed the way Sylvia looked at him every couple of minutes, and began to wonder if perhaps Sylvia had found love at Sunny Days.

Sylvia smiled at Emma and Arabella. "Thank goodness Crystal Davis is gone. That Decker woman still isn't talking to me, but some of the others have come around."

"Could it be that she was a little upset the time you substituted salt for sugar in the bowl on her table?" Earl cocked a bristly white eyebrow at Sylvia.

"Oh, that." Sylvia waved a hand dismissively. "All in good fun, you know."

"Do you still think that Crystal is the one most likely to have killed Jessica?" Arabella said. "She had to have really been suffering, poor thing. Most of the items she stole were useless to her—or at least she wasn't making any use of them by stuffing them in that cupboard. It must have been some kind of mental quirk—a compulsion she couldn't control. And to have Jessica make her life miserable because of it probably only made it worse."

"I've heard of people like that." Sylvia nodded. "They're like those birds that collect shiny objects."

"You mean magpies?" Earl said.

"If Crystal did kill Jessica, then it seems likely she also killed Gladys. To prevent her from telling anyone that she saw Crystal go out into the garden that afternoon."

"But how to prove it?" Arabella asked.

"If we could find her car . . . see if there's been damage done. The police have been asking around all the local body shops, but what if Crystal's keeping it hidden in her garage?"

"Can we find out where she lives?"

"I don't see why not. I'll check online and see if she's listed."

"If you do discover something"—Arabella shook a finger at Emma—"you'd better go straight to Detective Walker and let him handle it. If we're right, Crystal has killed twice already. What's to stop her from doing it again?"

EMMA had no trouble finding Crystal's address the next morning. The difficulty was going to be in locating Crystal's car if it turned out she lived in an apartment building without assigned parking. She kept her fingers virtually crossed as she followed the directions she'd printed off the computer.

It turned out that Crystal had a small condo in a development called Sunny Farms. How ironic, Emma thought, to live at Sunny Farms and work at Sunny Days, especially when Crystal's life appeared to have been anything but sunny.

Each condo was a two-story town house with five units attached in a row. Crystal's was smack in the middle. There was no garage, but carports were across from each set of condos and were numbered the same as the units themselves. Emma checked the number on Crystal's place again and then turned around to find the matching number on the carport.

She found it easily enough. There was space for two cars. Unfortunately, both were empty. Had Crystal hidden her car somewhere else? Surely, Crystal knew the police would be looking for a vehicle with damage to the body. Would she take a chance on being stopped while out running errands?

Emma decided to check and see if Crystal was home. If Crystal was home, then she had most likely found somewhere else to keep her car. If she wasn't . . . well that wouldn't lead to much of anything conclusive. But it was still worth a try.

Emma climbed the three steps to the bright blue front door of Crystal's condo and rang the bell. She could hear it pealing inside. She waited hopefully . . . but nothing. The curtain in the square picture window didn't move, and no footsteps echoed down the hall.

Emma was turning away, with a deep sense of disappointment, when a young man on a bicycle pulled up to the town house next door. He propped the bike against the fence, pulled off his helmet and began to climb the front steps.

"Hello, there!" Emma called, waving at the young man.

He stopped on the landing and turned around with a curious look on his face. He had a mop of curly hair and enormous Elton John–style glasses.

"Do you know the woman who lives here?" Emma gestured toward Crystal's town house.

"You mean Crystal?"

"Yes. I'm trying to get in touch with her."

"You won't find her at home. I saw her loading up her car earlier. Packed that baby to the gills. Boxes, suitcases, clothes on hangers. The works. Looked like she was moving out, not going on vacation."

"Moving out, you say?"

The young man raised his eyebrows above the thick, dark frames of his glasses. "Don't know for sure. Just hazarding a guess considering the state of her car. Could be she was headed to Goodwill to make a donation."

"That doesn't seem likely."

"You're right. It doesn't."

"Did you get a good look at her car? Could you see if it had been damaged in any way?"

"Damaged? Not that I could see. I only saw the one side as she was pulling out, and far as I can recollect, it looked to be all in one piece."

"Do you know Crystal well?" The sun had come out from behind a cloud, and Emma shielded her eyes with her hand.

"Not particularly, no. She kept herself to herself as my Mamaw used to say."

"She wasn't friendly?"

"She wasn't unfriendly. We just didn't have many occasions to talk. Occasionally we'd run into each other by the recycling bin, but that was about it."

"Listen, could you do me a favor?"

The young man cocked his head. "Depends."

Emma scrabbled in her purse, pulled out a Sweet Nothings card, scribbled her cell phone number on it and handed it to him. "When Crystal comes back, would you mind giving me a call? I want to catch up with her."

The young man was about to pocket the card when he stopped and looked suspiciously at Emma. "Not a bill collector, are you?"

"Oh no. Just an . . . old friend."

"Doesn't seem to be any harm in it then. Sure." He tucked the card into his shirt pocket.

"Thanks."

Emma returned to her car and got behind the wheel. She was pulling away from Sunny Farms when she had a thought. If Crystal was responsible for the hit-and-run that killed Gladys on Tuesday night after the trunk show at Marjorie Porter's, how did she get to work on Wednesday? Had she taken a chance on her car not being spotted? Or, had she assumed the police investigation wouldn't have gotten that far so quickly? As soon as Emma had a moment, she was going to go back to Sunny Days and see if anyone remembered seeing Crystal pull into the parking lot Wednesday morning.

EMMA'S cell phone was ringing as she walked into Sweet Nothings. Arabella was already behind the counter showing a customer some vintage bed jackets. Emma ducked into the back room, retrieved her cell from the bottom of her purse and answered it.

"Hello?"

"Emma? It's Brian."

As usual, Emma's heart did a funny blip when she heard Brian's voice.

"Do you know what day tomorrow is?"

Emma frowned. "It's Saturday, isn't it?"

"That's right. And do you know what Saturday is?"

"Ummm, not really. It's a day off for some people, but we're open on Saturdays."

"Well down South here, we still call Saturday night, date night."

Emma felt her heart rate speed up. There was a humorous tone to Brian's voice, but she thought she detected a bit of nervousness, too.

"So I'm hoping you'll consider having dinner with me."

For one second, Emma thought of playing coy, but then she decided that that was not how she wanted her relationship with Brian to go. Instead she said, "I'd love to."

"Great."

Emma easily detected the note of relief in Brian's voice.

"How does L'Etoile sound?"

"Sure." L'Etoile was the fanciest restaurant in town. Emma and Brian had been once before when they celebrated the renovation of Sweet Nothings.

"I'll pick you up at seven o'clock," Brian said. "Oh, and Liz is loaning me her station wagon so you won't have to ride in my pickup truck."

Chapter 18

EMMA floated through the rest of the day. Her disappointment over not finding Crystal's car faded into thoughts of Brian's last kiss and hopes that he might kiss her again. Saturday night seemed an eternity away.

They were ready to close for the day when the door opened and Liz stuck her head in. "Hey." Her tone was serious and so was her expression.

Was something wrong? Emma looked at her friend in concern.

"Do you have time to get a cold drink? Matt's taken the kids riding. I need to talk to you."

She looked at Emma, her expression still grim.

"You two go ahead. I'll finish closing up." Arabella shooed them out the door.

They walked down to the Coffee Klatch in near silence, sticking to inane comments about the weather.

Emma could tell something was wrong. She just didn't know what it was.

The Coffee Klatch was nearly empty, and the hostess immediately showed them to a table. Before Emma could open her mouth, Mabel came up to them and slid two menus onto the table. "What'll it be?"

"Just some sweet tea," Liz and Emma said together.

"How's your boy doing?" Liz asked as Mabel continued to linger.

"He's growing like a weed." Mabel's face glowed with pride. "His teacher says he's real smart, too. Takes after his daddy, I expect." Mabel glanced around, but everyone was taken care of, and no new customers had entered. "Did you hear about that hit-and-run accident Tuesday night?" She nodded at Emma. "I know you like to keep your ear to the ground."

"Shame, wasn't it?" Liz said in dismissive tones.

Mabel didn't take the hint. "It seems so strange. First that woman drops dead at that party, and now this."

"Mabel!" the chef shouted.

"Hold your horses. I'll be right there." Mabel rolled her eyes but took off at a trot in the direction of the kitchen.

Liz looked at Emma for a long moment. Emma found herself squirming in her seat. She hadn't done anything wrong. Why was she feeling guilty?

"I guess I'd better come right out with it." Liz fiddled with the tassel on her purse. "I saw you in here the other day with that detective. You two looked pretty cozy. I could tell by the look on his face that he was interested in you."

Emma opened her mouth to protest, but Liz went on.

"I know it's none of my business, but Brian is my brother, and he means the world to me. And frankly, from what he's told me, you mean the world to him. I don't want to see him get hurt."

Once again Emma opened her mouth, but before she could get out a word, Liz was continuing.

"I know he's not real good at showing it," she said as she looked down at the table, "but he really cares for you. He's just scared." Liz looked at Emma, a pleading look in her eyes. "It's all on account of that miserable Amy. She destroyed his confidence. He's like a little boy looking over his shoulder all the time."

Emma reached out and took Liz's hand in hers. "Liz! I feel the same way about Brian. Honest. I met with Detective Walker to discuss Jessica Scott's death. Nothing more."

"Honest?"

"Pinky swear," Emma said, referring to their old childhood ritual.

"Okay." Liz's face cleared momentarily, but then she frowned again. "I talked to Bitsy," she said. "She's going to have to close Sprinkles unless business picks up." Liz twirled her napkin around and around. "I feel terrible. I know it wasn't my fault, but somehow I keep thinking maybe I made a mistake. Maybe I did pick a foxglove flower by accident." She ran a hand through her hair, leaving her blond bangs disheveled. "I've been so distracted lately." She gave a rueful smile. "Did I tell you Brian offered me a job?"

Emma managed to look surprised. "Really?"

Liz nodded. "I'm really grateful. Besides, he needs all the help he can get. His books are in a complete mess."

"That's great." Emma gave a big smile. "Listen, Liz, I know that what happened to Jessica wasn't your fault. We know someone went out to the garden and picked that flower on purpose. I'm willing to bet it was Crystal Davis." Emma explained about Crystal, her compulsive stealing and how Jessica made her life miserable. "And then when she thought Gladys Smit was about to reveal the fact that she saw Crystal go out into Deirdre's garden the night of the trunk show, she mowed the poor woman down."

Emma fell silent as Mabel slid two tall, frosted glasses of iced tea in front of them. She watched as Mabel retreated, and only when she reached the kitchen did Emma start talking again.

"I went to Crystal's place today to see if I could get a look at her car and check for any damage that might be consistent with hitting a . . . a body." Emma choked a little on the word. "Unfortunately she'd already packed up and taken off."

"Taken off? Where?"

"I don't know. I mean, she might be going on vacation, but her neighbor said the car was awfully packed."

Liz groaned. "What next, then? Are the police making any progress at all?"

"I know they're checking body shops. Angel told us they'd been out to talk to Tom Mulligan already."

"Isn't there something we can do?"

"I've been planning to visit Gladys Smit's neighbors. No one seems to know much of anything about her. I thought if we could prove she didn't have any enemies . . ."

"Why not go now?" Liz began reaching for her purse.

"Let's!" Emma pulled a few bills from her wallet and tossed them on the table. "It's on me."

Mabel's head nearly spun in a circle as Liz and Emma bolted from their table and beat a hasty retreat from the Coffee Klatch. They piled into Liz's car.

"Where to?"

Emma gave the directions, and in a short time they were approaching Gladys Smit's garden apartment complex.

"There's not much to recommend this place, is there?"

Liz said as they pulled up in front of the door with the Easter egg wreath. "Is this where she lived?"

Emma nodded.

"We were so lucky to be able to take over my parents' place and make it our own. Daddy was so generous." Liz stifled a sob.

Emma turned toward her in alarm. "What's wrong?"

"I'm worried we won't be able to keep up the mortgage. Matt still hasn't heard about that contract, but that doesn't stop the bills from coming in," she said with a slightly bitter tone. "We can't lose the place, we can't. Grandma and Grandpa O'Connell bought that land when they moved here from Ireland. They built a little house for themselves, and then when Mom and Dad took it over, they added on. And now Matt and I have renovated it completely. I'm afraid we spent too much, and I feel so guilty. We never should have taken out that second mortgage. The house was fine the way it was for my parents and grandparents. Matt and I should have left it as it was."

"Everything will work out okay," Emma said with more conviction than she felt.

Liz pulled a tissue from her purse, dried her eyes and opened her door. She smiled at Emma. "Thanks for listening."

Emma opened her own door. "Let's see if we can dig up any information on Gladys Smit."

They approached Gladys's door although they knew that any knock would go unanswered.

"That makes me feel so sad." Liz pointed at the dilapidated wreath.

"I know. I wonder what kind of a life she had."

"Pretty humdrum, I'd imagine. She probably worked

hard, came home and watched her favorite television shows and then did it all over again the next day. If it weren't for the fact that she saw someone go into Deirdre Porter's garden that afternoon, she'd probably have lived to a ripe old age."

"You never know, though. Maybe there was another reason she was killed, and it's not related to Jessica's murder. Maybe it really was a random accident."

"You don't believe that, do you?" Liz looked Emma straight in the face.

"No," Emma said in a subdued voice. "I don't. Somehow this all does relate to Jessica Scott's death. But we have to make sure that there wasn't another reason for someone wanting Gladys dead."

Liz nodded her head. "And then we can spoon-feed it to the police."

Emma looked up and down the narrow street. One or two cars were parked along the curb, but no one was out and about—no dog walkers, joggers or mothers with strollers. Not even a curtain twitching in any of the apartment windows. Emma bit her lip. "Do you suppose there's a rental office somewhere?" She turned to Liz.

"Bound to be." Liz looked right and left then stopped and squinted at something in the distance. "What's that over there?" She pointed toward a small clapboard building hardly bigger than a shack. "Can you read the sign?"

Emma shook her head. "No, it's too far away."

"Could it be an office of some kind?"

"Could be. Or a place where they keep the garbage cans."

Liz laughed. "Well, let's hope for the former."

As they got closer, Emma was able to read the sign. She grabbed Liz's arm. "It *is* the rental office. Let's just hope someone is there."

They pushed open the door.

An older woman sat behind an old-fashioned metal desk. She looked up when she heard the door open. Her gray hair was sparse but neatly permed, and her cardigan had been visibly darned several times.

"No vacancies. Best come back next month." She bent her head over the book open on her desk.

"We're not interested in renting," Emma said, looking around the small space. There was a leather love seat with black electrician's tape mending a tear on one of the cushions and an automatic coffeemaker on a table with the dregs of what looked like days-old coffee in the bottom of the pot.

The woman sighed, folded down the corner of the page in her book and closed it. "What are you doing here, then? This is the rental office. You have a problem with your bill, you've got to call corporate. Number's on the back of your statement."

"Actually, we're not here about that, either," Emma said, searching her mind for a way to introduce the topic of Gladys Smit.

"We're looking for one of your residents," Liz piped up. "Gladys Smit."

"I'm Emma Taylor." Emma held out her hand and Liz quickly followed suit.

"Liz Banning."

The woman smiled, and the way her face spasmed, it looked like smiling was something she hadn't done in a long time. "Name's Billy. Short for Wilhelmina. When Granny heard they'd named me that she accused Ma and Pa of getting way ahead of their station."

Emma and Liz laughed politely.

"We were looking for Gladys Smit. Did you know her?"

"Did I? Why? Something happened to her?"

Emma explained about the hit-and-run.

Billy put a trembling hand to her lips. "Oh dear. That's just awful. Awful." She fussed at the collar of her blouse.

"We were wondering if Gladys had any enemies that you know of?" Emma said.

"Someone who might have run her over on purpose," Liz added.

Billy shuddered. "It hardly bears thinking about." She shook her head. "I can't imagine anyone wanting to harm that poor girl—so quiet and polite. Always stopped in to say good morning and good afternoon and to see if there was anything I needed." She shook her head again. "No. It must have been an accident. I can't imagine anyone wanting to hurt such a gentle creature."

"Well!" Liz said as they retreated back to her car. "That rather settles that, doesn't it?"

"I would think so. Gladys was hardly the type to go around collecting mortal enemies. That leaves only two choices: the accident was just that—an accident, or the person who put the poisonous flower on Jessica's cupcake murdered poor, unsuspecting Gladys."

"That person most likely being Crystal Davis."

"We can't rule out some of the other people at the trunk show," Emma cautioned. "Lotte Fanning was apparently quite steamed at Jessica for getting that job at Sunny Days."

"That's true." Liz was thoughtful. "And who knows how many other people might have had a motive?"

"I don't think our detecting is nearly done."

"No. But I hope we figure this out before poor Bitsy goes under."

EMMA was taking Saturday morning off. Arabella was going to handle the shop herself, and Emma was going to do a very different sort of volunteering stint at Sunny Days.

To introduce the new administrator, they were holding a pancake breakfast for all the residents. Emma would be flipping flapjacks, but her main objective was to ask questions and eavesdrop. It had certainly proved fruitful in the past.

Although the breakfast was slated to start at 9:00 a.m., residents were already lined up outside the dining hall at 8:30 a.m. when Emma arrived. Emma noticed Sylvia and Earl about three quarters of the way down the line.

"How are you two this morning?"

"Eh. The arthritis in my knees is kicking up a bit, but I can't complain." Sylvia put a hand on Emma's arm. "Say, I heard this new administrator, Missy something-or-other, was one of the gals at our shape wear show."

"Yes, her mother is in the same crowd as Marjorie Porter."

Sylvia stuck her nose in the air. "Oh, la-di-da, indeed."

Earl gave a deep chuckle. "She still puts her pants on one leg at a time, like everyone else."

"And from what I hear, she definitely is the one wearing the pants." Sylvia huffed. "Alfred Porter, her husband, is something of a milquetoast. His brother, Wyatt, got all the spirit."

"Or, the spirits," Earl joked. "I heard he was arrested for drunk driving again."

Emma noticed someone waving at her out of the corner of her eye.

"Looks like I'm needed behind the assembly line. I'll see you two later."

Emma made her way through the increasingly restless crowd toward the long table at the front of the room. A handful of electric griddles were set out with pitchers of pancake batter next to them. Bacon sizzled in electric skillets, and aides were going around the room filling coffee cups and juice glasses.

Emma poured her first batch of pancakes. Two of them ran together slightly, but the rest were okay. As soon as the tops were covered in tiny bubbles, she flipped them over and cooked the other side. By the time they were done, a gentleman was already standing in front of her with his plate out. He winked at Emma as she flipped the four pancakes onto his dish.

Missy Fanning, the new administrator of Sunny Days, was wearing an apron, but as far as Emma could tell she was doing almost nothing to help. At the moment she was standing in the corner whispering with her mother, who looked as if she were dressed for afternoon tea as opposed to breakfast at a senior retirement community. Both of them sported the regulation strand of outsized pearls, diamond stud earrings and gold bangle bracelets.

Emma blew a lock of hair off her forehead and poured another batch of pancakes. An endless stream of plates appeared in front of her, and after forty-five minutes she began to wonder which was longer—the line of residents waiting for their breakfast or the Great Wall of China. At the moment she was putting her money on the Sunny Days seniors.

Finally the last plate had been filled. Emma looked around at the other limp volunteers standing behind their electric skillets. The woman next to her glanced over as Emma poured a fresh batch of batter.

"We might as well make some for ourselves," Emma said.

Emma slid the spatula under the edge of one of the pancakes. It looked to be a perfect golden brown. She scooped the four of them onto her plate and headed toward the table where the bacon, sausage and maple syrup were set out.

"There's a spot at my table." Eloise Montgomery breezed up behind Emma. She was wearing black slacks and a beige quilted satin jacket sashed at the waist. She was in great contrast to most of the other women, many of whom had come down in sweatshirts and jeans or even housecoats.

Emma helped herself to some rashers of bacon and poured a modest amount of syrup over her pancakes, then followed Eloise to a small table for two in the corner. Eloise unfurled her napkin and draped it across her lap. She picked up her fork but stopped with it halfway to her mouth.

"What do you think of Missy, our new administrator?" she asked before popping a crisp bit of bacon into her mouth.

Emma was slightly taken aback. "She seems nice enough. I understand she applied for the job before, but Jessica got it."

Eloise put her coffee cup down with a clang and rolled her eyes. "Jessica!" she said in dismissive tones. "That girl did nothing all day long but file her nails and take pleasure in making poor Crystal cater to her whims." She raised a penciled eyebrow. "Of course, now we know why Crystal was so willing to bear the brunt of Jessica's ill will." She picked up her coffee cup. "There must have been something terribly wrong with her to take all those things and hoard them like that."

"It is very bizarre." Emma tasted a bite of pancake. *Not bad.* "I heard that Jessica was the niece of the chairman of the board. I imagine that's why they never got rid of her."

Eloise threw her head back and laughed deeply. A few heads at the nearby tables turned in their direction.

Emma raised her eyebrows questioningly.

"Is that what they're saying?" Eloise dried her eyes with

the edge of her napkin. "That Jessica was Jim Calhoun's niece?"

Emma nodded, confused.

"She wasn't his niece."

"Then how—"

"She was his mistress. They were having an affair," Eloise added when Emma continued to stare at her.

"So that's why—"

Eloise nodded. "Jessica could do no wrong with Calhoun protecting her."

"No wonder Lotte Fanning was so mad when her daughter didn't get the administrator job and Jessica did."

Eloise laughed again—a hearty guffaw that had the heads at the other tables turning again. "Not only that." She sipped a bit of her ice water and dabbed at the end of her nose with a tissue she pulled from her sleeve. "Jessica stole Jim Calhoun right out from under Lotte Fanning's nose." She sat back in her chair with an air of triumph.

"What?" was all Emma was able to squeak out. She swallowed a bit of pancake a little too hastily and began to cough. She reached for her water glass. "But isn't Lotte married? I thought I noticed a wedding ring."

"Noticed? Honey, how could you miss that thing? There are enough stones in it to fill the Grand Canyon."

Emma nibbled a piece of her bacon and thought furiously. Maybe Lotte Fanning *was* the person who had murdered Jessica, not Crystal Davis. And perhaps Crystal's leaving town was purely coincidental. She was going to have to see if she could find out what kind of car Lotte drove.

Emma had finished her pancakes and was throwing her trash in the garbage bin when Missy rushed up to her.

"Thank you so much for volunteering today. Everyone

here at Sunny Days appreciates your sharing your valuable time with us."

Emma had noticed Missy going around to some of the other volunteers as well. She was shaking Emma's hand when Lotte came up to them.

"Missy, darling, I'm going to run out to the car and get that rug we bought for your new office." She had a set of car keys dangling from her right hand.

Perfect, Emma thought. She would follow her. She quickly ended her conversation with Missy, and as soon as Lotte had disappeared through the door, she made her way in the same direction.

Emma was about to leave the building when a middle-aged couple stopped her. "Can you tell us where 401B is?" He was frowning at a piece of paper that fluttered in his hand, as she clutched his arm worriedly.

"I'm sorry. I don't live here," Emma said abruptly and tried to edge around them.

"It says here"—the man gestured at the scrap of paper in his hand—"to go in the north entrance." He looked around the hall. "This is the north entrance, isn't it?"

"I'm sorry, I don't—" Emma was beginning to sweat. How long would it take Lotte to get to her car and retrieve the rug?

"You've got an employee badge on." The man pointed a nicotine-stained index finger at Emma's name tag.

"I'm a volunteer," Emma protested.

"Still. Can you tell me if this is the north entrance or not?"

"Honey, please." The woman tugged on his arm. "Let's go ask someone else."

She managed to distract him long enough for Emma to

slip past and out the door to the parking lot. She shaded her eyes with her hand and scanned the rows of cars. Lotte was coming toward her, a rolled-up area rug tucked under her arm.

Emma groaned. She'd missed her golden opportunity. She was about to go back inside when she remembered the keys swinging from Lotte's hand. There had been a Mercedes emblem on the fob. How many people visiting Sunny Days were likely to be driving a Mercedes?

Emma tried to look purposeful as she hovered in the doorway waiting for Lotte to go past. As soon as the coast was clear, she darted out the door and down the first row of cars. Most were American made except for a red Audi rather badly parked toward the end. Emma made her way up the next row and the next. Finally she spotted it. A dark blue late-model Mercedes Benz sedan.

It was bright and shiny and looked as if it had recently come from the car wash. Emma heard a car door slam a couple of rows away and looked up, startled, but the woman who got out of the car walked in the opposite direction and had her back to Emma.

Emma continued to circle Lotte's Mercedes. The left front bumper was intact, the headlight spotless without all the dead bugs that accumulated on Emma's. She momentarily closed her eyes and crossed her fingers and then made her way around to the right front bumper.

There was an enormous, sickening dent in it and the headlight was broken.

Chapter 19

"WE can't be positive it's Lotte's car," Arabella said when Emma arrived back at Sweet Nothings. "Or, that she didn't hit the side of her garage door trying to pull in." Arabella put down the peignoir she was mending. "I know that happened to me more than once when I was learning to drive."

"That's true," Emma admitted. "I wonder if you mentioned it to Francis, if he'd be able to get the Paris police to at least take the car in for examination."

"I know Francis always says that the TBI likes to give the local boys plenty of rein, but I don't suppose it would hurt to ask. As soon as I finish this piece, I'll give him a call. He doesn't start his watchman duties until seven o'clock." Arabella chuckled. "I do feel sorry for him having to do that night after night and still no sign of those bank robbers. Of course I'm glad for that, even if it does make for dull evenings for him."

Arabella continued with her mending, and Emma went to help a customer who had just walked in. By the time the woman left with two sets of the lingerie Emma had ordered from Monique Berthole, Arabella was finished with her project.

Arabella folded the peignoir, placed it on one of the armoire shelves and headed toward the back room. "I'll go call Francis now." She paused by Pierre's dog bed. "Come on, Pierre, time for your dinner."

Pierre scrambled to his feet, did a quick down dog and up dog and followed Arabella into the back room. Emma could hear the sound of dry dog nuggets hitting a metal bowl then moments later, the low murmur of Arabella's voice on the telephone.

Emma had her back to the stockroom door when Arabella emerged a few moments later. She waited for her aunt to say something, but when Arabella didn't, Emma turned away from the mannequin she'd been changing.

The look on Arabella's face had Emma flying to her side. "What's wrong, Aunt Arabella? What's happened? Is it Francis? Is he okay?"

Arabella remained white and speechless. Emma led her to a chair and made her sit down. Arabella's mouth moved, but no sounds came out.

"Can I get you some water?"

Arabella's hands jerked in her lap, and she shook her head no.

"Please tell me what's happened!"

Emma didn't know what to do. Should she call Arabella's doctor?

Finally, Arabella made a sound like a whimper. Emma bent closer to listen.

"It's Francis," Arabella finally said. "He's been taken

hostage by the bank robbers. They're threatening to kill him if the bank doesn't meet their demands."

EMMA insisted on driving Arabella home after they closed. She was still white and her hands were shaking. Emma hated leaving her alone, but she'd already made plans with Brian. Besides, Arabella insisted that Emma go and promised that she would call a friend if need be. Meanwhile, Arabella wanted to be near her phone and the television in case there were any developments, and as soon as she walked into the house she flipped on the local news station and sat down in front of the set.

As Emma walked back to her car her cell phone rang. She recognized Brian's number and her heart sank. Was he canceling their plans?

"I hope we're still on for tonight," Brian said when Emma answered.

She smiled. "Of course." She was really looking forward to an evening alone with Brian.

Emma quickly told Brian about how Francis had been taken hostage by the bank robbers. She could hear Brian's indrawn breath over the telephone.

"Do you think we ought to stay with Arabella instead? She must be terribly upset."

"I already asked her, and she insisted we keep our date," Emma said, suddenly feeling selfish. Maybe she should have insisted on staying with Arabella despite what Arabella said.

Emma looked up to find that Arabella had come into the hallway. She waved her hand at Emma as if shooing her out the door.

"I think she'll be fine," she said to Brian as she smiled at her aunt.

Arabella nodded vigorously.

"Arabella is certainly one tough cookie. If you're sure she'll be okay . . . I'm really looking forward to our dinner. I've shaved and everything."

Emma laughed. Brian always looked good, even when covered in plaster dust.

"I'll pick you up at seven o'clock if that's all right."

"Don't you dare cancel your plans on account of me," Arabella said when Emma had hung up. "What are you wearing?"

Emma mentally went through her closet. "I've got the proverbial little black dress." It was simple and basic and her go-to ensemble.

"You need something to give it some punch then. Come on." Arabella indicated that Emma should follow her down the hallway.

Arabella entered her bedroom and went straight to an enormous cherrywood jewelry armoire that was almost as tall as she was. Her hand hesitated over the drawers and then finally she pulled one open. "I think it's in here . . ." she mumbled as she sorted through the contents. "Yes. This is perfect. It will give your simple little dress some pizzazz."

Arabella pulled out a stunning turquoise necklace that Emma had never seen before. "This is what's known as a torsade. Torsade means twisted, and you can see the strands of turquoise beads are all twisted together."

"It's gorgeous," Emma said, imagining how spectacular it was going to look with her black dress. "But are you sure . . . ?"

Arabella waved a hand. "Don't worry. It wasn't all that expensive. I bought it at the Marché aux Puces, the flea market, when I was in Paris. I don't think the stall owner knew what he had." She shrugged.

Arabella seemed slightly less worried by the time Emma left. Nevertheless, Emma kept one ear cocked for her cell phone the whole time she was in the shower. She thought she heard her cell ringing as she was toweling off, but when she checked, it was completely silent with no voice mails and no text messages. Must have been her imagination.

Emma worked some product through her hair to style it and slipped into her dress. She couldn't wait to put on the necklace. As she suspected, it looked spectacular and took her simple black dress to a whole new level.

EMMA'S buzzer rang right at six forty-five. She opened her door to find Brian standing there clutching a bouquet. His eyes lit up when he saw her. He handed her the flowers.

"Thank you." Emma admired them before putting them in a vase with some water.

"God bless Liz for loaning me her car. I'd hate for you to have to suffer the indignity of arriving at L'Etoile, the best restaurant in Paris, Tennessee, in a pickup truck," Brian said as Emma followed him down the stairs.

Emma laughed. "Are you kidding? Half the vehicles in the parking lot are usually pickup trucks."

Still, she was glad she didn't have to vault into the truck in her short dress—although Brian always gave her a boost, and she enjoyed the feeling of his arms around her.

Nearly every space in the parking lot was filled when they got to L'Etoile. Saturday night was in full swing. L'Etoile was one of the only restaurants in town where you weren't asked do you want fries with that? The tables were set with fine white linen, the cutlery was real silver and the waiters wore dinner jackets with satin lapels and black bow ties.

Brian gave his name to the maître d', who discreetly consulted his seating chart. "Your table will be ready shortly. Would you like to wait in the bar?" He gestured toward the darkened nook where several couples were already seated.

Brian led Emma toward two stools at the end of the bar. There were two empty glasses on the counter.

The bartender grabbed the glasses and tossed the spent ice into the sink, where it rattled around like the ball on a roulette wheel before disappearing down the drain. He put two fresh napkins in front of Brian and Emma and raised his eyebrows.

"What would you like?" Brian turned to Emma.

"A glass of Chardonnay would be lovely."

Brian placed their order and swiveled his stool so he was facing Emma, their knees touching. "I've never seen this place so busy." He glanced at his watch. "I hope we don't have to wait too long. I'm starving."

Emma didn't mind waiting at all. Just being with Brian made her happy.

"Brian, my man," a deep voice boomed at them suddenly.

"Hey, John. What are you doing here?" Brian slid off his stool and shook hands with the slightly balding man. His suit was expensive—the expert tailoring subtly hiding a substantial paunch.

Brian turned to Emma. "This is John Jasper. He's a client of mine. I just finished the renovations on his place."

"Brian's a genius," the man boomed, holding out his hand to Emma. "I'm guessing you're Emma, right?" He pumped Emma's hand enthusiastically.

Was Brian telling people about her? Emma wondered. That was a good sign.

John looked around the crowded restaurant. "There's

room at our table. Why don't you join us? Lara and I would love to have you."

Emma closed her eyes, hoping that Brian would say thank you, but no thank you.

"Sure, we'd love to, wouldn't we?" He turned to Emma for confirmation.

She gave him a lukewarm smile and waited as John instructed the bartender to bring their drinks over to his table.

"Sorry about that," Brian whispered to Emma as they followed John through the crowded restaurant. "He's a really good client, and I didn't want to risk offending him. He's a good guy."

Emma squeezed his hand in reply. She would have to make the best of it.

They approached a table in the corner where a striking-looking woman was seated. She got up and smiled shyly as they neared the table.

"Lara," John said, his eyes glowing with pride, "you know Brian"—he gestured toward Brian—"and this is his Emma."

"Lovely to meet you." She held out a hand, and Emma took it. It was very soft and cool to the touch.

"They're going to join us for dinner. Restaurant's terribly crowded and who knows how long they'd have to wait for a table."

As Emma and Brian were taking their seats, the waiter appeared with their drinks. Emma took a sip of her wine and studied her new dinner companions. Lara had long, straight golden brown hair and green eyes. She was simply dressed in a tangerine-colored halter top and white, gauzy pants. She reminded Emma of the models she used to work with when she was a stylist in New York. She was considerably younger than her husband, appearing to be in her late twenties, and spoke with a slight accent that Emma couldn't quite place.

John slapped Brian on the back. "Your boy here rescued our place for us. Lara and I are big fans of mid-century modern, and when we found this place we were thrilled. But it was practically rubble. We weren't sure anyone would be able to restore it, but Brian did a fabulous job. The kitchen is completely new, but you can't tell it wasn't part of the original design." He turned toward Brian. "You tell her about it, Brian."

Brian looked slightly uncomfortable. "Primarily we used glass, aluminum and galvanized steel. But we kept with wood for the roof so it would blend better with the existing one. Redoing the whole thing would have been too costly and time-consuming."

"Now, Emma," John said when the waiter had taken their orders. He leaned back in the banquette, his arm draped across his wife's shoulders. "Tell us a little bit about yourself."

Emma gave everyone a short précis about her life in New York, her move back to Paris to help Arabella and her plans for Sweet Nothings.

"Your shop sounds lovely," Lara exclaimed. "I will have to come and visit." Her speech was only slightly accented, her English nearly perfect.

John took a glug of his drink and guffawed. "I'm all in favor of beautiful lingerie. You go and get yourself anything you want." He smiled indulgently at his wife.

Ka-ching, Emma thought. The evening wouldn't be a total waste if she snagged a new customer for Sweet Nothings.

"I've been away from Paris for years now. Hardly

recognized it when I got back." John paused as the waiter placed dishes in front of them. He looked at Emma. "I'd been working all over—New York, London, Hong Kong." He cut into his steak and forked up a large bite. "It's been fascinating, but now, in my position, I can afford to work from home most of the time. The blessings of the Internet!" He turned to Brian. "I saw in the paper that Wyatt Porter was picked up on another DUI. He was a couple of years ahead of me in school. He was wild even back then. Not like that older brother of his. What's his name?" He wrinkled his brow.

"Alfred? He's the mayor now."

"That's what someone told me. And why not? The position doesn't pay, and he sure doesn't need the money." John shook his head. "For a long time it looked as if there wasn't ever going to be a Porter heir. I think Constance was in her forties when Alfred came along. And then surprise, another boy, Wyatt. Of course he gets a pittance compared to what Alfred inherits." He gave a loud guffaw. "I started with nothing, and I'm proud to say that everything we have"—he squeezed his wife's shoulders—"I earned myself. Nothing wrong with hard work."

Emma and Brian murmured agreement. Conversation ebbed and flowed, and finally Emma was finishing the last bite of her chicken.

"Did you know Brian used to date my baby sister at UT?" John leaned back in his chair and surveyed his dinner companions.

Emma had no idea what to say, but she managed to plaster an interested look on her face as she waited for John to continue.

"It didn't last long. They weren't cut out for each other." He smiled smugly. "She's happily married now with a baby on the way." He threw a benign look in Brian's direction. "Then there was that other girl. What was her name?"

"Amy," Brian mumbled.

John gave a deep sigh, leaned back in his seat and stretched his legs out under the table. "When we first met Brian, we were really worried about him. This girl, Amy"— he looked to Brian for confirmation—"threw him over, and he was in quite a funk."

John glanced across the table at Lara, and they smiled at each other. "But then you came along!" John turned toward Emma so suddenly that she jumped. "We're so grateful to you for putting the smile back on Brian's face."

Emma glanced at Brian out of the corner of her eye. She thought his face was slightly red, and she looked down at her plate to hide the small smile that tugged at her lips.

"Okay, how about some dessert?" John said, as the waiter removed their plates. He clapped his hands together and rubbed them briskly.

Brian caught Emma's eye and gave an almost imperceptible shake of his head. Emma returned the gesture.

Brian made a big show of looking at his watch. "I'm so sorry, John, but we have to bolt. We're . . ."

"Catching a movie," Emma said smoothly.

"Oh, what are you going to see?" John looked disappointed.

"The . . . the . . ." Brian stumbled.

"That new foreign flick. I'm afraid I can't pronounce the title."

"Well, you two have a good time."

Brian began to signal for the waiter, but John stopped him.

"This is on me." He stood up. "It's been a real pleasure meeting you, Emma." He shook her hand.

Lara got up as well, but instead of shaking Emma's and

Brian's hands, she kissed them both on the cheek, European style.

"Thanks so much," Brian called over his shoulder as they made their way through the tables toward the front door.

Brian grabbed Emma's hand as they headed toward Liz's station wagon.

"Sorry about that." He stopped and turned Emma to face him. "I was looking forward to an evening alone with you, but I didn't want to turn John down."

"Don't worry about it." Emma linked her arm through his. "I understand."

"Since we didn't get dessert, how about some ice cream?"

"Sounds good to me."

Brian opened the passenger door for Emma.

He was getting behind the wheel when his cell phone rang.

"I'm so sorry," he said, digging in his jacket pocket. "I was sure I'd turned this beastly thing off." He pulled out the phone and glanced at the number. His features froze.

Emma couldn't miss the look on his face. "You'd better answer it."

Brian hesitated, and she insisted. "Please, go ahead."

Brian pushed the button and placed the phone against his ear. "Hello?"

As is so often the case with cell phones, Emma was able to hear every word.

"Brian? It's Amy," the voice echoing from the cell said.

"Amy?"

Emma tried to analyze the tone of Brian's voice. Hopeful? Happy? Excited? Or just plain curious?

"I wanted to tell you," Amy continued, "that Tony and I have called off the wedding. We've broken up." There was a pause. "I need to see you."

An entire rainbow of emotions passed over Brian's face as Emma watched. "I can't talk now. I'll call you later." He flicked the phone off and turned toward Emma.

"What are you going to do?" she asked.

"I don't know."

Chapter 20

BRIAN was quiet as they drove to get their ice cream. He pulled into the parking lot of the Dairy Queen and maneuvered into a space. There were a number of other cars in the lot with music blaring from their partially open windows.

"What will you have?" Brian asked as they approached the counter.

"A small vanilla cone." Emma really wanted sprinkles, but that seemed too unsophisticated after their meal at L'Etoile.

"I think we're a little overdressed," Brian said as he tugged at his tie to loosen it.

"That's for sure."

They took their cones back to the car and ate by the glow of the sodium lights.

"What do you think I should do about Amy?" Brian finally said.

"Amy?" Emma wasn't sure what to tell him.

"I don't really want to see her ever again. People talk about closure, but I'm not sure what that means."

"Well . . ." Emma was thinking fast. "Sometimes it's helpful to talk to the person and sort of . . . square things up." She thought about her ex-boyfriend Guy. There'd been no chance for closure with him—he'd been murdered before there was any opportunity for that.

"That makes sense." Brian sat still, his cone momentarily forgotten. "But I'm still not sure I want to see her again." He jerked as a dribble of cold ice cream slid down his hand.

"You don't have to decide right away."

"That's true. It isn't as if I don't already have a lot on my mind. I'm still awfully worried about Liz. Not only the money issue, but this whole business of that woman dying from the poisonous flower. She had a call from her old advisor at UT saying the police had been around asking questions about her and this Jessica Scott. Liz hardly knew her."

"Liz and I have uncovered another suspect." Emma told Brian about Lotte Fanning and the dent in her front bumper. "If Lotte can't come up with a plausible reason for it, I'm going to the police."

Brian was already shaking his head. "No. I don't want you talking to her. What if she is the murderer? What's going to stop her from killing you, too? Leave it up to the police. Please."

Detective Walker crossed Emma's mind, but she pushed the thought away.

"Promise me you'll stay far away from Lotte Fanning."

"Okay." Emma crossed her fingers behind her back.

"Promise?" Brian said again.

"Yes," Emma said with slightly more conviction.

"You've got some ice cream right by the side of your

mouth." Brian's voice grew husky. He wiped gently at the spot with his index finger.

Emma closed her eyes as Brian's face got nearer and his lips found hers.

EMMA woke up early on Sunday morning. She pulled back the curtains and peered out. Rain created rivulets down Washington Street, puddling in the gutters and lashing the shop windows. Emma let the curtain fall back into place. A good day to stay in bed.

But she was concerned about Arabella. She reached for her phone but then decided that instead she would pick up some croissants or whatever she could find at Kroger's, and go over to Arabella's for breakfast. Maybe it would be good to invite Sylvia, too. She and Arabella had become quite good friends, and Sylvia somehow always managed to bring everyone back down to earth. Emma grabbed her cell.

Sylvia answered almost immediately, and they arranged to meet at Arabella's in half an hour.

Emma pulled on a pair of yoga pants, a T-shirt and a zip-up sweatshirt. Once again she was glad she'd cut her hair short and needed to do little more than pull a comb through it. A dash of lipstick, and she was ready to go out the door.

The parking lot at Kroger's was fairly full, and there were quite a few people gathered around the bakery section. Emma snared some chocolate croissants and headed toward the cashiers.

Five minutes later she was knocking on Arabella's front door. The paperboy had thrown the *Post* onto the porch, but not quite far enough. When Emma picked it up, she noticed the edges were damp and curling.

Arabella opened the door moments later, and it was obvious she hadn't slept well . . . if at all. Her eyes were ringed with dark circles, and her usually well coiffed long, gray hair was pulled back willy-nilly into a slapdash ponytail.

"Oh, it is good to see you," she said as she hugged Emma. "I've spent a terrible night, imaging all sorts of horrors."

"Is there any news?" Emma asked as she followed Arabella into the kitchen. A pot of coffee was already sitting on the warmer. She tossed the newspaper onto the kitchen table.

"Tea?" Arabella opened a cupboard and pulled out a box of green tea bags.

"Thanks." Emma got a plate from the cupboard and arranged the croissants on it.

Arabella brought a mug of tea to the table and handed it to Emma. She was about to sit down when the front bell rang.

"Sylvia," Emma said in answer to Arabella's quizzical look. "I'll get it."

Sylvia was wearing a tightly belted black trench coat with the collar turned up and a broad-brimmed black fedora. Emma thought she looked a little like Boris from *Bullwinkle*.

"It's raining cats and dogs out there." Sylvia closed her umbrella and shook it vigorously. "Should I leave this out here?"

"No need. Arabella has an umbrella stand inside."

Sylvia stowed her umbrella and raincoat, and they headed back to the kitchen, where Emma got down another mug and poured Sylvia some coffee.

"Black." Sylvia held up a hand as Emma stood poised with sugar and milk.

"So." Sylvia took a big slurp of coffee. "Any news?"

"I talked to someone at the TBI last night." Arabella broke a tiny piece off her croissant and rolled it back and forth between her thumb and index finger. "They've heard from Francis. At least he's still alive." She swiped a tear from her cheek.

"Is the bank negotiating?" Sylvia broke her croissant in half and took a big bite.

"Yes. They said they've got a whole team on it." Arabella dropped the tiny bit of croissant back onto her plate. "I don't see why he can't retire. At his age—going undercover. Imagine!"

"Men." Sylvia dunked a bit of croissant into her coffee. "They're stubborn."

"You can say that again."

Arabella gave a tiny smile, which made Emma feel slightly better.

"Did I tell you?" Sylvia paused and wiped a smidge of chocolate from her lip. "That poor old dear who was taken to the hospital—"

"The one the police think someone tried to smother?"

"Yeah. That's the one. She's back at Sunny Days. I saw the ambulance pull in last night. And the state surveyors have been crawling all over the place. Poor Missy is being run off her feet. Somehow I think she imagined she'd be spending her time filing her nails like Jessica did."

"It's beginning to look as if Lotte Fanning might have killed to get her daughter that job."

"What?" Sylvia choked on her coffee.

Emma brought her up to date about the dent in Lotte's car and the fact that she'd been having an affair with Jim Calhoun before Jessica snagged him.

"Sounds like she's our woman."

Emma caught a glimpse of the front page of the *Post*

she'd brought in earlier. She spun the paper around to face her.

"Look at this." She pointed at one of the headlines. "It looks like the police are continuing their investigation." She read the first few lines of the article. "It says that they haven't found any garages locally that did bodywork on any cars that might have been involved in the hit-and-run that killed Gladys, so they've expanded their search outside the area to Memphis and Nashville."

"You've got to tell Detective Walker about finding that dent in Lotte Fanning's car," Arabella said.

"I know," Emma admitted with a sinking heart.

BY Monday morning the rain had stopped and pale sun peeked from between the clouds. Emma opened the door to Sweet Nothings. It wasn't time to open yet, and she needed to do a little accounting first. Arabella was a whiz at finding exquisite vintage pieces, but she was hopeless with numbers.

Emma was staring at some figures—at least they were getting better—when she heard Arabella enter. She joined her aunt in the stockroom for a cup of tea. Pierre headed straight for his dog bed. Obviously the car ride over had exhausted him and he was ready for his first nap of the day.

Pierre was snoring softly when they heard someone banging on the front door. Pierre levitated from the bed and was on all four paws, barking, before Emma could even blink.

She glanced at her watch and then at Arabella. "It's not time to open yet. Maybe it's a delivery?"

"Are you expecting something?"

Emma shook her head. "No."

They both began walking toward the door. Through the

glass they could see the shadow of a man. He was slightly bent over and wearing an old-fashioned hat.

Arabella squinted at the door. "It looks like Mr. Zimmerman from across the street." She glanced toward Pierre. "What on earth could he want? Pierre is right here and certainly not bothering his precious Bertha."

Arabella opened the door slowly and peered around the edge. "Yes? We're not open yet." She pointed to the large sign that was flipped to *closed*.

"I'm not here to go shopping." Zimmerman nearly spat out the words. "I can't imagine what use I would have for any of the things you sell. It's bad enough having to look at all that scanty stuff from my window across the street."

Emma saw Arabella's back stiffen. They did their best to keep their window displays classy and not provocative, but they *were* selling lingerie, after all.

"What can I do for you, then?" Arabella cracked the door a little wider. Pierre had stopped barking, but he was growling under his breath.

"That cur of yours . . ."

Arabella lifted her chin and gazed at Zimmerman through narrow eyes. "If you mean my championship French bulldog—"

"Call him what you will. He's nothing but a beast as far as I'm concerned."

"Pray tell. What did Pierre do to annoy you this time? He's been with me all morning."

"He got my Bertha in the family way!" Zimmerman said so vehemently that Emma could see his spit spraying the air.

Arabella clapped a hand to her mouth, and Emma had to stifle her own laugh.

"Bertha's got a bun in the oven, and it's all his fault." Zimmerman pointed a bony finger at Pierre.

Pierre lowered his head and skulked back toward his bed.

"That's ridiculous!" Arabella sniffed.

"How many times has he gotten loose and come over to my shop?" Zimmerman moved his face until it was only inches from Arabella's.

Arabella's eyes were blazing. "So what of it? They were never together for more than a few minutes."

"Don't take long for dogs," Zimmerman said smugly.

"I refuse to believe it."

"Well, we'll see, won't we? When Bertha delivers her litter, then we'll know. And if a single one of them pups looks at all like . . . like . . . him"—he pointed at Pierre—"then I'll drown the lot of them!"

"He wouldn't really do that, would he?" Emma said as they closed the door on Zimmerman's retreating back.

"I wouldn't put it past him. But don't worry. I'm quite certain Pierre had nothing to do with his precious Bertha's being *enceinte*. Obviously Bertha got out at one point and found herself a beau. And I'm certain it wasn't Pierre." She turned toward Pierre, who was lying on his dog bed, one eye closed and the other half open. "Right, Pierre?"

Arabella went to stand by the window. "Well, would you look at that!" she said suddenly.

"What is it?"

Emma went to stand by her aunt.

"Look." Arabella pointed to a couple walking down the sidewalk across the street.

"That's Les," Emma said.

"Yes." Arabella nodded briskly. "And that's Sally Dixon with him." Bright spots of red suffused her cheeks. "Of all the nerve." She was quiet for a moment. "Well, I suppose that does solve the problem of what to do about Les. Sally never forgave me for stealing Francis from her, as she put it."

"And now she's stolen Les from you by the looks of things." Emma peered out the window where Sally was walking arm in arm with Les.

"I'm glad," Arabella said, and Emma could tell she meant it. "I like Les and want him to be happy. If Sally Dixon makes him happy, then so be it."

MONDAY mornings weren't usually their busy times, but Emma was pleased to sell a 1940s rayon satin negligee that was in a very small size. Emma had been worried about finding someone whom it would fit. She also sold three pieces of shape wear to one of the members of Marjorie Porter's garden club. She'd missed the trunk show but had made a note to stop by Sweet Nothings. All in all, it was a very satisfactory morning.

"You know what?" Emma said to Arabella, who was rearranging some stock. "I think I'm going to put on my big girl panties and go to Detective Walker and tell him about that dent in Lotte Fanning's car. Hopefully he'll bring it in for examination."

"At the least, I imagine they'd go out and talk to her. If she is the killer it wouldn't hurt to make her a little nervous."

"Good point." Emma glanced at her watch. "If you can handle things, maybe I'll take a ride over there now."

"No problem, dear. Besides, Sylvia's due any minute."

Emma ran a comb through her hair and freshened her lipstick. It was obvious Walker found her attractive. She would have to use that to her advantage, selling him on this idea with as much vigor as she sold lingerie to the customers of Sweet Nothings.

The police station was on North Caldwell Street, and it

didn't take her long to get there. The flat brick building was hardly imposing, but Emma sat in her car for a minute, marshalling her thoughts. Finally she was ready and marched up to the front door and pulled it open.

Fortunately, Walker was in and more than willing to see her. A uniformed officer showed Emma the way down the hall.

Walker's office was small and cramped with stacks of folders spilling half off the chair pulled up in front of his desk. He jumped up when Emma entered.

He stared at her for a moment. "If you aren't a sight for sore eyes." He began to move the papers off the chair. "Please. Have a seat."

His desk was piled high with papers, too, but he'd cleared a spot in the middle where he had a piece of wax paper open with half of a large deli sandwich resting on it. He gestured toward it.

"Sorry. You've caught me on my lunch break."

"Please. Don't let me interrupt."

"I hope you mean that, because I'm starving. I got called out early this morning and never did manage breakfast." He picked up the sandwich and took a large bite.

"Are you still working on the hit-and-run case involving Gladys Smit?"

Walker finished chewing and took a big glug from a can of pop. "Yes. The case is still open, although we don't have much of anything in the way of leads at the moment."

"I think I might have a lead for you."

Walker raised his dark brows. "Really?" He picked up the last of his sandwich.

Here was where Emma began to get a little nervous. How was she to explain what she was doing skulking around in the Sunny Days parking lot looking for damaged cars? She should have thought this through before coming to the police station.

"I happened to park next to a car with a large dent in the front right bumper," Emma said with sudden inspiration. It certainly sounded better than what she'd really been doing.

"Where was this?" Walker swiped a napkin across his mouth.

"The Sunny Days retirement community."

"Did you get the license plate number?"

Emma could have kicked herself. If she'd taken down the number she wouldn't have to admit to knowing whose car it was.

"No, but I recognized the car."

A wary look came across Walker's handsome, dark features.

Emma felt the heat rising toward her face and tried desperately to control it. "There aren't many people in town who drive a late-model Mercedes."

"True. A pickup truck or an old beater, for sure. But a Mercedes?" Walker shrugged.

"It belongs to a Charlotte Fanning." Emma twisted a lock of hair around her finger. If she were wrong, and Charlotte was totally innocent . . . It was too late to back out now.

Walker pulled a pad of paper toward him and scribbled down the name. "We'll check into it."

"You won't mention that I—"

He shook his head. "We'll be discreet. Your name won't be mentioned at all. No one would ever come forward with information if we went around blabbing about where it came from." He leaned back in his chair, and it creaked loudly. "Probably have a lot more dead bodies on our hands, too."

Emma nodded.

"Listen." Walker leaned forward, folding his hands

together in front of him on his desk. "Would you like to maybe go out sometime . . ." He let the rest of the sentence dangle in the air.

Emma gave what she hoped was a rueful smile. "That would be lovely, but at the moment I'm seeing someone."

But was that true? she wondered. Brian still hadn't decided about meeting Amy one last time. What if she managed to get him back again?

Chapter 21

EMMA headed back to Sweet Nothings to finish out the afternoon. Around four o'clock she decided that she absolutely had to have a cupcake. Preferably one of Bitsy's carrot cake ones with the cream cheese frosting.

"Anyone up for a cupcake?" she asked Sylvia and Arabella.

"Sure, why not." Sylvia's deep rumbling voice came from behind the counter. "It's not as if I have to watch my figure anymore."

"I'll have one, too." Arabella smiled. "I'm still watching my figure, but that's about all I'm doing . . . watching!"

Emma grabbed her sweater and headed around the corner to Sprinkles. She was pleased to see that a handful of people were standing in front of the counter.

"Emma! So good to see you," Bitsy said when Emma got to the front of the line.

"It looks as if business is improving."

Bitsy made a face. "Slightly, but nothing like before. I had to take out a loan to make my mortgage payment this month."

"I have an idea," Emma said as something suddenly occurred to her. "I'll buy a couple of dozen from you and hand them out at Sweet Nothings along with your card. A lot of our clients come from Jackson or even Memphis or Nashville. They won't have heard all about the nasty business with Jessica and perhaps they'll stop by to take some cupcakes home."

Bitsy's face brightened. "It's worth a try."

Emma glanced at her watch. "It's kind of late now, but if you can bring two dozen by tomorrow morning, I'll see that they're given out."

"Great."

"Right now, though, I'll take a carrot cake"—Emma pointed to the last carrot cupcake in the case—"along with one coconut and one red velvet."

Bitsy retrieved the cupcakes and carefully placed them in a white paper bag. "Can you believe the police are still coming around asking questions?" she said as she folded the top of the bag over and handed it to Emma.

"Liz said they'd been out to UT talking to her old advisor, of all things."

Bitsy nodded. "Yes. I heard from an old sorority sister that they'd been contacted, too. I guess they've ferreted out the story about me and Jessica by now. But"—she put her hands together and held them out toward Emma—"See? No handcuffs. I haven't been arrested yet."

Emma carried her bag of cupcakes back to Sweet Nothings. She hoped her scheme would help turn Bitsy's business around. If she could hang on a little longer, the case would be solved, and it would be proven that she'd had nothing to do with Jessica's death.

When Emma got back to the shop, Arabella was changing a mannequin, and Sylvia was sitting on the love seat, resting.

"Isn't that the set we showed at Deirdre Porter's trunk show?" Sylvia pointed a finger in Arabella's direction.

"Yes, I believe it is." Arabella straightened the bow on the peignoir.

"You know what I'm wondering?" Emma looked at Arabella and Sylvia, who both shook their heads. "I'm wondering what happened at that trunk show to put the murderer over the edge. Because the whole thing couldn't have been planned in advance."

"True." Sylvia took a deep breath and coughed briefly. "They had no way of knowing that Deirdre would be serving Bitsy's cupcakes."

"Or that she'd have foxglove growing in her garden," Arabella added.

"You haven't heard any more about that Crystal Davis, have you?" Sylvia asked.

"No." Emma shook her head and took a bite of her cupcake. "I asked the guy next door if he would call me when she came back, but nothing. Of course, he may have forgotten."

"Or lost your number." Arabella had finished with the mannequin and was digging in the bakery bag for her red velvet cupcake.

"I think it's that Fanning woman." Sylvia finished her cupcake and tossed the wrapper in the trash can. "She's the one who has a dent in her car, after all."

"I did go and tell the police about that," Emma said. "Of course, Liz and Bitsy both said the police were still asking questions about *them*."

"Oh, did I tell you about my new gig?" Sylvia said.

"No," Arabella and Emma chorused.

"They talked me into volunteering at Sunny Days. I'm taking the bookmobile around. I kind of enjoy it. It gives me a chance to talk to some of the nursing residents. They're an interesting bunch. That old lady, the one who was in the coma, has been coming in and out of consciousness. She woke up a bit when I got there yesterday. Not that she had any interest in the books. Poor thing, I doubt she can see all that well. But she did tell me she used to be a nurse at the Henry County Hospital. Seemed to think she was still there. Kept calling me *doctor*."

BY the time she got up to her apartment after Sweet Nothings closed, Emma was almost too tired to cook. She put a pot of water on the stove to boil some eggs. She'd make some deviled eggs and throw together a salad. As she passed the refrigerator, she noticed the slip of paper from the fortune cookies she'd shared with Brian taped to the front. It had been a nice evening, and the thought made her smile.

Unfortunately thoughts of Jessica's and Gladys's murders intruded. Emma frowned. It all started at that trunk show. But what had caused the murderer to strike right then? She tried to remember everything that had happened, but it was all such a muddle. She was dropping the eggs into the boiling water when she thought about what Sylvia had told them about the old woman on the nursing floor. Someone had tried to smother her. Why? As far as Sylvia had been able to find out, she had almost no family and certainly no money to leave. Nursing care cost hundreds of dollars a day. Even if she'd had a small estate, it wouldn't take long for it to be eaten up.

Steam from the boiling pot wafted into Emma's face, and she stepped back from the stove. Could the three cases be connected somehow? Jessica's death and Gladys's hit-and-run and someone trying to kill this old woman?

As she washed and tore some lettuce leaves, she thought about the story Jessica had told at the trunk show. Jessica's story had been about a nurse. The old woman whom someone had inexplicably tried to kill had been a nurse. Could they possibly be one and the same?

She felt her heart race with excitement. She was onto something. Definitely. She had to call Liz right away and see what she thought.

Liz sounded quite glum when she answered the phone, but her tone perked up when she heard Emma's voice.

Emma explained about the ideas she'd had.

"I'm not sure I get it," Liz said when Emma had finished.

"What if Jessica was murdered because of that story about the babies being switched? Obviously it was never meant to come out. I imagine the mothers themselves carried the secret to their graves. And then all of a sudden, Jessica knows all about it from this old nurse who's now a resident at Sunny Days."

"But Jessica didn't know the women's names. Just a nickname—Cat, wasn't it?"

Emma silenced the timer pinging on the stove and turned the gas off under her eggs. "Yes. But presumably the nurse knows the names. Or at least the murderer must be afraid she does. And that's why they tried to smother her."

"But didn't Jessica say that the babies who had been switched were boys? There weren't any men at that trunk show."

"Maybe it was someone's brother or husband?" Emma

carried the pan of eggs to the sink and ran cold water over them.

"But why would anyone care after all these years?"

"Maybe there's money involved." Emma turned off the tap and fished the boiled eggs from the water. She started to put them on the counter, but one nearly rolled off. She grabbed it in the nick of time.

"Could be. So, what next?"

"I'd like to see if that nurse who is now at Sunny Days was working at the Henry County Hospital in 1954. That's the year the switch supposedly took place. I'm sure Sylvia can get her name for me."

"I'll go with you. I know someone who works in the human resources department there. She's the wife of a friend of Matt's. Maybe she'll help us out."

TUESDAY the shop was fairly calm. No outbursts from Mr. Zimmerman, no escapades by Pierre and no deliveries. Arabella was unusually quiet. Emma knew she was worried about Francis. With nothing new to report, the story had slipped from the front pages of the newspaper. Arabella was worried that Francis would be forgotten. Emma assured her that the police were no doubt working overtime to secure his release from the robbers.

Emma was a little concerned about leaving Arabella alone in the shop, but Liz was picking her up at eleven o'clock to swing by the Henry County Medical Center, as it was now known, to see if they could find out more about that nurse living at Sunny Days. Sylvia had managed to discover her name—Rosalind Newell. The nurse Jessica had talked about was named Rose—it seemed perfectly possible that that might be a nickname for Rosalind.

"Are you sure you'll be okay?" Emma asked as she slipped into her sweater.

Arabella made a face. "You worry way too much for such a young girl. I'll be fine. Besides, I'm dying to know what you'll find out."

Emma kissed her aunt on the cheek. A horn sounded outside Sweet Nothings—Liz. Emma went out the front door and slid into the passenger seat of Liz's station wagon.

"Don't you feel we're getting close to an answer?" Liz said as she pulled away from the curb.

"I hope so. I'm only concerned as to whether or not the records at the Henry County Medical Center go back to 1954."

"Fingers crossed," Liz said as she turned into the hospital parking lot. They parked Liz's car and headed toward the modern glass and steel entrance.

A blue-haired woman sat behind the information desk. She was wearing an old-fashioned flowered dress with a large starburst brooch on the right shoulder. Emma guessed they were both almost as vintage as the lingerie Arabella found for the shop.

"We're looking for the human resources department."

The woman scribbled some directions on a piece of paper with Henry County Medical Center printed at the top and handed it to Emma.

They followed the rights and lefts until they came to their destination. "Cross your fingers again," Liz said to Emma, "that Tammy hasn't gone out to lunch."

A pleasant young woman behind the desk looked up inquiringly as they entered. Liz approached her with a smile.

"I'm Liz Banning, and I was wondering if Tammy Cole is here."

"I think I saw her a minute ago," the girl said, picking up the telephone on her desk.

She spoke a few words into the receiver then looked up at Liz. "She'll be right out."

A woman with short blond hair came down the hallway. She was tall and trim with an athletic gait. She smiled when she saw Liz.

"Liz!" They shook hands. "Good to see you. How are Matt and the kids?"

"Fine, just great." Liz turned toward Emma. "This is my friend, Emma."

"Come on down to my office." Tammy waved an arm, and her cluster of bracelets tinkled melodically.

"What can I do for you?" she asked when they were seated in her rather cramped office.

"We're trying to find out whether or not a nurse by the name of Rosalind Newell worked here in 1954," Liz said.

"Rosalind Newell? Does this have anything to do with all that stuff that's been going on at Sunny Days? Your father's there, isn't he?"

"Yes, he is. And yes, it's somewhat related. And rather complicated."

Tammy leaned back in her chair. "Unfortunately the records from that far back are no longer here. They're in storage . . ."—she waved her hands around—"somewhere."

"I was afraid of that," Liz said as she picked up her purse.

The phone on Tammy's desk rang, and her hand went toward it reflexively.

"We won't keep you any longer. Come on over with Dan some night for a drink, okay?"

Tammy gave Liz a thumbs-up as they left her office.

"We didn't really expect to find out anything," Emma

said soothingly as they retraced their steps back down the corridor.

"True. Still, it would have been nice to have had confirmation."

They were going through the lobby when Emma grabbed Liz by the arm.

"Look!" She pointed at a series of gold plaques on the wall. Large gold letters at the top read *Employees of the Year.* "You don't suppose . . ."

Liz was already reading through the names.

"There!" She pointed toward the plaque for 1954.

Engraved in the gold was the name *Rosalind Newell.*

Chapter 22

"WHAT'S our next step?" Liz asked as she leaned on the counter at Sweet Nothings.

"Is there any way you can get in to see this nurse? Rosalind, you said her name was?" Arabella put down her mending and took off her silver-framed half-glasses.

"People are used to seeing you around Sunny Days. You might be able to pop into her room without being noticed."

"I don't know," Emma said. "They're quite careful about things like that up on the nursing floor."

"Say you're a friend or relative." Arabella smiled. "Use your charm." She patted Emma on the arm.

Emma made a face. "Very funny."

"You could go over now," Liz suggested. "I can stay here in case Arabella needs a hand."

"I'm afraid I can't pay more than minimum wage," Arabella quipped.

A shadow crossed Liz's face. "Right now even that would be a blessing."

"Still no news on Matt's contract?" Emma frowned. She'd hoped that Liz's situation would have improved by now.

Liz shook her head. "No. Soon, though. Hopefully by the end of the week. He's pretty sure he's got it, but you know how these things go."

"Well, are you going or not?" Arabella put the piece she'd been working on under the counter and turned to Emma. "I can't wait to hear what you find out."

"I guess I'll go then."

Emma was thinking hard as she walked to her car. Should she try to sneak into Rose's room or claim to be a relative? By the time she'd slid behind the wheel of the Bug, she'd decided that honesty was the best policy. Besides, she wasn't much of an actress and was likely to be busted by the first person to come along.

Emma parked at the back of the Sunny Days lot. She really, really didn't want to do this. She should have sent Liz instead. She dragged her feet as much as possible, but eventually she still found herself at the front door of the retirement community. She threw back her shoulders, raised her chin, pushed open the front door and approached the front desk.

The woman sitting there smiled helpfully.

Emma tried to control the quaver in her voice. "I'm here to visit Rosalind Newell. She's on fourth-floor nursing."

The woman's expression of interest turned to boredom. She pointed toward the elevators. "Take the elevator to the fourth floor."

Emma's stomach did a little victory leap. She couldn't believe it was going to be this easy! She stabbed the elevator button and waited impatiently as the car crawled downward from the fourth floor.

The doors opened and Emma stepped inside. They closed so slowly she found herself clenching her teeth in frustration. She really felt as if she were about to find the one thread that would unravel this whole mystery. If she could only manage to get to the fourth floor!

Finally, the car began its slow ascent. Emma studied the numbers on the indicator, trying to focus on what questions she would ask Rosalind Newell when she got there. According to Sylvia, she was in room 403, which was a right off the elevator and a left turn at the end of the corridor.

Emma wiped her palms on her slacks as the elevator doors swung open. The corridor was quiet and empty. She tried to step out as boldly as possible. As if she belonged. Of course it didn't matter, since there was no one there to see her.

She followed Sylvia's directions and took a right off the elevator and headed down the hall. Room 403 was easy enough to find. Emma counted off the rooms . . . 397 . . . 399 . . . 401 . . . and finally she was approaching number 403.

She was almost there when a woman came out of the room opposite, carrying a tray and pushing the door closed with her hip. She was wearing blue and white scrubs and a pair of scuffed clogs. She looked up in alarm when she saw Emma.

"Can I help you?"

Emma swallowed the huge lump that had formed in her throat. She ran her hand casually through her hair. "I'm stopping in to see how Rose is doing." She indicated the doorway to room 403.

The woman eyed her suspiciously. "Did you check in at the desk?"

"Downstairs?" Emma asked, confused.

The woman shook her head vehemently and her frizzy brown curls bobbed this way and that. "No." She pointed toward the end of the corridor. "At the nurse's station." She must have noticed Emma's confused look. "When you got off the elevator," she clarified.

"Oh," Emma said in a very small voice. "No one was there."

"Come with me." The woman motioned with her head toward the other end of the hallway. "I think the doctor's issued orders that Miss Rose isn't to have any visitors for the near future." She marched officiously down the corridor, and Emma had no choice but to follow.

The woman who now sat behind the desk opposite the elevator, which had been empty when Emma got off, was, if possible, even more severe looking. Her eyes were narrowed to slits, and her lips were sucked in so tightly it looked as if they had been stitched shut by an expert plastic surgeon.

"Can I help you?" she asked as Emma approached the desk. Her lips barely moved, and her eyes retained their suspicious mien.

Emma was horrified when her voice came out several octaves higher than normal.

"I came to see Rosalind Newell. She's a . . ."—she hesitated for a bare second—"friend of the family."

The woman's fingers were already poised on the keys of her computer. She tapped for several seconds, paused, then looked up from the monitor at Emma.

"No visitors. It says so right here." She tapped the monitor with her knuckle.

Emma's shoulders slumped. "Does it say when she'll be

able to have visitors?" Maybe the orders were only for a day or two.

The woman peered at the screen, hit the down arrow and squinted some more. "Doesn't say. Probably not for a while. It's best if you call first." She plucked a business card from the holder on her desk and handed it to Emma.

Emma tried to smile, but her mouth refused to cooperate. "Thank you." She tucked the card into her purse.

The elevator ride down felt twice as fast, and before she knew it, she was being spit out into the lobby.

The sun was in Emma's eyes as she walked back toward her car, but she thought she saw something on her windshield, stuck under the wiper. It couldn't be a ticket; she was legally parked in the Sunny Days parking lot. Perhaps it was one of those annoying flyers for car washes or detailing firms.

As she got closer, she could see that the item was a pale blue. It looked more like an envelope than a flyer. Emma's curiosity grew with each step.

Finally she reached her car. It was an envelope—stuck securely under her windshield wiper blade. She eased it out carefully. It looked and felt expensive. She ripped open the flap. Who on earth would have left a letter for her like this?

As Emma slid the piece of notepaper out of the envelope, a delicious perfume rose from within. She inhaled deeply. She couldn't identify the scent, although she knew she had smelled it before. Now she was really curious. Not only had someone stuck a note on her car, it was written on obviously expensive scented notepaper.

Emma removed the paper the rest of the way and opened it up. The top of the sheet was cut off at a slight angle. And instead of elegant, delicate handwriting, the note was printed in block capital letters.

Even more shocking was the message:

Mind your own business now . . . before it's too late.

EMMA'S hands shook all the way back to Sweet Nothings. Who could have done such a thing? Obviously, she'd alarmed the murderer. Was it Lotte Fanning? Had she somehow discovered that Emma was the one who told the police about her car?

She pulled into the Sweet Nothings parking lot, kicking up gravel and nearly skidding. She parked the car, and when she got out, she realized it was horribly crooked. Fortunately, it didn't matter. All she wanted to do right now was to show the note to Arabella and down a big glass of her revivifying sweet tea.

"This is excellent paper," Arabella said as she held Emma's mystery note up to the light. She pointed at a spot on the pale blue vellum. "Here's the watermark." She showed Emma where *Tiffany & Co.* was pressed into the paper. Arabella grabbed the envelope from the counter. "It's here, too." She pointed to the spot near the opening where the raised letters of *Tiffany & Co.* could be seen.

"I wonder why the paper's been torn," Emma said. "It's not as if it's been ripped off a pad or something."

Arabella smiled. "They had to cut off the monogram." She rubbed the robin's egg blue paper between her fingers. "This is the kind of good stationery you would always have monogrammed. Whose ever it is probably had a die made. Tiffany keeps them on file so you can engrave your stationery, calling cards, invitations and the like."

"What about the scent? Does Tiffany sell scented notepaper?"

Arabella shook her head. She held the sheet of vellum

up to her nose and sniffed. "Chanel No. 5." She took another sniff. "Definitely Chanel No. 5." She shook her head again. "No. We used to perfume our own paper so that it would carry our own signature scent. A few drops on a cotton ball placed inside the box was enough to do the trick."

Arabella's face clouded over. "This scares me, though." She waved the paper around and Emma caught a hint of the perfume. "This is a threat, even if it is on scented Tiffany notepaper."

"Maybe Lotte Fanning got wind of the fact that I was the one who told Detective Walker about the dent in her car."

"I think you should show this to him." Arabella pointed to the note. "He needs to know about this. If Lotte is the murderer, and she's gotten a bee into her bonnet about you . . ." Arabella shivered.

They'd been careful to handle the paper by the edges, and Emma now wrapped it in some Sweet Nothings tissue and put it in a bag.

Emma pulled her cell phone from her pocket and dialed the police station. Walker was out, but the secretary said Emma ought to be able to catch him if she came by early the next morning.

EMMA was up early Wednesday morning. She wanted to be sure to catch Walker before he was called out of the office or decided to go out for some breakfast.

Washington Street was quiet. Most of the shops were dark and shuttered, although a light was on in Let Us Cater to You, and the Coffee Klatch was already open for patrons needing that early morning cup of coffee.

A number of Crown Vics were still in the parking lot at the police station when Emma arrived. She hoped that meant that Walker would be there and not out investigating a case somewhere.

Walker was almost hidden by a stack of folders and papers when Emma arrived in his office. She couldn't tell if they were the same papers as last time or different ones. It didn't look as if Walker would dig himself out before the next century.

He jumped up immediately when he saw Emma, a hopeful look crossing his face like a sudden ray of sunshine.

"Have a seat," he mumbled around a bite of granola bar. He waved it toward Emma. "Sorry, haven't had a chance to eat so I grabbed this from the vending machine. To what do I owe this pleasure?"

Emma put the Sweet Nothings bag on Walker's desk. He glanced at the label, and Emma could have sworn he blushed slightly. She removed the tissue-wrapped note from within and handed it to Walker.

He raised his thick dark brows.

"It's a note I found under the windshield wiper on my car."

"A note?" he said somewhat indistinctly, having just taken a bite of his snack.

Emma nodded. "A threatening note."

"Ah," Walker said with relish. "A threatening note."

He carefully unwrapped the tissue and, holding the note with the tips of his fingers by its very corners, began to read the printing on the robin's egg blue stationery.

His dark brows drew together. "Do you have any idea what this means?" He brandished the paper, and Emma got a slight whiff of Chanel No. 5. "Why would someone leave this on your car?"

She tried not to squirm under his direct gaze. "I have no idea."

Walker's eyes narrowed slightly. He didn't believe her. Emma raised her chin and leveled her glance at his. He sighed and looked away.

"Can you dust it for fingerprints?"

Walker shrugged. "Sure, but chances are the person who owns this fancy notepaper doesn't have their prints on file. Most felons aren't partial to scented stationery. At least in my experience."

He steepled his fingers and looked over their tops at Emma. "Could this"—he gestured toward the note he had rewrapped in the tissue—"be some kind of love triangle? You stole someone's boyfriend, and this is her way of getting back?"

Emma's spine stiffened. "Certainly not!"

"Okay, okay, just asking." Walker held up a hand. "No need to get so upset. It's only that in these cases, it's usually personal, you know?"

Emma relaxed slightly. She twisted a lock of hair around her finger. "I don't suppose you've heard anything about that car with the dented fender . . ."

Walker looked confused for a moment, and then his face cleared. "I have the file here somewhere." He began sifting through the masses of paperwork on his desk. Finally he held a manila folder triumphantly. He paged through it.

"Seems the car was involved in a fender bender. Flecks of paint from another car were found, but no traces of anything that would lead us to believe it had been involved in a hit-and-run."

"What kind of traces . . ."

Walker glowered at Emma. "Hair, skin, blood . . . traces like that."

Emma shuddered. She was sorry she'd asked.

"So there's no chance it could have been the car that was involved in that hit-and-run."

Walker shook his head vigorously and tapped the folder. "Nope. At least not according to this report."

He put his elbows on the desk and leaned his chin on his clasped hands. He leveled a stern gaze at Emma. "I certainly hope"—he glanced at the note on his desk—"that you will leave the detective work to the police." His voice took on a husky tone. "Who knows what this crackpot letter writer might do? I'd hate for anything to happen to you. Even if you won't let me take you out." He made a comically sad face.

"If I find out anything, I promise to come right to you," Emma reassured him.

"That's not quite what I had in mind." Walker gave an exasperated sigh. "I don't want you to go around poking your nose into things. It could be dangerous. Despite the fancy stationery, despite the high-class-smelling perfume, this person"—he tapped the note—"might mean business."

Emma shuddered. The same thought had occurred to her.

She thanked Walker and made her way down the hall back to the front door. Emma felt a deep sense of disappointment as she left the Paris police station. If Lotte wasn't responsible for the hit-and-run, then who was?

Chapter 23

WHEN Emma got back to Sweet Nothings, the shop was perfumed with the scents of vanilla, lemon, strawberry and other delicious flavors.

Emma paused and took a deep breath. "It smells fabulous in here."

Arabella pointed at a display of miniature cupcakes from Sprinkles. "Bitsy dropped these off after you left."

"They look heavenly."

"The strawberry shortcakes are divine." Arabella sighed. She leveled a glance at Emma. "I had to taste one to be sure they were okay."

"Of course." Emma smiled. She knew Arabella loved her sweets.

"I've been offering them to customers along with Bitsy's card. She phoned a few minutes ago to say the shop was filling up for the first time in days."

"That's good news, at least."

"And your news . . ." Arabella fiddled with a silk strap that had slipped over the shoulder of one of the mannequins.

Emma made a face. "Not good. Walker said he'd try dusting the note for prints, but he wasn't optimistic."

"Oh well." Arabella took a pin from her pocket and shortened the offending strap. "How about the dent in Lotte's car?"

Emma made another face. "No luck there. According to Walker, the car was involved in a fender bender, not a hit-and-run. No sign of . . ." She hesitated, not wanting to offend her aunt.

"Blood or guts?" Arabella supplied.

Emma swallowed. "Exactly."

"Disappointing, isn't it?" Arabella brushed at the shoulders of the mannequin and straightened the bodice on the aqua silk gown. "I was quite convinced Lotte was our culprit. It's easy to imagine a woman who is edging past her prime giving in to murderous impulses when she finds her lover has taken up with a younger woman."

Emma nodded glumly. "If not Lotte, then who?"

"We still don't know where that Crystal woman has gone." Arabella undid the buttons on the bed jacket that graced their other mannequin and eased it off.

"The young guy who lived next door promised to call if she came back. It is odd that she took off like that."

The front doorbell jangled, and they both jumped. Pierre got up from his nap and sauntered toward the door.

A man stuck his head around the edge of the open door. "Can I come in?"

"Brian!" Emma and Arabella exclaimed together.

Emma took a mental inventory of the state of her physical affairs—she hadn't run a brush through her hair since that morning, but the benefit of short hair was that it tended to stay fairly neat. She took a surreptitious swipe at her nose with a tissue to remove any shine and straightened the slim belt that cinched the waist of her dress.

Instead of his usual work clothes, Brian had on gray slacks, a navy blazer and an open-necked blue shirt. Emma felt her heart give an extra beat.

"Looks like you're off to something important." Arabella slipped a 1940s ecru satin and lace gown over the denuded mannequin and gently eased it into place.

Brian shrugged, and Emma thought he looked uncomfortable. If she wasn't mistaken, she could have sworn his face turned slightly red. "Nothing much." He looked down at his well-polished shoes. "Don't tell Liz I told you because she probably wants to tell you herself, but Matt got that contract he was after."

"Wonderful!" Emma exclaimed. "I'm sure she's relieved."

"She sure is. Said it's a real load off her mind."

"I'll pretend to be surprised when she tells me." Emma grinned at Brian.

He ducked his head. "Thanks." He glanced at his watch. "Listen, Emma, do you have a second?" He gestured toward the door of the shop. "There's something I want to talk to you about."

"Sure. I'll be right back," Emma called over her shoulder to Arabella as Brian led her out the front door.

They found a park bench in front of the Taffy Pull and sat down.

Brian ran a finger around the collar of his shirt. "I've decided to go see Amy," he blurted out.

Emma was startled. "Oh," was all she could think to say.

"She claims she wants closure." He looked at Emma out of the corner of his eye. "I mean she just walked out one

day saying it was over between us. There'd been no indication . . ." He swallowed hard.

"How do you feel?" Emma asked with trepidation.

Brian threw his hands in the air. "I don't ever want to see
her again, but if this will stop her calling me all the time."
He put his head in his hands.

"Then you should go." She put her arm around his
shoulders.

"I don't want you to think . . ."

Emma shook her head. "I understand. Really," she said
when Brian continued to hesitate.

Brian gave a gigantic sigh and began to get up. "Guess
I'll be going then. I'll call you when I get back, okay?"

Emma smiled. "I'll be waiting." She stood and watched
as Brian headed to his car and then turned and went back
to Sweet Nothings.

"What was that all about? Or can't you tell me?" Arabella
said when Emma returned to the shop.

Emma couldn't help it. A tear escaped and dribbled down
her cheek. She brushed at it impatiently. "Brian is off to see
his ex, Amy. For closure." She smiled at her aunt. "I'm trying
not to imagine Amy winning him back."

"She won't." Arabella pulled a tissue from the box on
the counter and handed it to Emma. Emma wiped her eyes
and nose under Arabella's watchful eye. Her aunt's face
looked drawn and tired, and there were circles under her
eyes.

"Has there been any news about Francis?" Emma felt a
sudden pang of guilt. Arabella had her own worries.

A shadow crossed over Arabella's face, and her shoulders
sagged. She shook her head. "No. Apparently there's been
no word from the kidnappers for several days. It doesn't look
good."

"Oh no!" Emma rushed to her aunt's side and put her arms around her. She could feel Arabella's shoulders shake.

The door opened, and they jumped apart. Arabella squared her shoulders, lifted her chin and glided toward the woman who had entered. "Welcome to Sweet Nothings," she said with barely a tremor in her voice.

Emma looked on in admiration. She knew Arabella was a strong woman. Hopefully that strength would get her through this. If only the police would rescue Francis!

Emma took her laptop into the stockroom and set it up on Arabella's desk. She wrinkled her nose as she turned it on. She had some bookkeeping to do—not her favorite task. She stifled a yawn as she scrolled through the figures. Sweet Nothings was inching its way into the black despite her mistaking the cost of those items from Monique Berthole. Emma still felt guilty about that, although the lingerie was selling well and they were almost out.

Emma was entering some deposits into her spreadsheet when her cell phone rang.

"Hello," she said without thinking, as she continued to peruse the figures in front of her.

"Is this . . ." The voice hesitated. It sounded like a young man.

Emma glanced at the caller ID display, but she didn't recognize the number. Was this some kind of prank caller?

"Is this Emma?"

"Yes."

"You gave me your card and told me to call this number."

"Oh?"

"You said you wanted to know if that woman who lived next door, Crystal, came back."

Now Emma was all ears. She had a sudden vision of a

young fellow with curly hair and gigantic Elton John–style glasses. She sat up straighter in her chair. "Yes, I did say that."

"Good, because that's why I'm calling. She's come back."

"Is she there now?"

"Let me check."

There was silence then the sound of footsteps in the background retreating and then returning. "Yes, she's here now. Saw her car outside. She's taking stuff out of it and bringing it back in. I remember when she left it was packed to the roof."

Emma glanced at her watch. The shop was quiet. If Arabella could spare her, she could run over there right now and catch Crystal before she disappeared again.

EMMA hated leaving Arabella alone when she was feeling so down. Hopefully tracking down Crystal Davis wouldn't take more than an hour.

Emma pulled into the drive leading to the Sunny Farms town house condominiums. She passed the small clubhouse, the blue-tinted pond with a fountain spouting halfheartedly in the middle, and finally turned into the row where Crystal lived. A car was parked outside the center town house. Emma recognized Crystal's bright blue door. Hopefully that was Crystal's car.

She drove past the silver Ford Focus and pulled up to the curb beyond. The trunk of the car was open, and the front door of the town house was slightly ajar. It looked as if Crystal was in the process of unpacking.

Emma held her breath as she approached the right side of the Focus. She stood and stared for several long seconds. The right headlight was smashed, and the fender had a huge

dent in it. Crystal had obviously hit something . . . or someone . . . with the car. Emma shuddered. She glanced toward
the door to the condo, but there was no sign of Crystal. She
jumped when a voice came toward her from behind the
Focus, as Crystal backed away from the trunk, a large box
in her hands.

"What are you doing?" Crystal demanded.

Emma was at a loss for words. She sent up a prayer for
inspiration.

"I wanted to ask you some questions about Sunny Days."

Crystal's face puckered into a frown. "That's all over
with. We agreed. I left like I said I would." She clutched the
box in front of her protectively.

Emma struggled with her conscience. She hated upset-
ting people—she had been brought up not to—but being
nice wasn't going to get her the answers she was after.

"How did you get that dent in your fender?" She tilted
her head toward Crystal's front bumper.

Crystal's face turned white, and she dropped the carton
she was holding. Emma heard the sound of glass or china
breaking as the box hit the ground.

"I didn't do it. And you can't say I did. That happened
before." She pointed at the front of her car.

"Why did you run away, then?"

"I knew the police were looking for a car that had been
damaged, and I was afraid they wouldn't believe me. I went
to stay with my sister, but with her and Ray and the four
boys living in a single-wide, she said I had to leave and take
my chances, so I came home."

"How did you get the dent, then?"

"I don't know."

Emma frowned in disbelief. "You don't *know*?"

Crystal shook her head vehemently. "I come out to the

parking lot after work, and what do I find? A big old dent in my front bumper that wasn't there that morning. No note on the windshield or nothing."

"Can you prove it happened before Gladys's death?"

Crystal tossed her head. "I don't see why I have to prove anything to you, but I don't want you running around telling people I did it." She pointed at the car. "It was the day I loaned it to Jessica. Her own car was in the shop, and she needed to run an errand at lunchtime. She swore up and down that the dent wasn't there when she brought the car back." Crystal snorted. "I didn't believe her, but I couldn't prove it, could I? Besides, she was my boss, and I didn't know what she might do. She'd already made my life hell enough as it was."

"Well, I don't suppose I can ask Jessica to confirm that, can I?" Emma ran a hand through her hair in frustration.

"We had a big argument about it. You can ask anybody. I'm sure everyone in the place heard us. I was that mad."

EMMA returned to Sweet Nothings and thought about what Crystal had said as she served the day's customers. Arabella had left early saying she was tired. Emma was beginning to worry about her in earnest.

She had offered to volunteer at Sunny Days that evening, or she would have gone straight to Arabella's to check on her. She gave Arabella a quick call before closing up the shop, and Arabella insisted she was fine and that all she really needed was an early night.

Emma didn't really believe her, but she knew Arabella hated being fussed over. Besides, it was movie night at Sunny Days, and Emma had agreed to help make popcorn.

They were showing an old movie, *Roman Holiday* with Audrey Hepburn, that she'd always wanted to see, so she planned to grab a seat in back and stay for the show.

The parking lot was nearly empty, and Emma scooted into a spot up front near the door. Clouds had rolled in, and she felt a few drops of rain splatter on her arms as she dashed into the building. The halls were quiet as Emma headed toward the activity room. The residents at Sunny Farms ate early and had finished dinner over an hour ago. They were probably resting prior to the evening's program.

A woman was already fiddling with the popcorn machine in the activity room when Emma got there. Emma recognized her as one of Sunny Days' longtime volunteers. She was tall and very slim with graying hair curled tightly to her head and a pair of reading glasses slipping down her nose.

"Do you know how this thing works?" she asked as Emma entered the room.

Emma peered into the depths of the popcorn machine.

"I'm Grace, by the way." The woman gave Emma a sideways smile.

Emma spied a manual sticking out from under the machine and pulled it out. She read through the directions quickly.

"First, we need to briefly preheat the machine. No more than ten or fifteen seconds." She located the heat switch and turned it on.

"Here's the oil and the popcorn." Grace handed Emma a packet and a pair of scissors.

Emma cut open one side of the packet and squeezed the coconut oil into the kettle. It began to melt almost on contact. Then she slit open the packets of popcorn and salt, added them and activated the motor that turned the agitator, which kept the kernels from sticking. Shortly thereafter the sound of popping filled the room. As soon as the popping slowed, Emma turned off the heat and dumped out the kettle. A heat lamp would keep the popcorn warm while they dished it out.

The low murmur of voices floated down the hall, followed shortly by footsteps.

"Brace yourself," Grace said with a smile.

Within minutes the room was buzzing with seniors lining up to get their bag of popcorn. Emma and Grace took turns filling the small bags and handing them out. Emma helped a few residents in wheelchairs position themselves in the area that had been left open for them.

"Doing your good deed for the day, kid?" Sylvia came up behind Emma.

Emma smiled. Earl was right behind Sylvia, leaning heavily on his silver-headed walking stick.

"Nice to see a pretty, young face around here." He patted Emma on the shoulder.

Sylvia slapped him on the arm playfully. "Let's go find a seat. It looks like we've got a full house tonight."

They moved off as the lights began to blink, signaling the start of the movie.

There was a short delay as first Missy Fanning and then a bearded young man with a strand of beads around his neck fiddled with the computer and projection equipment, but finally the credits to *Roman Holiday* were rolling on the screen. Emma edged her way around the assembled residents toward an empty row in the back. She settled into a seat just as the movie began.

Emma thought it was a charming movie, and she was glad she'd stayed. Gregory Peck was handsome enough to put today's young actors to shame, and Audrey Hepburn was lyrical in her performance as the runaway princess.

Emma watched, rapt, as Hepburn had her hair cut into the pixie style she made famous. Emma put a hand to the back of her neck. No wonder Arabella always said Emma's hairdo reminded her of Hepburn.

Emma was thoroughly engrossed in the movie when she heard voices behind her. She swung around in annoyance. It was Missy Fanning talking to Grace in a loud whisper. Emma tried to turn her attention back to the movie, but their conversation kept intruding. Suddenly several words caught her ear, and she began to listen in earnest.

She leaned back in her chair slightly while pretending to watch the movie.

"She wasn't doing things by the book, that's for sure," Missy said in a whiny voice. "I've had the surveyors breathing down my neck to fix half a dozen things Jessica should have taken care of a long time ago."

Grace made soothing noises.

"I don't know what she did all day. File her nails?"

Grace's voice dropped even lower, but by leaning back, Emma was able to hear her.

"Well, I heard it was those long lunches with Jimmy Calhoun that were taking up her time."

Emma could almost hear the smirk in her voice.

Missy made a gagging sound.

"The residents liked her, though."

"Hmmmph." Missy bristled. "I heard they were getting fed up with her for not doing anything about the stealing that was going on."

The movie suddenly got louder, and Emma was afraid she would miss what Missy and Grace were saying. She quietly pushed her chair back as far as she dared.

"Do you know," Missy continued, "that weeks ago Gladys Smit reported having seen Crystal come out of one of the resident rooms shortly before the resident reported some of their personal property having been stolen?"

"Really?"

"Yes. And Jessica didn't do a thing about it. Too lazy, I expect."

They moved away then, and Emma missed the rest of their conversation. But she'd already heard more than enough. If Crystal knew that Gladys Smit had reported her—and having access to all the administrative records in Jessica's office, it was perfectly possible—then she had an excellent reason for running Gladys over.

Maybe that dent in Crystal's car wasn't so innocent after all.

Chapter 24

ARABELLA looked as if she'd hardly slept when she arrived at Sweet Nothings the next morning. Emma was about to say something when she bit her tongue. She knew Arabella hated being fussed over.

"Still no news?" She tried to keep her tone neutral.

Arabella shook her head, and her bun slipped to one side. Emma had never known Arabella to take anything but the greatest care with her appearance. Now Emma was really getting worried. Perhaps she'd have a word with Sylvia later and get her opinion.

"Did you enjoy *Roman Holiday*?" Arabella asked as she poured water into the coffeemaker.

"Yes, but you won't believe what I found out."

Arabella paused with the carafe of water in her hand.

"Apparently Gladys Smit, our hit-and-run victim, had reported seeing Crystal come out of a resident's room with something she'd stolen. She told Jessica, and Jessica made a note of it in Crystal's file but didn't do anything about it."

"That's not surprising, knowing Jessica. But it does give Crystal a motive for murder."

"And with that suspicious dent in her car . . ."

"But wasn't she out of town when you found that threatening note on your car?" Arabella pressed the start button, and coffee began gurgling out of the machine and into the pot. "Besides, Crystal doesn't strike me as the type to own Tiffany stationery."

"True." Emma frowned. "But no one really knows where she went. She could have easily snuck back. And maybe she stole the stationery from one of the residents?"

"I'll bet you're right." The coffee hadn't quite stopped perking, but Arabella was already reaching for the half-empty pot and filling her mug.

She really must have had a bad night, Emma thought. She followed Arabella out to the showroom and began turning on lights. She hadn't done her usual cleaning the night before, so she retrieved the glass cleaner from under the counter and began wiping down the glass. They would do it again halfway through the day. It was amazing how many fingerprints could be amassed in such a short time.

Arabella was quiet, sitting in the corner, mending a piece of black lace on a peignoir. The clock ticked over to ten a.m., and Emma went to flip the sign from *closed* to *open*. Just as she turned away, the door began to open.

The scent of masculine aftershave wafted into the store. It must have alerted Arabella, because she glanced up. Emma had her back to the door, and the look on Arabella's face made her whirl around.

A tall man with dark hair tinged with white at the temples and a thick mustache entered the shop.

Arabella jumped to her feet, heedless of the negligee in her lap, which slipped to the floor.

"Francis."

The man smiled and the dimples on either side of his mouth deepened.

For a moment, Arabella stood stunned, then she began to move forward. She buried her face in Francis's chest, and he put his arm around her. Finally, Arabella tilted her head back. "Where . . . When . . . How did you?"

Francis laughed. "How about you pour me a glass of that famous sweet tea of yours, and I'll tell you all about it."

Arabella bustled into the stockroom, her face and demeanor completely transformed.

Was this love? Emma thought with a shock. Would she and Brian someday have something similar?

"Is Arabella okay?" Francis asked as soon as Emma's aunt had left the room.

Emma paused for a moment. How much should she tell him? "She's been very worried." Somewhat of an understatement, Emma thought ruefully.

Francis nodded. "That was my biggest concern the whole time. I hated to think of Arabella having a single bad moment." He clenched his lips, and Emma could have sworn his eyes were wet with tears.

Arabella came back with the tea and poured each of them a glass. She held up her glass. "This is a wonderful moment." She smiled at Emma and then, with a special glint in her eye, at Francis.

Francis took a big sip of his tea. "Best sweet tea in the South." He smiled at Arabella, and it was as if they were the only ones in the room. Emma wondered if she ought to find some reason to leave the two of them alone.

"Now you must tell us what happened," Arabella said firmly.

Francis ducked his head. "It really was nothing. I don't know where to begin."

"The beginning is always a good place," Arabella said crisply.

Francis threw his head back and laughed. "Okay, the beginning it is. The dullest job on the face of the earth—security guard at a bank. I had to go to the drugstore and get some special insoles for my shoes because my feet were killing me making the rounds every night." Arabella and Francis smiled at each other, and again Emma wondered if she ought to sneak off. She was feeling decidedly de trop.

"Then . . ."—Francis paused for a drink of his tea—"the robbers finally showed up."

Arabella shivered, and Francis draped an arm over her shoulder and squeezed her tight. Emma suddenly felt very much alone.

"I let them go about their business, watching carefully from outside. I'd alerted my colleagues, but their instructions were to keep their distance unless I told them otherwise." Francis took a deep breath and continued. "One of them must have spotted me as they were leaving, because next thing I knew, they'd grabbed me and relieved me of my gun." He shrugged apologetically. "I guess maybe I'd better retire soon. My reaction time isn't what it used to be."

Arabella gasped. "Was it . . . terrible?"

Francis shook his head. "They fed me, made sure I had water, and I bunked down on a couple of blankets on the floor. Not exactly the Hilton, but it wasn't as bad as all that." He smiled at Arabella as if to reassure her.

"But how did you get away?"

"Criminals are basically stupid, no matter how smart they think they are. Eventually they couldn't resist the rewards of their spoils—drugs, alcohol. I waited until they were all either stoned or drunk, and I slipped out a window. They didn't tie me up. They were too arrogant to think I might try to escape." He gave a deprecating smile. "As far as they were concerned, I was an old copper, put out to pasture, and nothing they had to worry about."

Arabella's spine stiffened. "Little did they know!"

"Well, you should have heard my knees creaking when I sneaked out that window. Then my damn sciatica started acting up." Francis put a hand to his back.

Arabella smiled a conspiratorial smile. "Sciatica is the worst."

Emma decided this was the perfect opportunity for her to slip away. Neither Francis nor Arabella noticed when she picked up her glass of tea and sidled toward the stockroom.

Half an hour later, Emma was still working on some bookkeeping when a shadow fell across the desk. She looked up to find Sylvia standing there.

"How's it going, kid?"

"Okay. Did you hear? Francis escaped the robbers."

Sylvia grunted. "Arabella couldn't take off fast enough after lover boy. I told her I'd take over for her for the afternoon."

"It seems you have a boyfriend of your own." Emma closed the lid of her computer and smiled up at Sylvia.

Sylvia smiled in return. "Yeah, Earl and I get along. We make a great card-playing team, that's for sure." Sylvia fingered the large topaz ring she wore on her right hand. "Have you made any progress in our latest case?"

Emma shrugged. "I don't know what to think. Crystal

has a dent in her car that is consistent with the hit-and-run that killed Gladys. And I found out that Gladys reported Crystal to Jessica for stealing, although nothing ever came of it."

"Sounds like a good motive to me."

"I thought so. Of course Crystal claims that she loaned the car to Jessica at lunch one day, and when she went out to the parking lot that evening, voilà, there was a dent in the car."

"Of course, she *would* say that." Sylvia took a puff of oxygen from the tank that was never far away.

"She claimed to have had a big argument about it with Jessica. I wonder if anyone at Sunny Days heard her."

"I didn't, but I can easily ask around. Maybe someone else did."

The bell over the front door jangled as someone pushed it open. "I'll go see who that is."

Emma got up from her chair. She sniffed. She could have sworn she noticed the scent of vanilla. Someone's perfume, perhaps?

"Hello?" A voice came from the outer room.

"Hello," Emma answered as she walked into the showroom. "Liz!" She stopped short. Liz was nearly hidden behind a tower of white bakery boxes.

Liz peered around the edge of the stack in her arms. "I stopped by Bitsy's, and she asked if I could deliver these." Liz eased the boxes onto the counter. "She said the promotion is going great, and business has really picked up."

"I hear you have some good news, too."

Liz grinned. "Yes. Did Brian tell you? Matt got that contract. And someone else contacted him yesterday about a proposal for another project."

"That's great." Emma untied the string on the top box

and peeked inside. Gorgeous, miniature carrot cupcakes were nestled inside. "These look delicious." She stuck out her lower lip. "But they're not as pretty without your flowers."

A shadow crossed over Liz's face. "I know, but she wouldn't dare risk it." Liz looked down at her hands. They were gardener's hands with short, serviceable nails. "The police have been around again asking more questions. They think I blamed Jessica for the things that went missing from my father's room."

Emma was about to sample one of Bitsy's cupcakes, but her appetite suddenly deserted her. "That's ridiculous! Besides, whoever killed Jessica must have killed Gladys Smit as well."

"The police are treating that as a hit-and-run—a random act. Criminal, certainly, but not related to Jessica Scott's death."

Emma felt like stamping her foot in frustration. "I can't believe they don't see the connection." She was quiet for a moment. "I guess we'll have to *make* them see it."

EMMA didn't want to wait for Sylvia or Earl to pick up news around Sunny Days. The look on Liz's face had Emma worried. She had to do something now. She'd phoned the volunteer coordinator at Sunny Days, and luckily, they needed someone to help with games that very evening.

As soon as she and Sylvia closed the door to Sweet Nothings, Emma headed toward the retirement community. She had the strangest feeling that she was going to uncover something important—something that would put them on the right track. She hoped her intuition would be proved correct.

Emma glanced at her watch as she pulled into the parking lot at the retirement home. She had to hurry; she was running a little late.

Residents were already assembled in the activity room when Emma got there. The scent of popcorn permeated the air, and the crowd of women and a handful of men sat around munching from small paper bags.

Missy Fanning looked considerably less cool and collected than Emma suspected she would have liked. The collar of her white blouse was wilted, and sweat stains created dark arcs under her arms. She rushed over when she saw Emma.

"Thank goodness you're here. The residents at that table over there"—she pointed toward a group of three people seated together—"want to play euchre and need a fourth. Do you know the game?" She batted her heavily mascara-laden eyelashes at Emma, as if that would be the deciding factor.

"I've played a few times."

"Great!" Missy ran a hand across her chin where sweat beaded in the crease.

Emma moved toward the table Missy had indicated. She recognized Eloise Montgomery, who was dressed in an embroidered jacket and black pants, and had an elaborate pin studded with aqua terra jasper stones on her lapel. The other two people were unknown to Emma—a woman with striking white hair who was dressed as meticulously as Eloise, and a gentleman with a gentle mien and a droopy, mottled brown and gray mustache.

Emma slid into the empty seat and introduced herself. A deck of cards was on the table, separated into two piles. Emma remembered that in euchre, you only used the cards from nine through the face cards.

The gentleman, who had introduced himself as Robert,

asked if he should deal. Everyone was in agreement, and he reached a shaky hand toward one of the piles.

"So," Eloise said with obvious relish, "is there any news about Jessica's death?" She raked in the cards Robert had dealt in front of her. "Or that poor girl who was run over on her bicycle? She was an aide here. I didn't have much contact with her, but she was nice enough. A terrible end that was not deserved."

Emma studied her hand quickly. She shook her head. "Nothing much, really. The police still don't think the two deaths are connected."

Eloise snorted as she threw down a card. "That's ridiculous. Two people who both worked at Sunny Days suddenly snuffed out? I can't believe there isn't a connection."

Emma shrugged and tentatively proffered up a card. She wasn't going to win this game, that was for sure. But she didn't care. She was here for something very different. Robert put down a card, his face creased in concentration. His eyes darted between Eloise and Emma as if judging their reaction.

Deborah, the woman with the white hair, slid a card forward casually. She glanced around the room as if she were more interested in what other people were doing than in their card game.

"You do know that Crystal had a huge dent in the right front fender of her car," Emma said casually as she threw down the jack of spades. Clubs were trump, and this was the second-highest card in the deck.

Eloise made a sucking noise under her breath, and Emma knew it wasn't because she had thrown down the jack.

"Of course she says she loaned her car to Jessica at lunch and when she came out to the parking lot after work, the damage had been done," Emma said.

Eloise tossed out a card that had Robert, her partner, staring at her mutely.

"I heard the two of them arguing about it," Eloise said breathlessly as Deborah raked in the winning trick. "Crystal was furious." She leaned across the table toward Emma, and her gold inlaid pendant swung forward, nearly disturbing the cards. "Jessica kept saying she'd returned the car in perfect working order, but Crystal was having none of it."

"Really?" Emma glanced at her new hand of cards, but she was paying far more attention to Eloise's conversation.

"Frankly, I think Crystal had had her fill. Jessica treated her like a slave, then Jessica borrows her car and doesn't even have the decency to own up to the damage."

"That might be because Jessica was telling the truth," Deborah said as she carefully placed a king of diamonds in the center of the table. Her voice was quiet but deep and smoky.

Emma had to force herself to play it cool. "What makes you think that?" she said as she considered the cards in her hand.

"I happened to be looking out my window. I have a view of the parking lot." Deborah made a face. "I told my son I wanted an apartment in the back, but he never could do anything right. Anyway, as Jessica was pulling into the lot and getting out of Crystal's car, Lotte Fanning was leaving. She stood under the canopy—you know where the big Sunny Days sign is—and watched as Jessica let herself in that side door that's by her office."

Robert cleared his throat tentatively and glanced at Emma. "It's your turn."

"Oh." Emma threw down the first card she touched, and Robert, who was now her partner, gave her a startled look. She didn't care.

"Lotte stood there waiting and watching until Jessica was inside, then she got into her own car and drove around toward where Jessica had parked."

By now Emma was holding her breath.

"Yes?"

"And then she ran right into Crystal's front fender. It left a huge dent in both cars, at least as far as I could tell."

Emma sat, stunned.

That explained the dent in Lotte's car and also the one in Crystal's. What it didn't help explain was who had murdered Jessica and who had run Gladys Smit off her bicycle.

Chapter 25

EMMA was about to leave Sunny Days when Sylvia and Earl came up behind her.

"What's the matter, kid? You look like you've lost your best friend."

Emma gave a bitter laugh. "That's what it feels like. No, my best friend is fine." She thought of Liz and mentally crossed her fingers. Liz certainly did seem to be doing better these days. "But two of my murder theories got shot down."

"Now that's bad. Why don't you come back to my place and tell Auntie Sylvia all about it?"

Emma followed Sylvia and Earl down the corridor. All the residents were going back to their rooms after the game evening, and it was slow going maneuvering around the walkers and people in wheelchairs. Eloise Montgomery breezed past them, a cloud of French perfume trailing behind her.

"Make yourself at home." Sylvia opened the door to her apartment. "How about a cold drink?"

"Sure. But not vodka. I'm driving."

"Too bad. I've got some nice Stoli on ice."

Sylvia bustled out to the kitchen, and Earl made himself comfortable in the wing chair. Emma got the impression that it was his accustomed spot. Sylvia reappeared with a tray, a pitcher of lemonade and three glasses. She set it down on an end table and began to pour. She handed a glass to Emma.

Emma took a sip of lemonade and turned to Sylvia. "You know, it seems as if your cough is getting better." She gestured toward the tank parked in a corner of the apartment. "You're not using your oxygen as much."

Sylvia made a face that was halfway between a smile and a grimace. "I can't smoke in here, you know."

Earl jerked his head in Sylvia's direction. "She's got to sneak outside for a puff."

Sylvia nodded. "Yeah, and sometimes it's not worth the bother. By the time I get downstairs and out the door, the urge has passed."

"So you've given it up?"

"Not exactly, but I've sure cut down. Guess the doctor was right, and it wasn't doing my lungs any good." Sylvia was quiet for a moment. "But tell us what happened to your theories. I really thought you were onto something."

Emma explained about the dents in Lotte's and Crystal's cars and how she now knew they had nothing to do with Gladys Smit's murder.

"But why would Lotte ram Crystal's car? They don't have anything against each other, do they?"

"No, but Lotte obviously thought it was Jessica's car,

since she was the one driving it. And she certainly had something against Jessica."

Sylvia nodded sagely, her long, dangling earrings swinging to and fro. "Never mess with another woman's man," Sylvia declared. "You're asking for trouble."

"Especially a Southern woman's." Earl stroked his mustache thoughtfully.

"So you're back at square one, huh?"

Emma made a face. "Looks like it."

"I've got to think that story Jessica told about the old nurse had something to do with it. What do you think?" Sylvia tipped her glass toward Emma.

"I agree. I wish I could talk to her, but the doctor has ordered no visitors for the near future."

Sylvia slapped her knee. "I've got it. You can take my book cart and go around for me. They won't even look at you twice. I go in and out of all the rooms, and no one says a thing."

For a wild moment, Emma wondered if she would have to dress up as Sylvia, and she stifled a laugh. "Do you really think it would work?"

"Sure. We get new volunteers all the time. Besides, the staff have already seen quite a bit of you here volunteering."

"But I've already been up there, and they might remember that. I told them I was a . . . relative."

"Go at a different time. A new shift will be on." Sylvia turned toward the small wood cabinet next to her. "Let's see what the cards say." She opened the top drawer and pulled out a deck of tarot cards.

Earl leaned forward expectantly in his chair as Sylvia laid the cards out on the coffee table.

"I'm doing a simple five-card spread. That ought to give us some answers."

Emma found herself holding her breath as Sylvia's hand hovered over the cards.

"This is the Future card," she said, picking up the card on the far right of the middle row. Sylvia turned the card over and collapsed back in her chair as if she'd been shocked.

"What is it?" Emma felt her stomach churn, which was ridiculous since she didn't believe in Sylvia's tarot readings.

Sylvia showed the card to Earl. His bushy eyebrows shot up like rockets.

"The Tower," he said in a soft voice.

"What does it mean?" Emma asked.

Sylvia frowned. "There are many ways to interpret this card. Basically, though, it's about lies and the revelation of the truth."

"So maybe . . ."

Sylvia nodded. "Yes, I think the old nurse is going to be able to tell us the truth about this whole affair at last."

SYLVIA arrived at Sweet Nothings the next day shortly after lunch. She didn't have any bra fittings scheduled, but she was going to help Arabella in the shop while Emma took her turn at Sunny Days with the book cart.

"It's parked in the activity room," Sylvia said, as she settled in behind the counter. "Romances are on the top shelf, mysteries the second and nonfiction and everything else on the bottom."

"Do people have to sign for the books?"

"Nah. They're donated so it doesn't matter. Besides, people bring us more all the time."

Emma felt a combination of nervousness and excitement as she got into her car and began driving toward Sunny Days. There was a delicious cool breeze, and she rolled down all the windows and let it blow through her hair. She wished she were off on some adventure—preferably with Brian—instead of playing detective. Perhaps when this was all over, they'd be able to do something together again.

Emma hoped no one would say anything about her taking the book cart around. She was pretty sure Sylvia was right and no one would even notice.

She found it easily enough—tucked into the back corner of the activity room. It was a little unwieldy—like a grocery cart with a bum wheel—and she wondered how Sylvia managed to push it. Unfortunately, she had to follow Sylvia's route, which meant starting with the first floor. The nurse, Rosalind Newell, was on the fourth floor, and it would be quite a while before Emma was able to get there. She hoped no one would stop her before she did.

No one noticed that it wasn't Sylvia doing the rounds with the book cart. Staff nodded at Emma as she passed, and the residents were far more interested in what volume they were going to pick than who was dragging the cart around. Emma felt like groaning as they carefully examined each title before making a decision. In the end, it took her two hours to get to the fourth floor and the nursing unit.

Emma forced herself to take the rooms in order. Rosalind, or Rose, as Jessica called her, was in the middle of the hallway. Fortunately, most of the rooms' occupants were sleeping, and Emma was able to back the cart out without having to wait for someone to take an endless amount of time to make a decision.

Rose's room was across from the nurse's station, and Emma was relieved to see that a different woman sat behind the computer. She looked up long enough to nod at Emma before going back to the spreadsheet open on her monitor.

Emma eased the book cart into Rose's room. The recalcitrant wheels refused to cooperate, and it banged against the door frame. She held her breath, but the woman at the computer didn't even look up. The rest of the corridor was empty and quiet except for hissing and sighing noises from various machines.

Rose was propped up in bed, her brilliant white hair spread out across the pillow. Her blue eyes were open and sharp. Emma smiled as she approached the bed.

"Would you like something to read?"

Rose smiled sadly. "I'd love to, but the books are too heavy for me to hold. Can you believe that? I have to watch the idiot box if I want to do anything." She gestured with a thin hand crisscrossed with blue veins at the television mounted in the corner.

Emma was relieved to note that Rose's voice was quite strong. She'd been thinking and thinking about how to broach the story Jessica had told but had finally decided that she would simply have to rely on inspiration when the moment presented itself. Inspiration, alas, had deserted her.

"Is there anything I can get you? Some water?" A tray with the remains of lunch and a plastic glass with a straw sticking out was pushed to one side.

"Some water, please."

Emma held the straw to Rose's lips, and the woman took several small sips. She smiled. "Thank you."

Emma returned the glass to the tray. "Do you get many visitors?"

Rose smiled sadly. "Hardly any. I've outlived most of my friends, and I never did marry or have children, although I saw a lot of babies come into this world."

It was the opening Emma had been praying for. She perched on the edge of the plastic chair that was drawn up near the bed.

"You were a nurse." It was more statement than question.

Rose nodded, her hair swishing back and forth against the pillowcase. "For fifty years. At the Henry County Hospital—the old one before they redid everything." She closed her eyes for a minute. "Everything is so different now." She plucked at the bedcovers with her bony fingers.

Emma waited quietly.

"I loved helping the babies come into the world. So much joy and happiness." She was thoughtful for a moment. "But there was sadness, too. And babies who weren't wanted or who were a burden."

"I heard a story," Emma began. "From Jessica—she used to be the administrator here." Emma didn't know if Rose knew that Jessica was dead, and she didn't want to upset her. Not now, when she was so close to getting the information she needed. "She told us about a woman named Cat whose baby was stillborn. And another woman who was having her ninth or tenth child."

Rose closed her eyes. "I told her that story." She smiled at Emma. "It was a terribly stormy night. Not like the blizzards they get up north, of course, but enough to cause plenty of accidents when you're not used to it. Cars were sliding off the road everywhere. The ambulance came and went, I don't know how many times, and the emergency room staff were run off their feet. They needed all the doctors they could get their hands on, so I was left alone on the labor and delivery floor."

She gestured toward the glass of water, and Emma hastened to bring it to her. She took a long sip.

"Fortunately the storm didn't bring the babies out the way

they normally do, and I only had two patients that night." She ran her tongue over her lips. "There was Danny Brown's wife, Rachel. He's a farmer, and they already had a huge brood of children they could barely afford to keep clothed and fed. People always said the kids didn't get their first pair of shoes until one of the older ones grew out of theirs. I do know things were rough for them." She smiled at Emma. "A lot of people had it rough. They did their best." She sighed. "But I do know Rachel did not want another baby."

"And the other woman?"

"That was a completely different story. Cat's family had plenty of money, and they were ready to welcome this long-awaited baby with loving arms. He, because it did turn out to be a boy, would inherit a considerable fortune. Quite a contrast to hand-me-down shoes." Rose smiled ruefully.

"What happened?" Emma asked, even though she already knew the story from Jessica. She wanted to hear it in Rose's own words.

"Cat's baby was stillborn," Rose said succinctly. "He looked perfect—a solid seven pounds with well-formed features and a thatch of dark hair—but no matter what we did, we couldn't get him to breathe." She wiped at the tear that was sliding down the side of her face. "Fortunately, Cat had been heavily drugged, her labor was long and troublesome, and she wasn't aware of what was going on." Rose motioned for the water glass again.

After taking a sip she continued. "Rachel had given birth moments earlier to a very healthy boy who started to cry even before he was completely out. I'd been going back and forth between the two of them all night. The doctor had been called back down to the emergency room, and I was left to clean up. It was then that I had the idea."

Emma nodded encouragingly.

"What if we switched the babies? Why should Rachel take home a baby she didn't want, and Cat be sent home with empty arms? Rachel had had hardly any anesthesia so I was able to talk to her right away. She agreed. We would give her baby boy to Cat." She stopped to lick her lips again. "Cat would never know. I made up a new identification bracelet for Rachel's son, but when I was removing his, it broke and the beads scattered all over the floor. I was frantic. I didn't know when the doctors would come back or when Cat would awake. I had just finished when she began to stir." Rose closed her eyes as if picturing the scene. "I'll never forget placing that baby in Cat's arms. I knew in that moment that I'd done the right thing."

"So you never told her what happened?"

"No. Only Rachel and I knew the truth, and we'd sworn each other to secrecy."

She must have seen the look on Emma's face. "I know, you're wondering why I told Jessica the story." She shrugged. "I'd carried it with me for so long. Cat is dead, and so is Rachel. I didn't see any harm in it."

No harm, Emma thought. But Jessica had possibly been murdered because of it.

"What was Cat's real name?" Emma bit her lip, sitting on the edge of her seat.

"Time for your pills." A nurse bustled into the room, and Emma nearly swore out loud.

The woman took a small, pleated white paper cup from her tray and tipped the contents into Rose's outstretched hand. Rose dutifully swallowed the pills. Emma thought the nurse would leave, but she picked up one of Rose's frail wrists and held her finger over Rose's pulse while she glanced at the watch on her other hand. She gently laid Rose's hand back down on the blanket and patted it.

"Did you pick out some good books?" she asked in a cheerful voice, motioning toward Emma's book cart.

Emma and Rose exchanged a look.

"I'm still trying to decide," Rose said.

The nurse nodded briskly and headed toward the door. "If you need anything . . ." she called over her shoulder.

Finally she was gone. Emma and Rose listened to her progress down the hallway.

"I'm afraid I've been a terrible bore," Rose said, her fingers plucking at the sheets again.

Emma shook her head. "Not at all. It's a fascinating story. But you haven't told me Cat's real name."

"Oh dear." Rose turned her head this way and that on her pillow. "It's not really my story to tell. But I suppose it wouldn't do any harm." She gave Emma a pleading look. "Cat was short for Constance. Constance Porter."

Chapter 26

EMMA'S mind was reeling as she left Sunny Days. What she'd learned meant that Alfred Porter, Marjorie's husband, wasn't really a Porter after all. He was the son of Danny and Rachel Brown. And that meant he wasn't the legitimate heir to the Porter fortune; his younger brother, Wyatt, was.

Would that be enough to motivate Marjorie to murder? Emma thought it would. Marjorie was extremely proud of her own background and that of her husband. Knowing that she was actually married to the son of a poor farmer might have been more than she could bear. Combined with the fact that the money would now go to Wyatt and not be passed on to her precious son, Peyton. Murdering Jessica and attempting to smother Rose was a desperate ploy to keep the story from spreading any further and the mysterious "Cat" from being identified as her mother-in-law, Constance

Porter. Then when she realized Gladys Smit had seen her go out to the garden, she had to get rid of her as well.

Emma sat behind the wheel of the Bug, uncertain what to do next. Should she go to Detective Walker with the information? Would he believe her? He hadn't shown much interest in her theories before. Perhaps she'd go home first and call Arabella and see what she thought.

Emma pulled out of the parking lot of Sunny Days and headed back to her apartment over Sweet Nothings. She remembered that her refrigerator was almost bare, so she stopped at Kroger's to pick up a few things. By the time she got home, she couldn't wait to call Arabella and tell her what she'd discovered.

Emma's phone was ringing as Emma walked up the stairs to her apartment. She dumped her grocery bags down on the steps and retrieved her cell from her purse.

"Hello?"

It was Arabella.

"You won't believe who stopped by."

"Who?" Emma said as she fished her apartment keys out of her handbag.

"Marjorie Porter. She wants us to do another trunk show for her. Isn't that wonderful?"

Emma froze with her hand halfway to the doorknob. "Marjorie's there now?"

Emma tried to take a breath, but it stuck in her throat. Her aunt was alone with a vicious killer. Marjorie had killed two people already and had almost killed Rose. Emma didn't doubt she would do it again.

"Why don't I come over and we'll all talk about it?" She tried to keep the fear out of her voice.

"Are you okay, honey? You sound sort of funny."

"It's probably because I'm standing in the stairwell."

There was an extended silence that suggested Arabella didn't believe her.

"Can you come, or are you busy?"

"I'll be right there. I have to put my groceries away."

"Wonderful. See you soon." Arabella clicked off.

Emma's hands were shaking as she opened her door. She shoved the entire bag of groceries into the refrigerator—she didn't want to waste the time putting everything away. She had to get to Arabella's before anything happened. She would call Detective Walker on her way over.

ARABELLA and Marjorie were sitting in Arabella's living room, calmly drinking sweet tea, when Emma arrived, Pierre curled up contentedly at Arabella's feet. She wondered for a moment if she'd been mistaken. Maybe Marjorie wasn't the killer after all, and she was here at Arabella's for a legitimate purpose. She looked so proper with her legs crossed at the ankle and tucked to the side and one of Arabella's lacy napkins perched on her lap. Marjorie was a Porter and a Davenport, and the mayor's wife. Was it really possible she was also a killer?

Emma edged onto the sofa, eyeing Marjorie warily. Marjorie gave Emma a smile and patted her hand.

"So glad you could come. Arabella and I have been having the most wonderful chat, haven't we?" She smiled at Arabella.

Emma glanced at her aunt. Something was wrong. She looked slightly dazed. Was she that in awe of having Marjorie Porter in her own parlor?

"Let me pour you some tea." Marjorie grabbed the pitcher, which was closest to her, and filled a glass for Emma. "Your aunt does make the most delicious sweet tea."

Emma accepted the glass and took a long swallow. Her throat was parched.

"There's cake if you'd like." Marjorie pointed at an angel food cake sitting on a porcelain platter.

"Thanks." Emma hadn't eaten dinner yet, and she was hungry.

"Marjorie made the cake, and it's absolutely lovely."

Pierre lifted his head and gave a sniff but put it down again. He knew Arabella wasn't going to feed him table scraps.

Emma looked up sharply. Was Arabella slurring her words? Something was dreadfully wrong. Had she had a stroke?

"We've been discussing the idea of another trunk show," Marjorie said, sipping her tea delicately.

Emma tried to concentrate on Marjorie's words, but Marjorie was fading in and out like a radio station with bad reception. What was happening to her?

"More tea?" Marjorie held the pitcher over Emma's glass.

Emma drank the refill greedily. Maybe the tea would revive her. She put her glass down and glanced at Arabella. Her eyes were closed, and her chin was resting on her chest. She was obviously fast asleep. Emma knew that work and the scare with Francis had taken its toll, but she'd never known Arabella to fall asleep in company before.

Her own eyes were getting heavy as well. The living room was slightly stuffy. Was that making them all sleepy? She glanced at Marjorie, who looked as perky as ever. She was vaguely aware of Marjorie getting up and going into the kitchen. Perhaps she was putting the tea and cake away? Emma fought the urge to lean her head back and drift to sleep. She couldn't imagine what had come over her and Arabella. She remembered some of the things she'd read about carbon monoxide poisoning and wondered if that was what was happening. But surely Marjorie would be affected, too.

Marjorie! Emma forced her eyes open and struggled to straighten up. This was no ordinary tea party. Marjorie was a murderer, no matter how good her manners, and Emma was now quite certain she had come here to drug her and Arabella. But why?

Marjorie came back out from the kitchen with her purse over her arm. She looked at Emma and smiled—a smile that chilled Emma to the bones.

"Feeling a little sleepy, are you?"

Emma opened her mouth but the words wouldn't form.

"I've drugged your tea, and your aunt's as well. I saved Constance's pain pills when we cleaned out her house after she died. Thought they might come in handy someday. It was easy enough to grind them up. I added them to the tea after I'd poured my own glass."

"Why?" Emma managed to mumble, although her tongue felt as thick as one of the porterhouse steaks in the window of the Meat Mart.

"I was at Sunny Days for a board meeting, and I noticed your car there. Missy Fanning told me you were taking around the book cart. I checked each of the floors until I found you up on four talking to Rosalind Newell. I knew then that you were going to learn the whole story." She fiddled with the clasp on her handbag. "I imagined you would tell your aunt the news as soon as possible. Maybe you'd already called her from your car. I couldn't take any chances."

"So what are you going to do—"

"What am I going to do?" Marjorie gave that chilling smile again. "There's a pan of oil sitting on a burner on

Arabella's stove. It will look as if she was about to fry some chicken and got distracted." Marjorie glanced at her watch. "In ten or fifteen minutes the oil will begin to smoke, then it will catch fire. The fire will spread and . . ." She shrugged her shoulders. "I don't think I have to fill in the details for you, do I?"

She brushed at some invisible lint on her dress and straightened her belt. "Arabella is fast asleep, and you will be, too, soon. I wouldn't worry too much—you'll be overcome by the smoke long before the fire reaches the parlor." She glanced at the gold and diamond wristwatch on her arm again. "And now I really must be going."

"I've already called the police," Emma managed to blurt out.

"Really? Why don't I believe you?"

Emma tried to get up from her chair to stop Marjorie, but her limbs felt liquid and useless. She watched, helplessly, as Marjorie slid out the front door and closed it behind her. Arabella was still sound asleep. Emma tried to call to her, but her voice came out barely louder than a whisper. Hardly loud enough to wake someone who had been drugged. She strained to hear any outside noises. Surely the police would be here any minute. She'd tried to explain it all to the receptionist—Walker had been in a meeting and not in his office—but she'd been so frantic she was afraid she'd sounded terribly garbled. She hoped the receptionist hadn't put her down as some kook looking for attention.

She could smell the oil on the stove now. It was getting hotter by the second. Pierre was on his feet, his nose in the air, sniffing furiously. Any minute and the pan would explode into flames. A deep sob caught in Emma's throat. She had to do something. But first she had to shut her eyes— just for a moment. They were so heavy, and she was so tired.

Emma had no idea how much time had passed, but a cool breeze fanning her face woke her. Her eyes flew open as awareness of what had happened flooded back like the tide coming in. She could clearly smell the hot oil along with billows of smoke accompanied by the crackle of flames. She tried to move, but her limbs felt weighted down. She looked up and was surprised to see Marjorie whisk past her.

"I got halfway down the block when I remembered I'd forgotten this." She held up the prescription bottle she'd retrieved from between Arabella's sofa cushions. "Mustn't leave any evidence behind for the police to find. This way the police will think Arabella had become a bit dotty, you know"—she tapped the side of her head—"and left a pan of oil on the burner, and sadly, the two of you were overcome with smoke before you could do anything."

The thought that Arabella might be posthumously accused of carelessness roused Emma to a new level of anger. She managed to throw off her lethargy long enough to get to her feet and lurch toward Marjorie.

The air was thick with smoke, and Emma could see the orange glow of flames licking at the walls of the kitchen. In her drugged state, she was no match for Marjorie, but she had to try.

She swung at the older woman, but Marjorie sidestepped Emma's punch easily enough. Pierre barked furiously and nipped at Marjorie's ankles, but she dodged him, too.

Marjorie sighed. "You really should make it easier on yourself. Sit back down, let the drugs lull you to sleep and you'll never know what happened." She motioned toward Arabella, who had slid down in her chair and was sleeping soundly. "Like your aunt." She tucked the medicine bottle into her purse. "And now, I really must be going." Marjorie started toward the door.

Emma knew she had only a few seconds to act. She lunged at Marjorie, but the drugs had made her clumsy, and she fell heavily on top of the other woman.

Marjorie made a sound like *ouf* as the air was knocked out of her body by Emma's weight. She went down heavily, striking her head on the edge of the marble mantel on her way.

Emma rolled to her side and struggled to her hands and knees. There was a sizeable gash in Marjorie's head, her eyes were closed and she wasn't moving. By now the room was filling with smoke, and Emma had to stay close to the ground to breathe. Adrenaline had chased away some of the effects of the drugs, and she was able to crawl to the chair where Arabella still sat, dozing peacefully, unaware of what was going on.

Emma tried waking her, but Marjorie's potion had had more of an effect on her elderly aunt. Emma looked over her shoulder toward the kitchen where the bright orange glow had intensified, and she could see flames shooting into the hallway. It was now or never.

Emma grabbed Arabella by the ankles and pulled. She hoped that alone would wake her aunt, but it had no effect. Very gently, she pulled her aunt down until her back and head were on the seat of the chair, and her legs were sprawled indecently in front of her. Emma was stumped as to how to get her off the chair completely without banging her head. She looked around the room. Pillows! She dragged herself to the sofa and pulled one of the cushions off. Maneuvering it over to Arabella's chair seemed like the most difficult task she had ever faced—on par with a triathlon. She managed to place the pillow at the base of the chair, then she grabbed Arabella's ankles again and began to pull.

Just as Arabella's head was about to slide off the chair,

Emma stopped. She was running out of time. Smoke was thick in the air, and the flames were no longer contained in the kitchen but were racing down the hall toward the parlor, licking at Arabella's floral wallpaper. Pierre was standing by the door barking furiously. She had to hurry. The drug Marjorie had given her was starting to wear off, but she was still as limp as an overcooked piece of spaghetti.

She gave Arabella's feet a final tug, quickly putting one hand under her aunt's head as she slid off the chair and onto the cushion Emma had placed there. Emma managed to struggle to her feet. She gave a glance at Marjorie, who was still out cold, sprawled in the path of the onrushing flames. If she were able, she'd come back and get her, but Arabella was her first priority.

Emma once again grabbed Arabella by the ankles and yanked. It was hardly a dignified position, but her aunt was in no condition to complain. Emma managed to get her to the front door just as an enormous explosion sounded and the kitchen windows were blown out by the heat and fire. She got Arabella onto the porch and collapsed beside her. She gave a momentary thought to Marjorie trapped inside with the flames, but the little energy she'd been able to muster had deserted her.

Emma breathed in the fresh air, vaguely conscious of the sound of sirens in the distance. Pierre stood over her, alternately licking her face and yowling at the sounds of the approaching fire trucks and police cars.

Emma tried to get back on her feet, but it was too difficult. She let her head drop back against the porch floor and gave in to the slumber that washed over her.

Chapter 27

WHEN Emma awoke she had no idea where she was. She looked around, but her surroundings were completely unfamiliar.

"Where am I?" Her throat was parched from the smoke, and her lips felt thick and chapped.

"We're taking you to the Henry County Medical Center to have you looked over. You breathed in quite a bit of smoke." The paramedic smiled down at Emma.

Emma struggled to sit up. "Aunt Arabella. How is my aunt? I have to go to her."

The paramedic placed a gentle hand on her shoulder and eased her back against the gurney. "Your aunt is fine. They took her ahead of you, and she should be at the hospital by now. Her vitals were good and steady, so I don't think you have anything to worry about."

Emma moved her head restlessly on the pillow. "What about Pierre?"

The paramedic raised his eyebrows.

"My aunt's dog. She'd die if anything happened to him."

"The French bulldog? A very nice young man by the name of Brian came by. He said he'd take care of the dog. I hope that's okay?"

"Yes, that's fine." It was so like Brian to show up when he was needed. The thought helped to still some of the shaking that had seized hold of her, and she lay back against the pillows and tried to relax. Everything was going to be okay.

Arabella's house! Memory was flooding back, and Emma recalled the flames inching their way out of the kitchen and down the hall.

"My aunt's house!"

Once again the paramedic urged her to lay back and relax. "The firemen are working on it now. She will definitely need a new kitchen, but I heard the chief say they would be able to save the rest of the structure. A few more minutes and the fire would have been in the timbers. They got there in the nick of time."

The ambulance pulled into the emergency bay at the Henry County Medical Center, and Emma was whisked out and into the emergency room. Doctors and nurses hovered over her, taking vitals, drawing blood and performing various other tests.

"You're very lucky." A young doctor with unkempt dark hair looked at Emma over the top of his clipboard. "You've survived without any significant damage." He leaned forward and examined a cut on Emma's arm. "Just a scrape. I'll have the nurse clean it and put a bandage on it."

"What about my aunt?" Emma started to swing her legs over the side of the bed.

"Whoa." The doctor put out a hand. "Not so fast. I gather your aunt is the woman who was brought in right ahead of you? I'll check."

He stuck his head out of the cubicle and conferred with someone in the cubicle opposite.

"Your aunt said to tell you she's fine." He gave Emma a big grin.

She sank back against the pillows in relief. As long as Arabella was okay, nothing else mattered.

Emma had barely settled back in bed when another thought struck. "What about Marjorie?" She twisted the sheet between her hands. "She was in the house with us. She fell and hit her head."

The doctor frowned. "I don't know anything about that. You'll have to check with the police when you get out." He tapped Emma on the shoulder. "Now, I'll get a nurse to see to that gash on your arm."

No sooner had the doctor exited than the cubicle curtain was swept aside again and Detective Walker poked his head inside.

"Okay if I come in?"

Emma pulled the sheet up to her chin. "Sure."

Walker perched on the edge of the plastic chair and pulled a notebook from his pocket. He shook his head at Emma. "I thought you told me you were done detecting?"

"I . . . I . . ."

"It's a good thing you called me and left that message. Although at first, everyone thought it was some kind of joke."

"I was really shaken up . . . I . . ."

Walker held up a hand. "Perfectly understandable. Fortunately we were still able to get there in time." He glanced around the emergency room cubicle. "We're trying to put some facts together on the fire at your aunt's house." He glanced at his feet and cleared his throat delicately. "Marjorie Porter was found dead in Arabella's parlor. There was a large wound in the side of her head."

Poor Marjorie, Emma thought for a fleeting moment before remembering that Marjorie had murdered two people in cold blood.

Emma explained, somewhat incoherently, she was sure, about Marjorie, the murders, the pot of oil on the stove and subsequent fire. Walker's face was bland throughout her recital, but she could sense his incredulity.

He snapped his notebook shut. "All this will have to be looked into, of course."

"Of course." Emma went limp. She may have solved the murders to her satisfaction, but not, obviously, to Detective Walker's.

A nurse bustled in with discharge papers. "Doctor says you're fine to go." She handed Emma a sheaf of computer-generated pages. "Here are some things you need to look for after you get home."

Emma promised to read them over carefully.

"Can I give you a lift?" Walker asked hopefully.

"Thanks, but I've already called a friend."

Walker nodded and slipped out the door.

As soon as Emma was dressed, she headed to Arabella's cubicle, where they were getting ready to move her to a room.

"It's only a precaution," the doctor said, tucking his clipboard under his arm. "We'd like to keep her under observation for twenty-four hours, then she'll be released."

Arabella insisted she'd be fine, and Emma gratefully headed toward the hospital exit. The events of the evening were beginning to take their toll, and she ached from head to toe. Her throat was still raspy, and her chest felt tight, the way it does when you're coming down with bronchitis. She thought perhaps a hot bath would help.

Emma had called Sylvia before leaving the emergency room, and she was waiting in her ancient Cadillac outside the front portico of the hospital. Emma got in, buckled up securely and mentally made the sign of the cross as Sylvia eased off the brake and pulled away from the curb.

"I talked to Eloise Montgomery," Sylvia said as she pulled onto the street. "She used to work at the Toggery before she retired and moved to Sunny Days. She's willing to help out at the store while your aunt is out of commission."

"That's wonderful." Emma leaned back against the seat and closed her eyes as Sylvia missed sideswiping a parked car.

"She's coming in tomorrow so you can take a day off and rest up. Quite the adventure you had." Sylvia sounded slightly wistful. Emma was glad Sylvia hadn't been there as well. She wouldn't have wanted to have to drag both of them out of Arabella's burning house.

Sylvia dropped Emma off in front of Sweet Nothings. As Sylvia pulled away, Emma waved good-bye and then gratefully climbed the stairs to her apartment. Her clothes reeked of smoke, and she dropped them straight into the hamper while she ran a hot bath and added a glug of scented bubble bath.

Emma groaned as she sank into the warm, deep water. She put her head back and allowed her eyes to close. When she woke, the water was barely lukewarm. She shivered slightly as she wrapped up in her robe and put on her slippers.

She was opening the refrigerator when she heard scratching on her door. She stopped and listened. It sounded like a dog. Before she could move, the bell rang.

Emma glanced at the clock. Nearly ten o'clock.

Emma pulled her robe tighter around her and peered through the peephole. It was Brian! She glanced toward her bedroom, but there was no time to change. She pulled open the door, knowing her face was turning pink.

Brian didn't seem fazed by her unusual attire. Nor was Pierre, who greeted Emma as if it had been months since they'd seen each other instead of mere hours. He danced around her one final time then dashed off to explore the rest of the apartment.

"I stopped by the hospital, and they said you'd already been released. I needed to check on you with my own eyes."

Emma felt a warm glow at Brian's words. She bent down and scratched Pierre who had returned from his explorations.

"Pierre seemed so down in the dumps, I thought maybe he would be happier staying with you. I hope that's all right."

"That's fine." Pierre had flipped onto his back, and Emma rubbed his rather round stomach. "I've got some cold lemonade if you'd like."

"Sounds great." Brian made himself at home on the couch.

Emma was glad to escape to the kitchen briefly to get control of herself. She glanced longingly toward her bedroom and the closet. If only she weren't trapped in her ancient bathrobe! She carried the pitcher of cold lemonade and two glasses out to the living room where she set them on the coffee table. She took a seat next to Brian and poured them each a glass.

"Delicious," Brian declared after his first sip. He looked at Emma thoughtfully over the rim of his glass.

"I wanted to tell you about my visit with Amy." Brian

put his glass down on the coffee table and swiveled toward Emma.

"Oh," Emma said in a very small voice.

"We talked"—he scowled—"and I made sure she understood that it was over between us." He looked down at his hands. "I told her there was someone else. I hope that's the case."

Emma smiled, unable to say much of anything.

Brian turned toward Emma "You smell delicious," he said as he leaned closer.

"Bubble bath," Emma mumbled as he put his lips over hers.

SEVERAL days later, Emma opened the front door to Sweet Nothings and was surprised to see Arabella already there, behind the counter organizing stock with Sylvia.

She hurried toward her aunt. "Aunt Arabella! Should you be back already?"

Arabella waved a hand. "Oh, pooh. I'm absolutely fine, and I couldn't stand to rest another single minute. You have no idea what horrors daytime television subjects one to." She looked around Sweet Nothings and smiled. "I couldn't wait to get back behind the counter."

Emma gave Arabella a hug. "I'm so glad you're back. Sylvia and I missed you, didn't we?"

"We sure did."

Emma could have sworn she saw the glint of tears in Sylvia's eyes.

"What I really hated is having missed all the drama and gossip that must have been swirling around town while I was stuck at home watching stupid reality shows that couldn't hold a candle to the real thing." Arabella tucked her purse behind the counter.

"Well, the Porter influence has helped to smooth things over, as you can guess, so things haven't been quite as dramatic as they might have been."

Arabella snorted. "That and the fact that Alfred is mayor. Of course it was Marjorie everyone was afraid of, not her husband."

"But Detective Walker is still investigating," Emma said. "Her car has been impounded, and there was a large dent in the right front fender. Marjorie had left it locked in the garage and was driving one of their other cars. Tests will most likely show she was the one who hit Gladys Smit that night. I don't know if they will ever prove that she added the foxglove flower to Jessica's cupcake, but they know she set that fire in your kitchen."

"My poor kitchen!"

"How are you managing?"

"So far okay, but I haven't told you my exciting news." Arabella blushed pinkly.

"Oh?"

"Francis has been temporarily assigned to an investigation in Paris. He's rented a charming little cottage." Arabella looked up at Emma, her eyes wide. "I will have my own room, dear. Don't worry."

Emma laughed. "Of course you will."

Sylvia snorted and winked at Emma but didn't say anything.

"And my house should be fully repaired by the time his lease is up." Arabella looked slightly sad at the thought. "I wonder what will happen to old man Porter's money now that they know Alfred isn't really a Porter."

"I imagine it will give the lawyers something to fight over for the next couple of decades."

"Yes, they'll be the ones who really gain from it, I should imagine."

Emma opened the cash register and took out the old receipt tape, which was now showing a pink stripe down the center, and although it matched the décor at Sweet Nothings, it meant that the roll was about up.

"I think it's time for a change, don't you?" Arabella was looking at one of the mannequins.

"Maybe the pale green Olga," Sylvia suggested. "We've had it in stock for quite a while. Maybe it's time we gave it a push."

Arabella was rummaging in the armoire when Pierre levitated from his dog bed and attacked the front door furiously.

"What on earth?" Arabella turned toward Emma.

Emma shrugged. "Delivery, maybe?"

"Not expecting anything, are we?" Sylvia pulled the tape measure from the drawer and hung it around her neck like a stethoscope.

"Pierre, that's enough," Arabella scolded. "He seems more excited than alarmed."

A knock on the door sent Pierre into fresh fits of barking.

Emma opened the door cautiously. "Yes?"

Mr. Zimmerman from across the street was standing on the mat. He didn't have his dachshund Bertha with him, but he was holding a cardboard box from which emanated tiny squeaks and squeals.

"Bertha had her puppies." His face softened. "I know what I said, but they've turned out to be adorable little things."

He put the box down on the floor, and Emma, Arabella and Sylvia crowded around. The seething mass of puppy bodies inside the box moved as one.

"Small litter," Zimmerman said. "She had three, and I'm keeping one. The one with the black-and-white ears." He picked up one of the puppies by the scruff and held it up for them to see. "Looks like his daddy no matter what you think."

Pierre preened proudly.

"He certainly does," exclaimed Arabella, leveling a stern look at Pierre.

"Any of you ladies want the other two? I'd hate to see them go to strangers."

Emma looked at the two remaining puppies while marveling at Zimmerman's change of heart. Each puppy was a strange amalgamation of different parts from Pierre and Bertha that somehow had ended up creating an adorable combination.

She lifted the female from the box and held her close. The puppy nuzzled Emma's neck then burrowed close and drifted off to sleep.

Without thinking Emma burst out with, "I'll take this one."

Zimmerman's face lifted in a smile, completely transforming his normally dour countenance.

"I kind of like this little guy." Sylvia held the other puppy up to her face and rubbed her cheek on its soft, silken fur.

"It's settled, then." Zimmerman eased the pup with the black-and-white ears back in the box.

"Looks like we've got ourselves some puppies," Sylvia said as the door closed behind Zimmerman.

"And Pierre is a father." Arabella gave the dog a slightly softer look.

There was another knock on the door.

"What now?" Arabella said.

Emma opened the door to find Brian standing there.

"I just stopped by on my way to the hardware store to see how you ladies are—" He glanced at the puppies cavorting around while Pierre watched complacently from his dog bed. "Good heavens, what do you have here?"

Emma laughed and explained about Pierre's romantic exploits.

"Which one is yours?"

Emma picked up the female pup. "This one."

"She's beautiful. Pierre, you rascal." Brian shook a playful finger at the French bulldog. He stroked the puppy's soft fur gently. "What are you going to name her?"

"I don't know. I've always loved the name Grace."

Brian cocked his head to one side and regarded the puppy. "I don't know." He looked at Emma and smiled and the dimple in his right cheek deepened. "What if we have a daughter someday and want to call her Grace? Maybe we should save that name?"

Emma felt heat flame into her face. "Oh . . . yes . . . maybe . . . you're right," she mumbled incoherently before Brian stopped her by putting his lips over hers.

Emma was too wrapped up to notice that Sylvia and Arabella had discreetly slipped from the room.

She relaxed in Brian's arms as the puppy licked the end of her nose. The future was suddenly looking very bright.

Penguin Group (USA) Online

What will you be reading tomorrow?

Patricia Cornwell, Nora Roberts, Catherine Coulter,
Ken Follett, John Sandford, Clive Cussler,
Tom Clancy, Laurell K. Hamilton, Charlaine Harris,
J. R. Ward, W.E.B. Griffin, William Gibson,
Robin Cook, Brian Jacques, Stephen King,
Dean Koontz, Eric Jerome Dickey, Terry McMillan,
Sue Monk Kidd, Amy Tan, Jayne Ann Krentz,
Daniel Silva, Kate Jacobs...

You'll find them all at
penguin.com

Read excerpts and newsletters,
find tour schedules and reading group guides,
and enter contests.

Subscribe to Penguin Group (USA) newsletters
and get an exclusive inside look
at exciting new titles and the authors you love
long before everyone else does.

PENGUIN GROUP (USA)
penguin.com